GREAT
SOLDIERS' TALES

Other titles in our
Great Short Stories series
include:

GREAT RACING STORIES

Edited & Introduced by
Dick Francis & John Welcome

FOOLS, KNAVES AND HEROES
Great Political Short Stories

Edited & Introduced by
Jeffrey Archer & Simon Bainbridge

GREAT LAW & ORDER STORIES

Edited & Introduced by
John Mortimer

GREAT SOLDIERS' TALES

Edited & Introduced by

Field Marshal Lord Carver

BELLEW PUBLISHING
London

To my comrades in arms

This collection first published in Great Britain
in 1990 by Bellew Publishing Company Limited
7 Southampton Place, London WC1A 2DR

ISBN 0 947792 52 X

Phototypeset by Input Typesetting Ltd, London
Printed and bound in Great Britain by
Billings & Sons

CONTENTS

Acknowledgements

The publishers wish to thank Eric Tripp for all his help with research.

Grateful acknowledgement is made to the Estate of H. E. Bates and Laurence Pollinger Ltd for permission to reprint the story *The Beginning of Things* from *The Stories of Flying Officer X*, published by Jonathan Cape Ltd; to Mrs Ann Monsarrat for the story *I Was There* from *The Ship That Died of Shame,* published by Pan Books (© The Estate of Nicholas Monsarrat 1958); to the Peters Fraser & Dunlop Group Ltd for permission to reprint the story *Gold From Crete* by C. S. Forester; to Miles Noonan for the stories *Shades of Greys* and *Reunion* from *Tales from the Mess,* published by Hutchinson & Co. Ltd (© 1983 Miles Noonan); to Alexander Baron and Lemon Unna & Durbridge Ltd for the story *Old Beethoven* from *The Human Kind,* first published by Jonathan Cape Ltd in 1953 (© Alexander Baron); to Irwin Shaw for the story *Hamlets of the World* from *Mixed Company,* first published in Great Britain by Jonathan Cape Ltd in 1952 (© Irwin Shaw).

Whilst all reasonable attempts have been made to contact the original copyright holders, the Publishers would be happy to hear from those they have been unable to trace, and due acknowledgement will be made in future editions.

All royalties will go to The Royal British Legion and The Army Benevolent Fund.

INTRODUCTION

THESE are not the tales of great soldiers – 'Of Alexander . . . of Hector and Lysander and such great names as these', nor are they 'of all the world's great heroes'; but they are works of fiction (although some are based on actual events) attempting to depict the experiences of fighting men, mostly soldiers, but some sailors and airmen. Some individually, and all taken together, illustrate the contrast between what Alfred de Vigny dubbed *Servitude et Grandeur Militaire*: the slavery and glory of military life. In that book he wrote: 'It is true that the existence of the Soldier is (after the death penalty) the most painful relic of barbarism that remains among men; but also that nothing is more worthy of the interest and the affection of the Nation than this devoted family which sometimes brings it glory.'

The reader will find that contrast illustrated in this collection. There are certainly relics of barbarism in some of the stories: in the bloodthirstiness and apparent callousness of the soldiers portrayed in Rudyard Kipling's *With the Main Guard*; in the cynicism of the gambling men in the trenches in C. E. Montague's *The First Blood Sweep*, and in the black humour of Miles Noonan's *Reunion*. But underlying that aspect of military life is the need for the fighting man to cocoon himself against emotions which could prevent him from executing effectively the prime duty of his calling: to be prepared both to kill and to be killed. One of the principal fears of the fighting man, particularly on the first occasion on which he faces actual combat, is how he will perform: how he will stand in the eyes of his comrades. In modern society glory and honour are not attributes which appear to find favour; but today's soldier, sailor or airman is just as concerned as was his predecessor down the ages that he should be well regarded by his fellows; be worthy of the company of which he is a member, whether or not it enjoys ancient traditions; and that his good service should be recognized. He may not regard those feelings as striving for glory and honour; but that is what they are, although not to such an absurdly exaggerated degree as displayed by Brigadier Gerard in Conan Doyle's *How the Brigadier Captured Saragossa*.

The feelings of a young man in his first experience of war is a favourite theme, as is the contrast between the youth's enthusiasm, his keenness to experience action and to win his spurs in some feat of courage and derring-do, and the caution and cynicism of the veteran who has seen it all before. The old soldier knows only too well that such boyish eagerness can only too easily lead to an early death and the loss of a leader of potential promise. This contrast is well portrayed in Prosper Mérimée's *The Storming of the Redoubt* and Tolstoy's *The Raid*. The theme of Jeffery E. Jeffery's *Five-Four-Eight* comes close to it, describing the keenness of the young artillery officer to be with his battery when it is in a tight spot, instead of in the comparative safety of the staff, although the idea that life on the staff is always cushy and free of danger is dispelled by Boyd Cable's *The Gilded Staff*.

The variety of forms of courage is another favoured theme. Brigadier Gerard's almost incredible exploits portray one extreme. The strong, silent courage of Captain Crowe in C. S. Forester's *Gold from Crete* is as much moral as it is physical, a very special form of courage which is particularly applicable to war at sea. The clear acceptance of responsibility in a situation where there is a risk of losing a ship, or several ships, and all the crew, demands moral courage of a high order, and, when the senior officer in his flagship shares the risk with every other sailor, it demands great physical courage also. This type of courage is needed by commanders at all levels, especially of ships, aircraft and tanks. Members of their crews generally have no option but to conform to their commander's will. Other commanders, particularly in the infantry, face a more difficult task. They have to persuade their soldiers to face heavy fire, and perhaps advance into it, without protection from armour or from a hole in the ground. The commander must himself set a personal example of bravery and resolution if he is to succeed in that testing task. Ambrose Bierce's *The Affair at Coulter's Notch* provides a dramatic example of such leadership, all the greater for the peculiar circumstances in which it took place.

In contrast to that is the courage needed by a man on his own, without the support of comrades to whom he must set an example. The pilot of a single-seater aircraft needed such courage, and H. E. Bates's *The Beginning of Things* provides a perceptive insight into the pilot's mind. Bartimeus's *The Survivor* looks at another aspect of lonely courage and endurance, a rare experience for a sailor who is usually in a group, in good times and bad.

But military life is not all action under fire. In both war and peace it involves long periods of inaction, of waiting, of moving from one place to another, being involved in all the vicissitudes, the joys and sorrows, the comedy, irony and tragedy of human life. Miles Noonan's *Shades of Greys* displays a light touch of humour, while Irwin Shaw's *Hamlets of the World* combines irony with tragedy. Conflicts of loyalty are very much part of military life – the pull between one's duty to higher authority and one's duty to care for the interests, welfare and lives of one's subordinates and comrades. Few armies have faced such difficult choices as the French in the Second World War, the subject of Irwin Shaw's story; while it was the conflict between his military duty to one side in the American Civil War and the interests and safety of his wife and child that provides the tragic and dramatic element of Ambrose Bierce's tale.

Military life in war, but also in peacetime, is spent in a community, generally set apart from that of civilians, often separated also from family or the presence of women. When that also involves shared hardships and danger, a strong bond of comradeship prevails – the smaller the group, the stronger the bond. The veteran, when he leaves the service, often misses that bond and looks back with nostalgia to it. This is a well-worn theme in all accounts of military life, represented in this collection by Rudyard Kipling's *With the Main Guard*, Nicholas Monsarrat's *I Was There* and Alexander Baron's *Old Beethoven*. Tall stories abound in the reminiscences of old soldiers: Boyd Cable's *The Diving Tank* is a good example of its kind. H. G. Wells's *The Land Ironclads*, also an early story about tanks, was a remarkable prophecy. Published in 1903, it preceded the appearance of the tank on the battlefield by thirteen years. It was prophetic not only in its forecast, even if dramatically exaggerated, of a development which was to have a profound impact on land warfare, but also in seeing that the day of the horse on the battlefield was disappearing, and that, with it, much of the romance of war would fade. No longer would it be possible to think of campaigning as a sport, an extension of fox-hunting, as the gallant Tony Quarme did in *Five-Four-Eight*. All those sentiments attached to horses, whether in barracks, camp or on the battlefield, with the sounds and smells associated with them, and the thrills of action on horseback, would go and could not be, it was thought, compensated for by any attachment to a machine. In the Second World War that did prove to be the case, although some men became almost as attached to their machines – even sentimental about them – as their forbears had been (or at least some of them) to their animals.

There are those who regret the departure of romance from war; but there must be many more, including those who have experienced battle, who welcome the fact that it would not today be possible for a modern Rupert Brooke to write, as he did in August 1914, 'Now, God be thanked Who has matched us with His hour,/ And caught our youth, and wakened us from sleeping'. In that, and other poems written that year, he welcomed the advent of war as a release from the unromantic course of everyday life and what he and many contemporaries saw as the sordid intrigues behind the compromises involved in national and international politics. 'Blow out, you bugles, over the rich Dead!' he wrote, and 'Honour has come back, as a king, to earth,/ And paid his subjects a royal wage;/ And Nobleness walks in our ways again;/ And we have come into our heritage.' I suppose that there may have been some young sailors, soldiers and airmen who nursed those sentiments as they set off for the Falkland Islands in 1982, but, if so, they probably kept them to themselves. If they had expressed them publicly, they would not have met with the same degree of approval which would have been accorded to their predecessors.

After two world wars with their vast numbers of casualties, both military and civilian, and now with the introduction of nuclear as well as chemical weapons, nobody wants to glorify or romanticize war. In spite of that, cinema and television screens regularly portray the tough guy winning by the use of violence, even if the outcome is tilted towards a victory of brain over brawn.

Modern stories of war, or of the military life, tend therefore towards disillusionment with the portraits of earlier ages which glamorized the military profession. Tolstoy, whose touching tale *The Raid* follows that road, developed it at much greater length in his famous novel *War and Peace*. He calls into question both the general purpose of war and the traditional methods by which, in the nineteenth century, it had been waged, while reminding us that the pattern of life, weaving together the separate threads of individual lives, on the battlefield and off it, continues, whatever the princes and generals may decide.

To the reasonable, educated person in the closing years of the twentieth century, it appears absurd that nations should try to settle the differences between them by resort to war – to killing each other's citizens. It seems doubly absurd in our age of nuclear weapons, the use of only a fraction of the world-wide stock of which could bring human, and perhaps also animal, life on the planet to an end. That absurdity is enhanced when it appears that all nations are threatened by changes to the environment brought about by human activity which was intended to be for the good of the human race – to provide it with more food and better material circumstances. Could not war as a means of settling international differences go the same way as has duelling as a means of settling individual ones; of defending one's honour, as men did in Brigadier Gerard's day?

Sadly, one has to admit that it is the very qualities that sailors, soldiers and airmen admire and foster most that also tend to encourage nations, or elements of them, to go to war; intense loyalty to one's own tribe, one's kith and kin, those who were born in the same area, speak the same language, dress in the same way, observe the same traditions, religious or other; and the smaller the tribe or group, the more intense the loyalty. Others, outside it, are then regarded with hostility or contempt, until, in the extreme case, they are not thought of as human beings at all. Rudyard Kipling's soldiers *With the Main Guard* thought that way. Willingness to endure every hardship, to face any danger, even unto death, in support of that loyalty is admired not only by fighting men themselves, but by almost everyone, except the devoted pacifist. Christian churches revere martyrs who died for *their* faith in conflict with the faith of others. When one looks round the world at the conflicts which have raged even since the end of the Second World War, some of which still continue, one is forced to realize that it is these ancient animosities, with deep roots in the past, which are their main cause. Economic differences may aggravate them, but are not such a basic motive.

Understanding this – that it is the very existence of separate nation-states which is the fundamental cause of war – rational pacifists have sought their abolition and have looked to some form of world government as the ultimate guarantee of peace. But experience of the two moves towards that – the League of Nations and its successor the United Nations – does not appear to offer much real hope in that direction, although the organizations have performed useful functions, as the United Nations continues to do. The tribal instinct, starting at the family, is too strong and, at present, the emphasis on the small grouping is, if anything, stronger than it was a century ago, in spite of certain developments in Europe.

The fiction of an age reflects the ethos of that time, as these tales reflect the commonly accepted ideas of the period in which they were written. I would like to have included some tales of earlier periods, but the short story, as a literary form, did not develop until the nineteenth century, and my attempts to find tales to cover Marlborough's and Wellington's times have been unsuccessful.

Nobody telling a story of war today is likely to write anything like Jeffery's description of Tony Quarme's ride in *Five-Four-Eight*: 'The rush of wind in his ears, the thud of iron-shod hoofs on sound old turf, the thrill that is born of speed, made him forget for a moment the war, his enemy, his mission. He was back in England on a good scenting morning in November. Hounds were away on a straight-necked fox, and he had got a perfect start . . . This was not humdrum soldiering – cold and hunger, muddy roads and dreary marches. It was Life.' We want no more romanticizing of war: no more encouragement to young men, like Ensign Alanin in Tolstoy's *The Raid*, to fling their lives away recklessly for the sake of glory, so that the old soldier, as he does in that tale, is forced to say: 'Of course it's a pity. He was afraid of nothing; how can anyone do so? Still young and foolish – and so he has paid for it.' Men will still have to face death in defence of their country's interests, and have to be encouraged to do so; but let it be more from a sense of duty, a sense of repaying the debt they owe to others, than of romance. Let us leave romance to other fields of human endeavour, but not deny ourselves the pleasure of being reminded, in the pages that follow, that men and women of previous generations have found romance in the ranks of fighting men.

THE LAND IRONCLADS

H. G. Wells

THE young lieutenant lay beside the war correspondent and admired the idyllic calm of the enemy's line through his field-glass.

'So far as I can see,' he said at last, 'one man.'

'What's he doing?' asked the war correspondent.

'Field-glass at us,' said the young lieutenant.

'And this is war!'

'No,' said the young lieutenant; 'it's Bloch.'

'The game's a draw.'

'No! They've got to win or else they lose. A draw's a win for our side.'

They had discussed the political situation fifty times or so, and the war correspondent was weary of it. He stretched out his limbs. 'Aaai s'pose it *is*!' he yawned.

Flut!

'What was that?'

'Shot at us.'

The war correspondent shifted to a slightly lower position. 'No one shot at him,' he complained.

'I wonder if they think we shall get so bored we shall go home?'

The war correspondent made no reply.

'There's the harvest, of course . . .'

They had been there a month. Since the first brisk movements after the declaration of war things had gone slower and slower, until it seemed as though the whole machine of events must have run down. To begin with, they had had almost a scampering time; the invader had come across the frontier on the very dawn of the war in half-a-dozen parallel columns behind a cloud of cyclists and cavalry, with a general air of coming straight on the capital, and the defender horsemen had held him up, and peppered him and forced him to open out to outflank, and had then bolted to the next position in the most approved style, for a couple of days, until in the afternoon, bump! they had the invader against their prepared lines of defence. He did not suffer so much as had been hoped and expected: he was coming on it seemed with his eyes open, his scouts winded the guns, and down he sat at once without the shadow of an attack and began grubbing trenches for himself, as though he meant to sit down there to the very end of time. He was slow, but much more wary than the world had been led to expect, and he kept convoys tucked in and shielded his slow-marching infantry sufficiently well to prevent any heavy adverse scoring.

'But he ought to attack,' the young lieutenant had insisted.

'He'll attack us at dawn, somewhere along the lines. You'll get the bayonets coming into the trenches just about when you can see,' the war correspondent had held until a week ago.

The young lieutenant winked when he said that.

When one early morning the men the defenders sent to lie out five hundred yards before the trenches, with a view to the unexpected emptying of magazines into any night attack, gave way to causeless panic and blazed away at nothing for ten minutes, the war correspondent understood the meaning of that wink.

'What would you do if you were the enemy?' said the war correspondent, suddenly.

'If I had men like I've got now?'

'Yes.'

'Take those trenches.'

'How?'

'Oh – dodges! Crawl out half-way at night before moonrise and get into touch with the chaps we send out. Blaze at 'em if they tried to shift, and so bag some of 'em in the daylight. Learn that patch of ground by heart, lie all day in squatty holes, and come on nearer next night. There's a bit over there, lumpy ground, where they could get across to rushing distance – easy. In a night or so. It would be a mere game for our fellows; it's what they're made for . . . Guns? Shrapnel and stuff wouldn't stop good men who meant business.'

'Why don't *they* do that?'

'Their men aren't brutes enough; that's the trouble. They're a crowd of devitalized townsmen, and that's the truth of the matter. They're clerks, they're factory hands, they're students, they're civilized men. They can write, they can talk, they can make and do all sorts of things, but they're poor amateurs at war. They've got not physical staying power, and that's the whole thing. They've never slept in the open one night in their lives; they've never drunk anything but the purest water-company water; they've never gone short of three meals a day since they left their feeding-bottles. Half their cavalry never cocked leg over horse till it enlisted six months ago. They ride their horses as though they were bicycles – you watch 'em! They're fools at the game, and they know it. Our boys of fourteen can give their grown men points . . . Very well – '

The war correspondent mused on his face with his nose between his knuckles.

'If a decent civilization,' he said, 'cannot produce better men for war than – '

He stopped with belated politeness. 'I mean – '

'Than our open-air life,' said the young lieutenant.

'Exactly,' said the war correspondent. 'Then civilization has to stop.'

'It looks like it,' the young lieutenant admitted.

'Civilization has science, you know,' said the war correspondent. 'It invented and it makes the rifles and guns and things you use.'

'Which our nice healthy hunters and stockmen and so on, rowdy-dowdy cow-punchers and nigger-whackers, can use ten times better than – *What's that?*'

'What?' said the war correspondent, and then seeing his companion busy with his field-glass he produced his own: 'Where?' said the war correspondent, sweeping the enemy's lines.

'It's nothing,' said the young lieutenant, still looking.

'What's nothing?'

The young lieutenant put down his glass and pointed. 'I thought I saw something there, behind the stems of those trees. Something black. What is was I don't know.'

The war correspondent tried to get even by intense scrutiny.

'It wasn't anything,' said the young lieutenant, rolling over to regard the darkling evening sky, and generalized: 'There never will be anything any more for ever. Unless – '

The war correspondent looked inquiry.

'They may get their stomachs wrong, or something – living without proper drains.'

A sound of bugles came from the tents behind. The war correspondent slid backward down the sand and stood up. 'Boom!' came from somewhere far away to the left. 'Halloa!' he said, hesitated, and crawled back to peer again. 'Firing at this time is jolly bad manners.'

The young lieutenant was uncommunicative for a space.

Then he pointed to the distant clump of trees again. 'One of our big guns. They were firing at that,' he said.

'The thing that wasn't anything?'

'Something over there, anyhow.'

Both men were silent, peering through their glasses for a space. 'Just when it's twilight,' the lieutenant complained. He stood up.

'I might stay here a bit,' said the war correspondent.

The lieutenant shook his head. 'There's nothing to see,' he apologized, and then went down to where his little squad of sun-brown, loose-limbed men had been yarning in the trench. The war correspondent stood up also, glanced for a moment at the businesslike bustle below him, gave perhaps twenty seconds to those enigmatical trees again, then turned his face toward the camp.

He found himself wondering whether his editor would consider the story of how somebody thought he saw something black behind a clump of trees, and how a gun was fired at this illusion by somebody else, too trivial for public consumption.

'It's the only gleam of a shadow of interest,' said the war correspondent, 'for ten whole days.

'No,' he said presently; 'I'll write that other article, "Is War Played Out?" '

He surveyed the darkling lines in perspective, the tangle of trenches one behind the other, one commanding another, which the defender had made ready. The shadows and mists swallowed up their receding contours, and here and there a lantern gleamed, and here and there knots of men were busy about small fires. 'No troops on earth could do it,' he said . . .

He was depressed. He believed that there were other things in life better worth having than proficiency in war; he believed that in the heart of civilization, for all its stresses, its crushing concentrations of forces, its injustice and suffering, there lay something that might be the hope of the world; and the idea that any people by living in the open air, hunting perpetually, losing touch with books and art and all the things that intensify life, might hope to resist and break that great development to the end of time, jarred on his civilized soul.

Apt to his thought came a file of the defender soldiers and passed him in the gleam of a swinging lamp that marked the way.

He glanced at their red-lit faces, and one shone out for a moment, a common type of face in the defender's ranks: ill-shaped nose, sensuous lips, bright clear eyes full of alert cunning, slouch-hat cocked on one side and adorned with the peacock's plume of the rustic Don Juan turned soldier, a hard brown skin, a sinewy frame, an open, tireless stride, and a master's grip on the rifle.

The war correspondent returned their salutations and went on his way.

'Louts,' he whispered. 'Cunning, elementary louts. And they are going to beat the townsmen at the game of war!'

From the red glow among the nearer tents came first one and then half-a-dozen hearty voices, bawling in a drawling unison the words of a particularly slab and sentimental patriotic song.

'Oh, *go* it!' muttered the war correspondent, bitterly.

It was opposite the trenches called after Hackbone's Hut that the battle began. There the ground stretched broad and level between the lines, with scarcely shelter for a lizard, and it seemed to the startled, just-awakened men who came crowding into the trenches that this was one more proof of that inexperience of the enemy of which they had heard so much. The war correspondent would not believe his ears at first, and swore that he and the war artist, who, still imperfectly roused, was trying to put on his boots by the light of a match held in his hand, were the victims of a common illusion. Then, after putting his head in a bucket of cold water, his intelligence came back as he towelled. He listened. 'Gollys!' he said; 'that's something more than scare firing this time. It's like ten thousand carts on a bridge of tin.'

There came a sort of enrichment to that steady uproar. 'Machine-guns!'

Then, 'Guns!'

The artist, with one boot on, thought to look at his watch, and went to it hopping.

'Half an hour from dawn,' he said. 'You were right about their attacking, after all . . .'

The war correspondent came out of the tent, verifying the presence of chocolate in his pocket as he did so. He had to halt for a moment or so until his eyes were toned down to the night a little. 'Pitch!' he said. He stood for a space to season his eyes before he felt justified in striking out for a black gap among the adjacent tents. The artist coming out behind him fell over a tent-rope. It was half past two o'clock in the morning of the darkest night in time, and against a sky of dull black silk the enemy was talking search-lights, a wild jabber of search-lights. 'He's trying to blind our riflemen,' said the war correspondent with a flash, and waited for the artist and then set off with a sort of discreet haste again. 'Whoa!' he said, presently. 'Ditches!'

They stopped.

'It's the confounded search-lights,' said the war correspondent.

They saw lanterns going to and fro, near by, and men falling in to march down to the trenches. They were for following them, and then the artist began to get his night eyes. 'If we scramble this,' he said, 'and it's only a drain, there's a clear run up to the ridge.' And that way they took. Lights came and went in the tents behind, as the men turned out, and ever and again they came to broken ground and staggered and stumbled. But in a little while they drew near the crest. Something that sounded like the impact of a tremendous railway accident happened in the air above them, and the shrapnel bullets seethed about them like a sudden handful of hail. 'Right-ho!' said the war correspondent, and soon they judged they had come to the crest and stood in the midst of a world of great darkness and frantic glares, whose principal fact was sound.

Right and left of them and all about them was the uproar, an army-full of magazine fire, at first chaotic and monstrous and then, eked out by little flashes and gleams and suggestions, taking the beginnings of a shape. It looked to the war correspondent as though the enemy must have attacked in line and with his whole force – in which case he was either being or was already annihilated.

'Dawn and the Dead,' he said, with his instinct for head-lines. He said this to himself, but afterwards by means of shouting he conveyed the idea to the artist. 'They must have meant it for a surprise,' he said.

It was remarkable how the firing kept on. After a time he began to perceive a sort of rhythm in this inferno of noise. It would decline – decline perceptibly, droop towards something that was comparatively a pause – a pause of inquiry. 'Aren't you all dead yet?' this pause seemed to say. The flickering fringe of rifle-flashes would become attenuated and broken, and the whack-bang of the enemy's big guns two miles away there would come up out of the deeps. Then suddenly, east or west of them, something would startle the rifles to a frantic outbreak again.

The war correspondent taxed his brain for some theory of conflict that would account for this, and was suddenly aware that the artist and he were vividly illuminated. He could see the ridge on which they stood, and before them in black outline a file of riflemen hurrying down towards the nearer trenches. It became visible that a light rain was falling, and farther away towards the enemy was a clear space with men – 'our men?' – running across it in disorder. He saw one of those men throw up his hands and drop. And something else black and shining loomed up on the edge of the beam-coruscating flashes; and behind it and far away a calm, white eye regarded the world. 'Whit, whit, whit,' sang something in the air, and then the artist was running for cover, with the war correspondent behind him. Bang came shrapnel, bursting close at hand as it seemed, and our two men were lying flat in a dip in the ground, and the light and everything had gone again, leaving a vast note of interrogation upon the night.

The war correspondent came within bawling range. 'What the deuce was it? Shooting our men down!'

'Black,' said the artist, 'and like a fort. Not two hundred yards from the first trench.'

He sought for comparisons in his mind. 'Something between a blockhouse and a giant's dish-cover,' he said.

'And they were running!' said the war correspondent.

'*You'd* run if a thing like that, with a search-light to help it, turned up like a prowling nightmare in the middle of the night.'

They crawled to what they judged the edge of the dip and lay regarding the unfathomable dark. For a space they could distinguish nothing, and then a sudden convergence of the search-lights of both sides brought the strange thing out again.

In that flickering pallor it had the effect of a large and clumsy black insect, an insect the size of an iron-clad cruiser, crawling obliquely to the first line of trenches and firing shots out of port-holes in its side. And on its carcass the bullets must have been battering with more than the passionate violence of hail on a roof of tin.

Then in the twinkling of an eye the curtain of the dark had fallen again and the monster had vanished, but the crescendo of musketry marked its approach to the trenches.

They were beginning to talk about the thing to each other, when a flying bullet kicked dirt into the artist's face, and they decided abruptly to crawl down into the cover of the trenches. They had got down with an unobtrusive persistence into the second line, before the dawn had grown clear enough for anything to be seen. They found themselves in a crowd of expectant riflemen, all noisily arguing about what would happen next. The enemy's contrivance had done execution upon the outlying men, it seemed, but they did not believe it would do any more. 'Come the day and we'll capture the lot of them,' said a burly soldier.

'Them?' said the war correspondent.

'They say there's a regular string of 'em, crawling along the front of our lines . . . Who cares?'

The darkness filtered away so imperceptibly that at no moment could one declare decisively that one could see. The search-lights ceased to sweep hither and thither. The enemy's monsters were dubious patches of darkness upon the dark, and then no longer dubious, and so they crept out into distinctness. The war correspondent, munching chocolate absent-mindedly, beheld at last a spacious picture of battle under the cheerless sky, whose central focus was an array of fourteen or fifteen huge clumsy shapes lying in perspective on the very edge of the first line of trenches, at intervals of perhaps three hundred yards, and evidently firing down upon the crowded riflemen. They were so close in that the defender's guns had ceased, and only the first line of trenches was in action.

The second line commanded the first, and as the light grew, the war correspondent could make out the riflemen who were fighting these monsters, crouched in knots and crowds behind the transverse banks that crossed the trenches against the eventuality of an enfilade. The trenches close to the big machines were empty save for the crumpled suggestions of dead and wounded men; the defenders had been driven right and left as soon as the prow of a land ironclad had loomed up over the front of the trench. The war correspondent produced his field-glass, and was immediately a centre of inquiry from the soldiers about him.

They wanted to look, they asked questions, and after he had announced that the men across the traverses seemed unable to advance or retreat, and were crouching under cover rather than fighting, he found it advisable to loan his glasses to a burly and incredulous corporal. He heard a strident voice, and found a lean and sallow soldier at his back talking to the artist.

'There's chaps down there caught,' the man was saying. 'If they retreat they got to expose themselves, and the fire's too straight . . .'

'They aren't firing much, but every shot's a hit.'

'Who?'

'The chaps in that thing. The men who're coming up – '

'Coming up where?'

'We're evacuating them trenches where we can. Our chaps are coming back up the zigzags . . . No end of 'em hit . . . But when we get clear our turn'll come. Rather! Those things won't be able to cross a trench or get into it; and before they can get back our guns'll smash 'em up. Smash 'em right up. See?' A brightness came into his eyes. 'Then we'll have a go at the beggars inside,' he said . . .

The war correspondent thought for a moment, trying to realize the idea. Then he set himself to recover his field-glasses from the burly corporal . . .

The daylight was getting clearer now. The clouds were lifting, and a gleam of lemon yellow amidst the level masses to the east portended sunrise. He looked again at the land ironclad. As he saw it in the bleak, grey dawn, lying obliquely upon the slope and on the very lip of the foremost trench, the suggestion of a stranded vessel was very strong indeed. It might have been from eighty to a hundred feet long – it was about two hundred and fifty yards away – its vertical side was ten feet high or so, smooth for that height, and then with a complex patterning under the eaves of its flattish turtle cover. This patterning was a close interlacing of port-holes, rifle barrels, and telescope tubes – sham or real – indistinguishable one from the other. The thing had come into such a position as to enfilade the trench, which was empty now, so far as he could see, except for two or three crouching knots of men and the tumbled dead. Behind it, across the plain, it had scored the grass with a train of linked impressions, like the dotted tracings sea-things leave in sand. Left and right of that track dead men and wounded men were scattered – men it had picked off as they fled back from their advanced positions in the search-light glare from the invader's lines. And now it lay with its head projecting a little over the trench it had won, as if it were a single sentient thing planning the next phase of its attack . . .

He lowered his glasses and took a more comprehensive view of the situation. These creatures of the night had evidently won the first line of trenches and the fight had come to a pause. In the increasing light he could make out by a stray shot or a chance exposure that the defender's marksmen were lying thick in the second and third line of trenches up towards the low crest of the position, and in such of the zigzags as gave them a chance of converging fire. The men about him were talking of guns. 'We're in the line of the big guns at the crest, but they'll soon shift one to pepper them,' the lean man said, reassuringly.

'Whup,' said the corporal.

'Bang! bang! bang! Whir-r-r-r!' it was a sort of nervous jump, and all the rifles were going off by themselves. The war correspondent found himself and the artist, two idle men crouching behind a line of preoccupied backs, of industrious men discharging magazines. The monster had moved. It continued to move regardless of the hail that splashed its skin with bright new specks of lead. It was singing a mechanical little ditty to itself, 'Tuf-tuf, tuf-tuf, tuf-tuf,' and squirting out little jets of steam behind. It had humped itself up, as a limpet does before it crawls; it had lifted its skirt and displayed along the length of it – *feet!* They were thick, stumpy feet, between knobs and buttons in shape – flat, broad things, reminding one of the feet of elephants or the legs of caterpillars; and then, as the skirt rose higher, the war correspondent, scrutinizing the thing through his glasses again, saw that these feet hung, as it were, on the rims of wheels. His thoughts whirled back to Victoria Street,

Westminster, and he saw himself in the piping times of peace, seeking matter for an interview.

'Mr. – Mr. Diplock,' he said; 'and he called them Pedrails . . . Fancy meeting them here!'

The marksman beside him raised his head and shoulders in a speculative mood to fire more certainly – it seemed so natural to assume the attention of the monster must be distracted by this trench before it – and was suddenly knocked backward by a bullet through his neck. His feet flew up, and he vanished out of the margin of the watcher's field of vision. The war correspondent grovelled tighter, but after a glance behind him at a painful little confusion, he resumed his field-glass, for the thing was putting down its feet one after the other, and hoisting itself farther and farther over the trench. Only a bullet in the head could have stopped him looking just then.

The lean man with the strident voice ceased firing to turn and reiterate his point. 'They can't possibly cross,' he bawled. 'They – '

'Bang! Bang! Bang! Bang!' – drowned everything.

The lean man continued speaking for a word or so, then gave it up, shook his head to enforce the impossibility of anything crossing the trench like the one below, and resumed business once more.

And all the while that great bulk was crossing. When the war correspondent turned his glass on it again it had bridged the trench, and its queer feet were rasping away at the farther bank, in the attempt to get a hold there. It got its hold. It continued to crawl until the greater bulk of it was over the trench – until it was all over. Then it paused for a moment, adjusted its skirt a little nearer the ground, gave an unnerving 'toot, toot,' and came on abruptly at a pace of, perhaps, six miles an hour straight up the gentle slope towards our observer.

The war correspondent raised himself on his elbow and looked a natural inquiry at the artist.

For a moment the men about him stuck to their position and fired furiously. Then the lean man in a mood of precipitancy slid backward, and the war correspondent said 'Come along' to the artist, and led the movement along the trench.

As they dropped down, the vision of a hillside of trench being rushed by a dozen vast cockroaches disappeared for a space, and instead was one of a narrow passage, crowded with men, for the most part receding, though one or two turned or halted. He never turned back to see the nose of the monster creep over the brow of the trench; he never even troubled to keep in touch with the artist. He heard the 'whit' of bullets about him soon enough, and saw a man before him stumble and drop, and then he was one of a furious crowd fighting to get into a transverse zigzag ditch that enabled the defenders to get under cover up and down the hill. It was like a theatre panic. He gathered from signs and fragmentary words that on ahead another of these monsters had also won to the second trench.

He lost his interest in the general course of the battle for a space altogether; he became simply a modest egotist, in a mood of hasty circumspection, seeking the farthest rear, amidst a dispersed multitude of disconcerted riflemen similarly employed. He scrambled down through trenches, he took his courage in both hands and sprinted across the open, he had moments of panic when it seemed madness not to be quadrupedal, and moments of shame when he stood up and faced about to see how the fight was going. And he was one of many thousand very similar men that morning. On the ridge he halted in a knot of scrub, and was for a few minutes almost minded to stop and see things out.

The day was now fully come. The grey sky had changed to blue, and of all the cloudy masses of the dawn there remained only a few patches of dissolving fleeciness. The world below was bright and singularly clear. The ridge was not, perhaps, more than a hundred feet or so above the general plain, but in this flat region it sufficed to give the effect of extensive view. Away on the north side of the ridge, little and far, were the camps, the ordered waggons, all the gear of a big army; with officers galloping about and men doing aimless things. Here and there men were falling in, however, and the cavalry was forming up on the plain beyond the tents. The bulk of men who had been in the trenches were still on the move to the rear, scattered like sheep without a shepherd over the farther slopes. Here and there were little rallies and attempts to wait and do – something vague; but the general drift was away from any concentration. There on the southern side was the elaborate lacework of trenches and defences, across which these iron turtles, fourteen of them spread out over a line of perhaps three miles, were now advancing as fast as a man could trot, and methodically shooting down and breaking up any persistent knots of resistance. Here and there stood little clumps of men, outflanked and unable to get away, showing the white flag, and the invader's cyclist infantry was advancing now across the open, in open order but unmolested, to complete the work of the machines. Surveyed at large, the defenders already looked a beaten army. A mechanism that was effectually ironclad against bullets, that could at a pinch cross a thirty-foot trench, and that seemed able to shoot out rifle-bullets with unerring precision, was clearly an inevitable victor against anything but rivers, precipices, and guns.

He looked at his watch. 'Half past four! Lord! What things can happen in two hours. Here's the whole blessed army being walked over, and at half past two –

'And even now our blessed louts haven't done a thing with their guns!'

He scanned the ridge right and left of him with his glasses. He turned again to the nearest land ironclad, advancing now obliquely to him and not three hundred yards away, and then scanned the ground over which he must retreat if he was not to be captured.

'They'll do nothing,' he said, and glanced again at the enemy.

And then from far away to the left came the thud of a gun, followed very rapidly by a rolling gun-fire.

He hesitated and decided to stay.

The defender had relied chiefly upon his rifles in the event of an assault. His guns he kept concealed at various points upon and behind the ridge, ready to bring them into action against any artillery preparations for an attack on the part of his antagonist. The situation had rushed upon him with the dawn, and by the time the gunners had their guns ready for motion, the land ironclads were already in among the foremost trenches. There is a natural reluctance to fire into one's own broken men, and many of the guns, being intended simply to fight an advance of the enemy's artillery, were not in positions to hit anything in the second line of trenches. After that the advance of the land ironclads was swift. The defender-general found himself suddenly called upon to invent a new sort of warfare, in which guns were to fight alone amidst broken and retreating infantry. He had scarcely thirty minutes in which to think it out. He did not respond to the call, and what happened that morning was that the advance of the land ironclads forced the fight, and each gun and battery made what play its circumstances dictated. For the most part it was poor play.

Some of the guns got in two or three shots, some one or two, and the percentage of misses was unusually high. The howitzers, of course, did nothing. The land ironclads in each case followed much the same tactics. As soon as a gun came into play the monster turned itself almost end-on, so as to minimize the chances of a square hit, and made not for the gun, but for the nearest point on its flank from which the gunners could be shot down. Few of the hits scored were very effectual; only one of the things was disabled, and that was the one that fought the three batteries attached to the brigade on the left wing. Three that were hit when close upon the guns were clean shot through without being put out of action. Our war correspondent did not see that one momentary arrest of the tide of victory on the left; he saw only the very ineffectual fight of half-battery 96B close at hand upon his right. This he watched some time beyond the margin of safety.

Just after he heard the three batteries opening up upon his left he became aware of the thud of horses' hoofs from the sheltered side of the slope, and presently saw first one and then two other guns galloping into position along the north side of the ridge, well out of sight of the great bulk that was now creeping obliquely towards the crest and cutting up the lingering infantry beside it and below, as it came.

The half-battery swung round into line – each gun describing its curve – halted, unlimbered, and prepared for action . . .

'Bang!'

The land ironclad had become visible over the brow of the hill, and just visible as a long black back to the gunners. It halted, as though it hesitated.

The two remaining guns fired, and then their big antagonist had swung round and was in full view, end-on, against the sky, coming at a rush.

The gunners became frantic in their haste to fire again. They were so near the war correspondent could see the expression of their excited faces through his field-glass. As he looked he saw a man drop, and realized for the first time that the ironclad was shooting.

For a moment the big black monster crawled with an accelerated pace towards the furiously active gunners. Then, as if moved by a generous impulse, it turned its full broadside to their attack, and scarcely forty yards away from them. The war correspondent turned his field-glass back to the gunners and perceived it was now shooting down the men about the guns with the most deadly rapidity.

Just for a moment it seemed splendid, and then it seemed horrible. The gunners were dropping in heaps about their guns. To lay a hand on a gun was death. 'Bang!' went the gun on the left, a hopeless miss, and that was the only second shot the half-battery fired. In another moment half-a-dozen surviving artillerymen were holding up their hands amidst a scattered muddle of dead and wounded men, and the fight was done.

The war correspondent hesitated between stopping in his scrub and waiting for an opportunity to surrender decently, or taking to an adjacent gully he had discovered. If he surrendered it was certain he would get no copy off; while, if he escaped, there were all sorts of chances. He decided to follow the gully, and take the first offer in the confusion beyond the camp of picking up a horse.

Subsequent authorities have found fault with the first land ironclads in many particulars, but assuredly they served their purpose on the day of their appearance. They were essentially long, narrow, and very strong steel frameworks carrying the engines, and borne upon eight pairs of big pedrail wheels, each about ten feet in diameter, each a driving-wheel and set upon long axles free to swivel round a common axis. This arrangement gave them the maximum of adaptability to the contours of the ground. They crawled level along the ground with one foot high upon a hillock and another deep in a depression, and they could hold themselves erect and steady sideways upon even a steep hillside. The engineers directed the engines under the command of the captain, who had lookout points at small ports all round the upper edge of the adjustable skirt of twelve-inch iron-plating which protected the whole affair, and who could also raise or depress a conning-tower set about the port-holes through the centre of the iron top cover. The riflemen each occupied a small cabin of peculiar construction, and these cabins were slung along the sides of and before and behind the great main framework, in a manner suggestive of the slinging of the seats of an Irish jaunting-car. Their rifles, however, were very different pieces of apparatus from the simple mechanisms in the hands of their adversaries.

These were in the first place automatic, ejected their cartridges and loaded again from a magazine each time they fired, until the ammunition store was at an end, and they had the most remarkable sights imaginable, sights which threw a bright little camera-obscura picture into the light-tight box in which the rifleman sat below. This camera-obscura picture was marked with two crossed lines, and whatever was covered by the intersection of these two lines, that the rifle hit. The sighting was ingeniously contrived. The rifle-man stood at the table with a thing like an elaboration of a draughts-man's dividers in his hand, and he opened and closed these dividers, so that they were always at the apparent height – if it was an ordinary-sized man – of the man he wanted to kill. A little twisted strand of wire like an electric-light wire ran from this implement up to the gun, and as the dividers opened and shut the sights went up or down. Changes in the clearness of the atmosphere, due to changes of moisture, were met by an ingenious use of that meteoro-logically sensitive substance, catgut, and when the land ironclad moved forward the sights got a compensatory deflection in the direction of its motion. The rifleman stood up in his pitch-dark chamber and watched the little picture before him. One hand held the dividers for judging distance, and the other grasped a big knob like a door-handle. As he pushed this knob about the rifle above swung to correspond, and the picture passed to and fro like an agitated panorama. When he saw a man he wanted to shoot he brought him up to the cross-lines, and then pressed a finger upon a little push like an electric bell-push, conveniently placed in the centre of the knob. Then the man was shot. If by any chance the rifleman missed his target he moved the knob a trifle, or readjusted his dividers, pressed the push, and got him the second time.

This rifle and its sights protruded from a port-hole, exactly like a great number of other port-holes that ran in a triple row under the eaves of the cover of the land ironclad. Each port-hole displayed a rifle and sight in dummy, so that the real ones could only be hit by a chance shot, and if one was, then the young man below said 'Pshaw!' turned on an electric light, lowered the injured instrument into his camera, replaced the injured part, or put up a new rifle if the injury was considerable.

You must conceive these cabins as hung clear above the swing of the axles, and inside the big wheels upon which the great elephant-like feet were hung, and behind these cabins along the centre of the monster ran a central gallery into which they opened, and along which worked the big compact engines. It was like a long passage into which this throbbing machinery had been packed, and the captain stood about the middle, close to the ladder that led to his conning-tower, and directed the silent, alert engineers – for the most part by signs. The throb and noise of the engines mingled with the reports of the rifles and the intermittent clangour of the bullet hail upon the armour. Ever and again he would touch the wheel that raised his conning-tower, step up his ladder until his engineers could see nothing of him above the waist, and then come down again with orders. Two small electric lights were all the illumination of this space – they were placed to make him most clearly visible to his subordinates; the air was thick with the smell of oil and petrol, and had the war correspondent been suddenly transferred from the spacious dawn outside to the bowels of this apparatus he would have thought himself fallen into another world.

The captain, of course, saw both sides of the battle. When he raised his head into his conning-tower there were the dewy sunrise, the amazed and disordered trenches, the flying and falling soldiers, the depressed-looking groups of prisoners, the beaten guns; when he bent down again to signal 'Half speed,' 'Quarter speed,' 'Half circle round towards the right,' or what not, he was in the oil-smelling twilight of the ill-lit engine room. Close beside him on either side was the mouthpiece of a speaking-tube, and ever and again he would direct one side or other of his strange craft to 'Concentrate fire forward on gunners,' or to 'Clear out trench about a hundred yards on our right front.'

He was a young man, healthy enough but by no means sun-tanned, and of a type of feature and expression that prevails in His Majesty's Navy: alert, intelligent, quiet. He and his engineers and his riflemen all went about their work, calm and reasonable men. They had none of that flapping strenuousness of the half-wit in a hurry, that excessive strain upon the blood-vessels, that hysteria of effort which is so frequently regarded as the proper state of mind for heroic deeds.

For the enemy these young engineers were defeating they felt a certain qualified pity and a quite unqualified contempt. They regarded these big, healthy men they were shooting down precisely as these same big, healthy men might regard some inferior kind of nigger. They despised them for making war; despised their bawling patriotisms and their emotionality profoundly; despised them, above all, for the petty cunning and the almost brutish want of imagination their method of fighting displayed. 'If they *must* make war,' these young men thought, 'Why in thunder don't they do it like sensible men?' They resented the assumption that their own side was too stupid to do anything more than play their enemy's game, that they were going to play this costly folly according to the rules of unimaginative men. They resented being forced to the trouble of making man-killing machinery; resented the alternative of having to massacre these people or endure their truculent yappings; resented the whole unfathomable imbecility of war.

Meanwhile, with something of the mechanical precision of a good clerk posting a ledger, the riflemen moved their knobs and pressed their buttons . . .

The captain of Land Ironclad Number Three had halted on the crest close to his captured half-battery. His lined-up prisoners stood hard by and waited for the cyclists behind to come for them. He surveyed the victorious morning through his conning-tower.

He read the general's signals. 'Five and Four are to keep among the guns to the left and prevent any attempt to recover them. Seven and Eleven and Twelve, stick to the guns you have got; Seven, get into position to command the guns taken by Three. Then we're to do something else, are we? Six and One, quicken up to about ten miles an hour and walk round behind that camp to the levels near the river – we shall bag the whole crowd of them,' interjected the young man. 'Ah, here we are! Two and Three, Eight and Nine, Thirteen and Fourteen, space out to a thousand yards, wait for the word, and then go slowly to cover the advance of the cyclist infantry against any charge of mounted troops. That's all right. But where's Ten? Halloa! Ten to repair and get movable as soon as possible. They've broken up Ten!'

The discipline of the new war machines was businesslike rather than pedantic, and the head of the captain came down out of the conning-tower to tell his men. 'I say, you chaps there. They've broken up Ten. Not badly, I think; but anyhow, he's stuck.'

But that still left thirteen of the monsters in action to finish up the broken army.

The war correspondent stealing down his gully looked back and saw them all lying along the crest and talking fluttering congratulatory flags to one another. Their iron sides were shining golden in the light of the rising sun.

The private adventures of the war correspondent terminated in surrender about one o'clock in the afternoon, and by that time he had stolen a horse, pitched off it, and narrowly escaped being rolled upon; found the brute had broken its leg, and shot it with his revolver. He had spent some hours in the company of a squad of dispirited riflemen, had quarrelled with them about topography at last, and gone off by himself in a direction that should have brought him to the banks of the river and didn't. Moreover, he had eaten all his chocolate and found nothing in the whole world to drink. Also, it had become extremely hot. From behind a broken, but attractive stone wall he had seen far away in the distance the defender-horsemen trying to charge cyclists in open order, with land ironclads outflanking them on either side. He had discovered that cyclists could retreat over open turf before horsemen with a sufficient margin of speed to allow of frequent dismounts and much terribly effective sharpshooting; and he had a sufficient persuasion that those horsemen, having charged their hearts out, had halted just beyond his range of vision and surrendered. He had been urged to sudden activity by a forward movement of one of those machines that had threatened to enfilade his wall. He had discovered a fearful blister on his heel.

He was now in a scrubby gravelly place, sitting down and meditating on his pocket-handkerchief, which had in some extraordinary way become in the last twenty-four hours extremely ambiguous in hue. 'It's the whitest thing I've got,' he said.

He had known all along that the enemy was east, west, and south of him, but when he heard land ironclads Numbers One and Six talking in their measured, deadly way not half a mile to the north he decided to make his own little unconditional peace without any further risks. He was for hoisting his white flag to a bush and taking up a position of modest obscurity near it until some one came along.

He became aware of voices, clatter, and the distinctive noises of a body of horse, quite near, and he put his handkerchief in his pocket again and went to see what was going forward.

The sound of firing ceased, and then as he drew near he heard the deep sounds of many simple, coarse, but hearty and noble-hearted soldiers of the old school swearing with vigour.

He emerged from his scrub upon a big level plain, and far away a fringe of trees marked the banks of the river.

In the centre of the picture was a still intact road bridge, and a big railway bridge a little to the right. Two land ironclads rested, with a general air of being long, harmless sheds, in a pose of anticipatory peacefulness right and left of the picture, completely commanding two miles and more of the river levels. Emerged and halted a few yards from the scrub was the remainder of the defender's cavalry, dusty, disordered, and obviously annoyed, but still a very fine show of men. In the middle distance three or four men and horses were receiving medical attendance, and nearer a knot of officers regarded the distant novelties in mechanism with profound distaste. Every one was very distinctly aware of the twelve other ironclads, and of the multitude of townsmen soldiers, on bicycles or afoot, encumbered now by prisoners and captured war-gear but otherwise thoroughly effective, who were sweeping like a great net in their rear.

'Checkmate,' said the war correspondent, walking out into the open. 'But I surrender in the best of company. Twenty-four hours ago I thought war was impossible – and these beggars have captured the whole blessed army! Well! Well!' He thought of his talk with the young lieutenant. 'If there's no end to the surprises of science, the civilized people have it, of course. As long as their science keeps going they will necessarily be ahead of open-country men. Still . . .'

He wondered for a space what might have happened to the young lieutenant.

The war correspondent was one of those inconsistent people who always want the beaten side to win. When he saw all these burly, sun-tanned horsemen, disarmed and dismounted and lined up; when he saw their horses unskilfully led away by the singularly not equestrian cyclists to whom they had surrendered; when he saw these truncated Paladins watching this scandalous sight, he forgot altogether that he had called these men 'cunning louts' and wished them beaten not four-and-twenty hours ago. A month ago he had seen that regiment in its pride going forth to war, and had been told of its terrible prowess, how it could charge in open order with each man firing from his saddle, and sweep before it anything else that ever came out to battle in any sort of order, foot or horse. And it had had to fight a few score of young men in atrociously unfair machines!

'Manhood *versus* Machinery' occurred to him as a suitable headline. Journalism curdles all one's mind to phrases.

He strolled as near the lined-up prisoners as the sentinels seemed disposed to permit, and surveyed them and compared their sturdy proportions with those of their lightly built captors.

'Smart degenerates,' he muttered. 'Anæmic Cockneydom.'

The surrendered officers came quite close to him presently, and he could hear the colonel's high-pitched tenor. The poor gentleman had spent three years of arduous toil upon the best material in the world perfecting that shooting from the saddle charge, and he was inquiring with phrases of blasphemy, natural in the circumstances, what one could be expected to do against this suitably consigned ironmongery.

'Guns,' said some one.

'Big guns they can walk round. You can't shift big guns to keep pace with them, and little guns in the open they rush. I saw 'em rushed. You might do a surprise now and then – assassinate the brutes, perhaps – '

'You might make things like 'em.'

'What? *More* ironmongery? Us? . . .'

'I'll call my article,' meditated the war correspondent, ' "Mankind *versus* Ironmongery," and quote the old boy at the beginning.'

And he was much too good a journalist to spoil his contrast by remarking that the half-dozen comparatively slender young men in blue pyjamas who were standing about their victorious land ironclad, drinking coffee and eating biscuits, had also in their eyes and carriage something not altogether degraded below the level of a man.

SHADES OF GREYS

Miles Noonan

ONE of the casualties of some heavy and confused fighting in Italy in 1943 was a trooper of the Royal Scots Greys. These cavalrymen of distinguished lineage had long since been converted to armour. They were commanded by Lieutenant Colonel Twisleton-Wykeham-Fiennes.

The trooper's tank had been brewed up by a German 88. He had got out with difficulty and removed himself to the nearest cover. The shifting state of the battle left him out of luck. He was overrun by German infantry and taken away as a prisoner.

The Germans, as was their custom with most of those of their captured opponents whom they regarded as possessing ethnic respectability, treated him as well as prevailing conditions allowed. They gave him water and a piece of black bread, and accepted him companionably as a sharer of their holes in the ground when concentrations of shelling and mortar fire from his friends came too close. During an interval of relative calm, he was escorted rearwards and delivered to a Panzer intelligence officer.

The trooper was equipped by both training and temperament to withstand the blandishments of interrogators seeking information. He had been taught repeatedly that the Geneva Convention required him to disclose to his captors no more than his name, rank and number. He did not find this restriction onerous. He was not by nature of a chatty disposition.

The Panzer intelligencer, genial and persuasive, spoke nearly fault-less English. He welcomed the trooper courteously, offered him a cigarette and a huge slug of Italian brandy, and congratulated him on getting out of his burning tank unwounded. He hoped that the trooper had not incurred too many painful scratches and abrasions whilst subsequently crawling to safety.

The trooper ignored the brandy, took the cigarette and gave his name, rank and number.

The intelligence officer became discursive about the good old days in the Western Desert. Warfare in a vast, barren arena, uncluttered by civilians, had been exciting and honourable. He himself had fought against the Scots Greys on a number of occasions. He had the greatest admiration for them. Had the trooper been in the Desert?

The trooper, who had, said nothing.

The intelligencer moved slickly to more recent occurrences. His respect for the regiment remained undiminished, he said, but they shared a weakness with most British units. Their radio security was, to put it bluntly, lousy. Did the trooper agree?

The trooper, who did, said nothing.

What these free-flowing conversationalists seemed not to have absorbed, said the intelligencer, was that the Germans operated an extraordinarily efficient tactical radio interception set-up. From this, and from various other sources which he wouldn't elaborate upon at the moment, he had assembled an almost complete picture of the command structure of the Scots Greys.

The trooper, who wasn't surprised, said nothing.

The intelligencer picked up some papers, neatly clipped together. In case his guest thought he was exaggerating, he said, it might be helpful to name names. He then read out an almost complete nominal roll that included the second in command, all the squadron commanders, most of the troop commanders, the adjutant, and the regimental sergeant major.

At the end of this offering he apologized charmingly for his remissness in letting his official duties override his responsibilities as a host. He pushed the brandy forward again and offered another cigarette.

The trooper left the brandy where it was and lit the cigarette. He had never been a man to confuse taciturnity with bad manners. This sort of hospitality, he felt, deserved acknowledgement. Continued silence would be churlish. He repeated his name, rank and number.

The intelligencer drew on his own cigarette, sat back and became confidential. The trooper would have noticed, he remarked, that, despite the comprehensive accuracy of the list of names that had been read out, there was an important omission. The commanding officer had not been mentioned. It was about this gap in their knowledge that he and his colleagues would value his new friend's advice.

There had, frankly, been differences of opinion in German intelligence circles about the identity of this colonel of tanks. He had originally been recorded under the name of Twisleton. He seemed later to have been replaced by someone called Wykeham. But no sooner had Wykeham been logged in on the order of battle than Twisleton was back. Any facile idea that Wykeham had been a *locum tenens*, looking after things while Twisleton was on leave or recovering from wounds, had been dissipated by later evidence that both Twisleton and Wykeham had been at work simultaneously, either in alternation or in tandem. Consideration of this interesting experiment in command technique had been clouded by the insertion of somebody named Fiennes, which no German could either spell or pronounce. Fiennes was obviously enmeshed with the first two, with whom for many purposes he appeared to be interchangeable.

After much thought and discussion, and the discarding of a number of farfetched hypotheses, the problem had been narrowed down to something manageable. Current argument ranged over three possible solutions: (a) the Scots Greys were commanded by a committee; (b) the regiment's RT discipline was more effective than had previously been believed. The use on the air of multiple aliases was undoubtedly confusing to their opponents; or (c) there was no such persons as Twisleton, Wykeham and Fiennes. The names were a front to mask the anonymity of an ingenious leader who was thought to be planning some unpleasant masterstroke.

Would the prisoner, after first please helping himself to another cigarette and if he so wished getting stuck into the brandy, care to comment?

The trooper lit up thoughtfully and considered the matter. He concluded that a truthful reply could bring no comfort to the enemy. 'If you're talking about the colonel,' he said laconically, 'I've never been able to work out what his name is either.'

THE STORMING OF THE REDOUBT (1829)

Prosper Mérimée

A MILITARY friend of mine who died of fever in Greece a few years ago once described to me the first engagement in which he had been involved. I was so struck by his account that I wrote it down from memory at the first opportunity. Here it is:

'I rejoined the regiment on the evening of 4 September. I found the colonel in the encampment. At first he received me fairly brusquely, but after he had read General B★★★★'s letter of recommendation his manner changed, and he spoke a few kind words to me.

'I was introduced by him to my captain, who had just that moment returned from a reconnaissance. The captain, whom I had little time to get to know, was a tall man with a dark complexion and a harsh, unattractive face. He had risen from the ranks, and had won his commission and his cross on the field of battle. His voice, which was hoarse and weak, contrasted oddly with his almost gargantuan stature. I was told that he owed this strange voice to a bullet that had pierced him clean through at the Battle of Jena.

'Learning that I was fresh from the military school at Fontainebleau, he pulled a wry face and said: "My lieutenant was killed yesterday."

'I realized that he meant, "You're going to have to take his place, and you're not up to it." An acid retort came to my lips, but I restrained myself.

'The moon rose behind the Cheverino redoubt, which was two cannon-shots distant from our encampment. It was large and red, as it often is when it rises. But that evening it seemed to me exceptionally large. For a moment the redoubt stood out, a black silhouette against the bright disc of the moon. It looked like the cone of a volcano during an eruption.

'An old soldier beside whom I was standing commented on the moon's colour.

' "It's very red," he said. "That's a sign that it will cost us dear to capture this precious redoubt we've heard so much about."

'I have always been superstitious, and this portent, especially coming at that particular moment, made a deep impression on me. I lay down but could not sleep. I got up and walked around for some time, looking at the immense line of camp-fires extending along the heights beyond the village of Cheverino.

'When I felt that my pulse had been sufficiently calmed by the fresh, keen night air, I returned to my place by the fire, wrapped myself carefully in my greatcoat, and closed my eyes, hoping not to open them again till daybreak. But sleep would not come to my aid. Imperceptibly my thoughts took a gloomy turn. I told myself I did not have a single friend among the hundred thousand men who covered that plain. If I was wounded I would be sent to a hospital and treated uncaringly by ignorant surgeons. I remembered all I had heard about surgical operations. My heart pounded violently, and mechanically I arranged my handkerchief and wallet against my breast, so as to act as a makeshift cuirass. I was dog-tired, yet every time I dozed off, some sinister thought would return with renewed force and wake me with a start.

'However, fatigue won out, and when reveille was sounded I was fast asleep. We fell in, the roll was called, then we piled arms again, and all the signs seemed to suggest that we were in for a quiet day.

'Around three o'clock an aide-de-camp arrived with a dispatch. We were again ordered to parade under arms. Our skirmishers spread out over the plain. We followed them slowly, and after twenty minutes we saw all the Russian outposts fall back and return into the redoubt.

'An artillery battery moved into position on our right flank, and another on our left, both well in advance of us. They began a heavy bombardment of the enemy, which met with a vigorous response, and the Cheverino redoubt soon disappeared behind thick clouds of smoke.

'Our regiment was almost protected from the Russian fire by an undulation of the ground. Their cannon-balls, few of which were intended for us (for they preferred to fire at our gunners), passed over our heads, or at worst showered us with earth and small stones.

'As soon as we were given the order to advance, my captain gave me a searching look, and I felt obliged to stroke my youthful moustache two or three times as nonchalantly as I was able. In fact, I was not afraid, my only concern being that someone might suppose I was afraid. Those harmless cannon-balls further contributed to my state of heroic calm. My pride told me I was in real danger, since I was under bombardment at last. I was delighted to find myself so unconcerned, and I thought of the pleasure I would derive from recounting the taking of the Cheverino redoubt, back in Madame de B★★★★'s salon in the rue de Provence.

'The colonel passed by our company. He spoke to me. "Well, it looks as if you're in for a stormy début."

'I gave him my most martial smile, brushing from my coat sleeve some dirt thrown up by a cannon-ball that had fallen thirty paces away.

'The Russians must have realized their cannon-balls were having little effect, because they started using shells, which could reach us more easily in the hollow where we were posted. A fairly large splinter knocked off my shako and killed a man standing beside me.

' "My compliments," said the captain as I rose from retrieving my shako. "You're safe now for the rest of the day."

'I had already come across this military superstition, which considers that the axiom *non bis in idem* is as valid on the battlefield as in a court of law. I proudly replaced my shako.

' "Rather a drastic way of getting you to raise your hat!" I said as cheerfully as I could. This poor joke struck me as excellent in the circumstances.

' "I congratulate you," continued the captain. "You'll come to no further harm, and you'll be commanding a company by this evening, for I can feel my number is up. Every time I've been wounded the officer beside me was hit by a spent bullet. And what's more," he added in an undertone, sounding almost ashamed, "their names all began with a P."

'I pretended to be unimpressed. Most people would have done the same; most people, too, would have been affected, as I was, by these prophetic words. As a raw recruit, I felt I could confide my feeling to no one, and that I must always appear calmly intrepid.

'After half an hour the Russian fire diminished appreciably. Thereupon we left our cover in order to march on the redoubt.

'Our regiment was composed of three battalions. The second was to outflank the redoubt from the entrance side; the other two were to make the assault. I was in the third battalion.

'Emerging from behind the sort of spur that had been protecting us, we were greeted by several volleys of rifle-fire, which inflicted only minor casualties among our ranks. The whistling of the bullets came as a surprise to me. I kept turning my head, eliciting some humorous comments from my comrades, who were more familiar with this sound than I was.

' "When all is said and done," I said to myself, "a battle isn't such a terrible thing."

'We were advancing at the double, preceded by skirmishers. Suddenly the Russians shouted "*Oura!*" three times – three distant cheers – then fell silent again and held their fire.

' "I don't like this silence," said the captain. "It bodes no good for us."

'I thought our own men were making rather too much noise, and I could not prevent myself from mentally comparing their tumultuous clamour with the enemy's imposing silence.

'We quickly reached the foot of the redoubt. The stockades had been shattered and the earth churned up by our cannon-balls. The soldiers threw themselves onto this latest scene of destruction, shouting "*Vive l'Empereur!*" louder than one would have expected of men who had already shouted so much.

'I raised my eyes, and never will I forget the sight I saw. Most of the smoke had risen, and remained hanging like a pall twenty feet above the redoubt. Through a bluish haze you could see the Russian grenadiers behind their half-destroyed parapet, with their rifles raised, motionless like statues. I can still see each soldier, his left eye fixed on us, his right eye concealed by his raised rifle. In an embrasure a few feet from us, a man stood by a field gun, holding a lighted fuse.

'I shuddered, and thought my final hour had come.

' "This is where the fun begins. Here goes!" cried the captain. Those were the last words I heard him speak.

'A roll of drums echoed around the redoubt. I saw all the rifles point down at us. I closed my eyes, and heard a dreadful crash followed by screams and groans. I opened my eyes again, surprised to find myself still alive. The redoubt was once again shrouded in smoke. I was surrounded by dead and wounded. The captain lay at my feet. His head had been shattered by a cannon-ball, and I was covered with his brains and blood. Out of my whole company only six soldiers and myself were left standing.

'A moment of stunned surprise followed this carnage. Placing his hat on the point of his sword, the colonel led the ascent of the parapet, shouting "*Vive l'Empereur!*" He was at once followed by all the survivors. I have virtually no clear recollection of what ensued. Somehow or other we entered the redoubt. We fought hand-to-hand amid smoke so thick that we could not see one another. I believe I struck home, for my sword had blood all over it. Finally I heard a shout of "Victory!" and, as the smoke dispersed, I saw that the floor of the redoubt was totally concealed by blood and corpses. The guns especially were buried beneath heaps of dead. About two hundred men in French uniforms stood around in disorganized groups, some loading their rifles, other wiping their bayonets. Among them were eleven Russian prisoners.

'The colonel lay on his back, covered in blood, on a shattered ammunition wagon near the entrance. Some soldiers were crowding around him. I approached.

' "Where's the senior captain?" he was asking the sergeant.

'The sergeant shrugged his shoulders eloquently.

' "And the senior lieutenant?"

' "This is the gentleman who arrived yesterday," said the sergeant imperturbably.

'The colonel smiled bitterly.

' "Well, sir," he said to me. "You are commander-in-chief. Have the entrance to the redoubt fortified at once with those wagons, the enemy is in force. But General C★★★★ will see to it that you are supported."

' "Colonel," I said, "are you seriously wounded?"

' "A b— goner, my boy. But the redoubt has been taken." '

HOW THE BRIGADIER CAPTURED SARAGOSSA

Sir Arthur Conan Doyle

HAVE I ever told you, my friends, the circumstances connected with my joining the Hussars of Conflans at the time of the siege of Saragossa, and the very remarkable exploit which I performed in connection with the taking of that city? No? Then you have indeed something still to learn. I will tell it to you exactly as it occurred. Save for two or three men and a score or two of women, you are the first who have ever heard the story.

You must know, then, that it was in the 2nd Hussars – called the Hussars of Chamberan – that I served as a lieutenant and as a junior captain. At the time I speak of I was only twenty-five years of age, as reckless and desperate a man as any in that great army. It chanced that the war had come to a halt in Germany, while it was still raging in Spain; so the Emperor, wishing to reinforce the Spanish army, transferred me as senior captain to the Hussars of Conflans, which were at that time in the 5th Army Corps under Marshal Lannes.

It was a long journey from Berlin to the Pyrenees. My new regiment formed part of the force which, under Marshal Lannes, was then besieging the Spanish town of Saragossa. I turned my horse's head in that direction, therefore, and behold me a week or so later at the French headquarters, whence I was directed to the camp of the Hussars of Conflans.

You have read, no doubt, of this famous siege of Saragossa, and I will only say that no general could have had a harder task than that with which Marshal Lannes was confronted. The immense city was crowded with a horde of Spaniards – soldiers, peasants, priests – all filled with the most furious hatred of the French, and the most savage determination to perish before they would surrender. There were eighty thousand men in the town and only thirty thousand to besiege them. Yet we had a powerful artillery, and our Engineers were of the best. There was never such a siege, for it is usual that when the fortifications are taken the city falls; but here it was not until the fortifications were taken that the real fighting began. Every house was a fort and every street a battlefield, so that slowly, day by day, we had to work our way inwards, blowing up the houses with their garrisons until more than half the city had disappeared. Yet the other half was as determined as ever, and in a better position for defence, since it consisted of enormous convents and monasteries with walls like the Bastille, which could not be so easily brushed out of our way. This was the state of things at the time that I joined the army.

I will confess to you that cavalry are not of much use in a siege, although there was a time when I would not have permitted anyone to have made such an observation. The Hussars of Conflans were encamped to the south of the town, and it was their duty to throw out patrols and to make sure that no Spanish force was advancing from that quarter. The colonel of the regiment was not a good soldier, and the regiment was at that time very far from being in the high condition which it afterwards attained. Even in that one evening I saw several things which shocked me; for I had a high standard, and it went to my heart to see an ill-arranged camp, an ill-groomed horse, or a slovenly trooper. That night I supped with twenty-six of my new brother-officers, and I fear that in my zeal I showed them only too plainly that I found things very different to what I was accustomed to in the army of Germany. There was silence in the mess after my remarks, and I felt that I had been indiscreet when I saw the glances that were cast at me. The colonel especially was furious, and a great major named Olivier, who was the fire-eater of the regiment, sat opposite to me curling his huge black moustaches, and staring at me as if he would eat me. However, I did not resent his attitude, for I felt that I had indeed been indiscreet, and that it would give a bad impression if upon this my first evening I quarrelled with my superior officer.

So far I admit that I was wrong, but now I come to the sequel. Supper over, the colonel and some other officers left the room, for it was in a farmhouse that the mess was held. There remained a

dozen or so, and a goat-skin of Spanish wine having been brought
in, we all made merry. Presently this Major Olivier asked me some
questions concerning the army of Germany and as to the part which
I had myself played in the campaign. Flushed with wine, I was
drawn on from story to story. It was not unnatural, my friends.
You will sympathize with me. Up there I had been the model for
every officer of my years in the army. I was the first swordsman,
the most dashing rider, the hero of a hundred adventures. Here I
found myself not only unknown, but even disliked. Was it not
natural that I should wish to tell these brave comrades what sort of
man it was that had come among them? Was it not natural that I
should wish to say, 'Rejoice, my friends, rejoice! It is no ordinary
man who has joined you tonight, but it is I, *the* Gerard, the hero of
Ratisbon, the victor of Jena, the man who broke the square at
Austerlitz'? I could not say all this. But I could at least tell them
some incidents which would enable them to say it for themselves.
I did so. They listened unmoved. I told them more. At last, after
my tale of how I had guided the army across the Danube, one
universal shout of laughter broke from them all. I sprang to my
feet, flushed with shame and anger. They had drawn me on. They
were making game of me. They were convinced that they had to
do with a braggart and a liar. Was this my reception in the Hussars
of Conflans? I dashed the tears of mortification from my eyes, and
they laughed the more at the sight.

'Do you know, Captain Pelletan, whether Marshal Lannes is still
with the army?' asked the major.

'I believe that he is, sir,' said the other.

'Really, I should have thought that his presence was hardly necessary now that Captain Gerard has arrived.'

Again there was a roar of laughter. I can see the ring of faces, the
mocking eyes, the open mouths – Olivier with his great black
bristles, Pelletan thin and sneering, even the young sub-lieutenants
convulsed with merriment. Heavens, the indignity of it! But my
rage had dried my tears. I was myself again, cold, quiet, self-
contained, ice without and fire within.

'May I ask, sir,' said I to the major, 'at what hour the regiment
is paraded?'

'I trust, Captain Gerard, that you do not mean to alter our hours,' said he, and again there was a burst of laughter, which died away as I looked slowly round the circle.

'What hour is the assembly?' I asked, sharply, of Captain Pelletan.

Some mocking answer was on his tongue, but my glance kept it there. 'The assembly is at six,' he answered.

'I thank you,' said I. I then counted the company, and found that I had to do with fourteen officers, two of whom appeared to be boys fresh from St Cyr. I could not condescend to take any notice of their indiscretion. There remained the major, four captains, and seven lieutenants.

'Gentlemen,' I continued, looking from one to the other of them, 'I should feel myself unworthy of this famous regiment if I did not ask you for satisfaction for the rudeness with which you have greeted me, and I should hold you to be unworthy of it if on any pretext you refused to grant it.'

'You will have no difficulty upon that score,' said the major. 'I am prepared to waive my rank and to give you every satisfaction in the name of the Hussars of Conflans.'

'I thank you,' I answered. 'I feel, however, that I have some claim upon these other gentlemen who laughed at my expense.'

'Whom would you fight, then?' asked Captain Pelletan.

'All of you,' I answered.

They looked in surprise from one to the other. Then they drew off to the other end of the room, and I heard the buzz of their whispers. They were laughing. Evidently they still thought that they had to do with some empty braggart. Then they returned.

'Your request is unusual,' said Major Olivier, 'but it will be granted. How do you propose to conduct such a duel? The terms lie with you.'

'Sabres,' said I. 'And I will take you in order of seniority, beginning with you, Major Olivier, at five o'clock. I will thus be able to devote five minutes to each before the assembly is blown. I must, however, beg you to have the courtesy to name the place of meeting, since I am still ignorant of the locality.'

They were impressed by my cold and practical manner. Already the smile had died away from their lips. Olivier's face was no longer mocking, but it was dark and stern.

'There is a small open space behind the horse lines,' said he. 'We have held a few affairs of honour there, and it has done very well. We shall be there, Captain Gerard, at the hour you name.'

I was in the act of bowing to thank them for their acceptance when the door of the mess-room was flung open and the colonel hurried into the room, with an agitated face.

'Gentlemen,' said he, 'I have been asked to call for a volunteer from among you for a service which involves the greatest possible danger. I will not disguise from you that the matter is serious in the last degree, and that Marshal Lannes has chosen a cavalry officer because he can be better spared than an officer of infantry or of Engineers. Married men are not eligible. Of the others, who will volunteer?'

I need not say that all the unmarried officers stepped to the front. The colonel looked round in some embarrassment. I could see his dilemma. It was the best man who should go, and yet it was the best man whom he could least spare.

'Sir,' said I, 'may I be permitted to make a suggestion?'

He looked at me with a hard eye. He had not forgotten my observations at supper. 'Speak!' said he.

'I would point out, sir,' said I, 'that this mission is mine both by right and by convenience.'

'Why so, Captain Gerard?'

'By right, because I am the senior captain. By convenience, because I shall not be missed in the regiment, since the men have not yet learned to know me.'

The colonel's features relaxed.

'There is certainly truth in what you say, Captain Gerard,' said he. 'I think that you are indeed best fitted to go upon this mission. If you will come with me I will give you your instructions.'

I wished my new comrades good night as I left the room, and I repeated that I should hold myself at their disposal at five o'clock next morning. They bowed in silence, and I thought that I could see, from the expression of their faces, that they had already begun to take a more just view of my character.

I had expected that the colonel would at once inform me what it was that I had been chosen to do, but instead of that he walked on in silence, I following behind him. We passed through the camp and made our way across the trenches and over the ruined heaps of stones which marked the old wall of the town. Within there was a labyrinth of passages, formed among the débris of the houses which had been destroyed by the mines of the Engineers. Acres and acres were covered with splintered walls and piles of brick which had once been a populous suburb. Lanes had been driven through it and lanterns placed at the corners with inscriptions to direct the wayfarer. The colonel hurried onwards until at last, after a long walk, we found our way barred by a high grey wall which stretched right across our path. Here behind a barricade lay our advanced guard. The colonel led me into a roofless house, and there I found two general officers, a map stretched over a drum in front of them, they kneeling beside it and examining it carefully by the light of a lantern. The one with the clean-shaven face and the twisted neck was Marshal Lannes, the other was General Razout, the head of the Engineers.

'Captain Gerard has volunteered to go,' said the colonel.

Marshal Lannes rose from his knees and shook me by the hand.

'You are a brave man, sir,' said he. 'I have a present to make to you,' he added, handing me a very tiny glass tube. 'It has been specially prepared by Dr Fardet. At the supreme moment you have but to put it to your lips and you will be dead in an instant.'

This was a cheerful beginning. I will confess to you, my friends, that a cold chill passed up my back and my hair rose upon my head.

'Excuse me, sir,' said I, as I saluted, 'I am aware that I have volunteered for a service of great danger, but the exact details have not yet been given to me.'

'Colonel Perrin,' said Lannes severely, 'it is unfair to allow this brave officer to volunteer before he has learned what the perils are to which he will be exposed.'

But already I was myself once more.

'Sir,' said I, 'permit me to remark that the greater the danger the greater the glory, and that I could only repent of volunteering if I found that there were no risks to be run.'

It was a noble speech, and my appearance gave force to my words. For the moment I was an heroic figure. As I saw Lannes's eyes fixed in admiration upon my face it thrilled me to think how splendid was the début which I was making in the army of Spain. If I died that night my name would not be forgotten. My new comrades and my old, divided in all else, would still have a point of union in their love and admiration of Etienne Gerard.

'General Razout, explain the situation!' said Lannes, briefly.

The Engineer officer rose, his compasses in his hand. He led me to the door and pointed to the high grey wall which towered up amongst the débris of the shattered houses.

'That is the enemy's present line of defence,' said he. 'It is the wall of the great Convent of the Madonna. If we can carry it the city must fall, but they have run counter-mines all round it, and the walls are so enormously thick that it would be an immense labour to breach it with artillery. We happen to know, however, that the enemy have a considerable store of powder in one of the lower chambers. If that could be exploded the way would be clear for us.'

'How can it be reached?' I asked.

'I will explain. We have a French agent within the town named Hubert. This brave man has been in constant communication with us, and he had promised to explode the magazine. It was to be done in the early morning, and for two days running we have had a storming party of a thousand Grenadiers waiting for the breach to be formed. But there has been no explosion, and for these two days we have had no communication from Hubert. The question is, what has become of him?'

'You wish me to go and see?'

'Precisely. Is he ill, or wounded, or dead? Shall we still wait for him, or shall we attempt the attack elsewhere? We cannot determine this until we have heard from him. This is a map of the town, Captain Gerard. You perceive that within this ring of convents and monasteries are a number of streets which branch off from a central square. If you come so far as this square you will find the cathedral at one corner. In that corner is the street of Toledo. Hubert lives in a small house between a cobbler's and a wine-shop, on the right-hand side as you go from the cathedral. Do you follow me?'

'Clearly.'

'You are to reach that house, to see him, and to find out if his plan is still feasible or if we must abandon it.' He produced what appeared to be a roll of dirty brown flannel. 'This is the dress of a Franciscan friar,' said he. 'You will find it the most useful disguise.'

I shrank away from it.

'It turns me into a spy,' I cried. 'Surely I can go in my uniform?'

'Impossible! How could you hope to pass through the streets of the city? Remember, also, that the Spaniards take no prisoners, and that your fate will be the same in whatever dress you are taken.'

It was true, and I had been long enough in Spain to know that that fate was likely to be something more serious than mere death. All the way from the frontier I had heard grim tales of torture and mutilation. I enveloped myself in the Franciscan gown.

'Now I am ready.'

'Are you armed?'

'My sabre.'

'They will hear it clank. Take this knife and leave your sword. Tell Hubert that at four o'clock before dawn the storming party will again be ready. There is a sergeant outside who will show you how to get into the city. Good night and good luck!'

Before I had left the room the two generals had their cocked hats touching each other over the map. At the door an under-officer of Engineers was waiting for me. I tied the girdle of my gown, and taking off my busby I drew the cowl over my head. My spurs I removed. Then in silence I followed my guide.

It was necessary to move with caution, for the walls above were lined by the Spanish sentries, who fired down continually at our advanced posts. Slinking along under the very shadow of the great convent, we picked our way slowly and carefully among the piles of ruins until we came to a large chestnut tree. Here the sergeant stopped.

'It is an easy tree to climb,' said he. 'A scaling ladder would not be simpler. Go up it, and you will find that the top branch will enable you to step upon the roof of that house. After that it is your guardian angel who must be your guide, for I can help you no more.'

Girding up the heavy brown gown, I ascended the tree as directed. A half-moon was shining brightly, and the line of roof stood out dark and hard against the purple, starry sky. The tree was in the shadow of the house. Slowly I crept from branch to branch until I was near the top. I had but to climb along a stout limb in order to reach the wall. But suddenly my ears caught the patter of feet, and I cowered against the trunk and tried to blend myself with its shadow. A man was coming towards me on the roof. I saw his dark figure creeping along, his body crouching, his head advanced, the barrel of his gun protruding. His whole bearing was full of caution and suspicion. Once or twice he paused, and then came on again until he had reached the edge of the parapet within a few yards of me. Then he knelt down, levelled his musket, and fired.

I was so astonished at this sudden crash at my very elbow that I nearly fell out of the tree. For an instant I could not be sure that he had not hit me. But when I heard a deep groan from below, and the Spaniard leaned over the parapet and laughed aloud, I understood what had occurred. It was my poor, faithful sergeant who had waited to see the last of me. The Spaniard had seen him standing under the tree and had shot him. You will think that it was good shooting in the dark, but these people use *trebucos*, or blunderbusses, which are filled up with all sorts of stones and scraps of metal, so that they will hit you as certainly as I have hit a pheasant on a branch. The Spaniard stood peering down through the darkness, while an occasional groan from below showed that the sergeant was still living. The sentry looked round and everything was still and safe. Perhaps he thought that he would like to finish off this accursed Frenchman, or perhaps he had a desire to see what was in his pockets; but whatever his motive he laid down his gun, leaned forward, and swung himself into the tree. The same instant I buried my knife in his body, and he fell with a loud crashing through the branches and came with a thud to the ground. I heard a short struggle below and an oath or two in French. The wounded sergeant had not waited long for his vengeance.

For some minutes I did not dare to move, for it seemed certain that someone would be attracted by the noise. However, all was silent save for the chimes striking midnight in the city. I crept along the branch and lifted myself on to the roof. The Spaniard's gun was lying there, but it was of no service to me, since he had the powder-horn at his belt. At the same time, if it were found it would warn the enemy that something had happened, so I thought it best to drop it over the wall. Then I looked round for the means of getting off the roof and down into the city.

It was very evident that the simplest way by which I could get down was that by which the sentinel had got up, and what this was soon became evident. A voice along the roof called 'Manuelo! Manuelo!' several times, and, crouching in the shadow, I saw in the moonlight a bearded head, which protruded from a trap-door. Receiving no answer to his summons the man climbed through, followed by three other fellows all armed to the teeth. You will see here how important it is not to neglect small precautions, for had I left the man's gun where I found it a search must have followed, and I should certainly have been discovered. As it was, the patrol saw no sign of their sentry and thought, no doubt, that he had moved along the line of roofs. They hurried on, therefore, in that direction, and I, the instant that their backs were turned, rushed to the open trap-door and descended the flight of steps which led from it. The house appeared to be an empty one, for I passed through the heart of it and out, by an open door, into the street beyond.

It was a narrow and deserted lane, but it opened into a broader road, which was dotted with fires, round which a great number of soldiers and peasants were sleeping. The smell within the city was so horrible that one wondered how people could live in it, for during the months that the siege had lasted there had been no attempt to cleanse the streets or to bury the dead. Many people were moving up and down from fire to fire, and among them I observed several monks. Seeing that they came and went unquestioned, I took heart and hurried on my way in the direction of the great square. Once a man rose from beside one of the fires and stopped me by seizing my sleeve. He pointed to a woman who lay motionless upon the road, and I took him to mean that she was dying, and that he desired me to administer the last offices of the Church. I sought refuge, however, in the very little Latin that was left to me. '*Ora pro nobis,*' said I, from the depths of my cowl. '*Te deum laudamus. Ora pro nobis.*' I raised my hand as I spoke and pointed forwards. The fellow released my sleeve and shrank back in silence, while I, with solemn gesture, hurried upon my way.

As I had imagined, this broad boulevard led out into the central square, which was full of troops and blazing with fires. I walked swiftly onwards, disregarding one or two people who addressed remarks to me. I passed the cathedral and followed the street which had been described to me. Being upon the side of the city which was farthest from our attack, there were no troops encamped in it, and it lay in darkness, save for an occasional glimmer in a window. It was not difficult to find the house to which I had been directed, between the wine-shop and the cobbler's. There was no light within, and the door was shut. Cautiously I pressed the latch, and I felt that it had yielded. Who was within I could not tell, and yet I must take the risk. I pushed the door open and entered.

It was pitch-dark within – the more so as I had closed the door behind me. I felt round and came upon the edge of a table. Then I stood still and wondered what I should do next, and how I could gain some news of this Hubert, in whose house I found myself. Any mistake would cost me not only my life, but the failure of my mission. Perhaps he did not live alone. Perhaps he was only a lodger in a Spanish family, and my visit might bring ruin to him as well as to myself. Seldom in my life have I been more perplexed. And then, suddenly, something turned my blood cold in my veins. It was a voice, a whimpering voice, in my very ear. 'Mon Dieu!' cried the voice in a tone of agony. 'Oh, mon Dieu! mon Dieu!' Then there was a dry sob in the darkness, and all was still once more.

It thrilled me with horror, that terrible voice; but it thrilled me also with hope, for it was the voice of a Frenchman.

'Who is there?' I asked.

There was a groaning, but no reply.

'Is that you, Monsieur Hubert?'

'Yes, yes,' sighed the voice, so low that I could hardly hear it. 'Water, water, for Heaven's sake, water!'

I advanced in the direction of the sound, but only to come in contact with the wall. Again I heard a groan, but this time there could be no doubt that it was above my head. I put up my hands, but they felt only empty air.

'Where are you?' I cried.

'Here! Here!' whispered the strange, tremulous voice. I stretched my hand along the wall, and I came upon a man's naked foot. It was as high as my face, and yet, so far as I could feel, it had nothing to support it. I staggered back in amazement. Then I took a tinder-box from my pocket and struck a light. At the first flash a man seemed to be floating in the air in front of me, and I dropped the box in amazement. Again, with tremulous fingers, I struck the flint against the steel, and this time I lit not only the tinder, but the wax taper. I held it up, and if my amazement was lessened, my horror was increased by that which it revealed.

The man had been nailed to the wall as a weasel is nailed to the door of a barn. Huge spikes had been driven through his hands and his feet. The poor wretch was in his last agony, his head sunk upon his shoulder and his blackened tongue protruded from his lips. He was dying as much from thirst as from his wounds, and these inhuman wretches had placed a beaker of wine upon the table in front of him to add a fresh pang to his tortures. I raised it to his lips. He had still strength enough to swallow, and the light came back a little to his dim eyes.

'Are you a Frenchman?' he whispered.

'Yes. They have sent me to learn what had befallen you.'

'They discovered me. They have killed me for it. But before I die let me tell you what I know. A little more of that wine, please! Quick! Quick! I am very near the end. My strength is going. Listen to me! The powder is stored in the Mother Superior's room. The wall is pierced, and the end of the train is in Sister Angela's cell, next the chapel. All was ready two days ago. But they discovered a letter, and they tortured me.'

'Good Heavens! have you been hanging here for two days?'

'It seems like two years. Comrade, I have served France, have I not? Then do one little service for me. Stab me to the heart, dear friend! I implore you, I entreat you, to put an end to my sufferings.'

The man was indeed in a hopeless plight, and the kindest action would have been that for which he begged. And yet I could not in cold blood drive my knife into his body, although I knew how I should have prayed for such a mercy had I been in his place. But a sudden thought crossed my mind. In my pocket I held that which would give an instant and painless death. It was my own safeguard against torture, and yet this poor soul was in very pressing need of it, and he had deserved well of France.

I took out my phial and emptied it into the cup of wine. I was in the act of handing it to him when I heard a sudden clash of arms outside the door. In an instant I put out my light and slipped behind the window-curtains. Next moment the door was flung open, and two Spaniards strode into the room – fierce, swarthy men in the dress of citizens, but with muskets slung over their shoulders. I looked through the chink in the curtains in an agony of fear lest they had come upon my traces, but it was evident that their visit was simply in order to feast their eyes upon my unfortunate compatriot. One of them held the lantern which he carried up in front of the dying man, and both of them burst into a shout of mocking laughter. Then the eyes of the man with the lantern fell upon the flagon of wine upon the table. He picked it up, held it, with a devilish grin, to the lips of Hubert, and then, as the poor wretch involuntarily inclined his head forward to reach it, snatched it back and took a long gulp himself. At the same instant he uttered a loud cry, clutched wildly at his own throat, and fell stone dead upon the floor. His comrade stared at him in horror and amazement. Then, overcome by his own superstitious fears, he gave a yell of terror and rushed madly from the room. I heard his feet clattering wildly on the cobble-stones until the sound died away in the distance.

The lantern had been left burning upon the table, and by its light I saw, as I came out from behind the curtain, that the unfortunate Hubert's head had fallen forward upon his chest and that he also was dead. That motion to reach the wine with his lips had been his last. A clock ticked loudly in the house, but otherwise all was absolutely still. On the wall hung the twisted form of the Frenchman, on the floor lay the motionless body of the Spaniard, all dimly lit by the horn lantern. For the first time in my life a frantic spasm of terror came over me. I had seen ten thousand men in every conceivable degree of mutilation stretched upon the ground, but the sight had never affected me like those two silent figures who were my companions in that shadowy room. I rushed into the street as the Spaniard had done, eager only to leave that house of gloom behind me, and I had run as far as the cathedral before my wits came back to me. There I stopped panting in the shadow, and, my hand pressed to my side, I tried to collect my scattered senses and to plan out what I should do. As I stood there, breathless, the great brass bells roared twice above my head. It was two o'clock. Four was the hour when the storming party would be in its place. I had still two hours in which to act.

The cathedral was brilliantly lit within, and a number of people were passing in and out; so I entered, thinking that I was less likely to be accosted there and that I might have quiet to form my plans. It was certainly a singular sight, for the place had been turned into a hospital, a refuge and a storehouse. One aisle was crammed with provisions, another was littered with sick and wounded, while in the centre a great number of helpless people had taken up their abode and had even lit their cooking fires upon the mosaic floors. There were many at prayer, so I knelt in the shadow of a pillar and I prayed with all my heart that I might have the good luck to get out of this scrape alive, and that I might do such a deed that night as would make my name as famous in Spain as it had become in

Germany. I waited until the clock struck three and then I left the cathedral and made my way towards the Convent of the Madonna, where the assault was to be delivered. You will understand, you who know me so well, that I was not the man to return tamely to the French camp with the report that our agent was dead and that other means must be found of entering the city. Either I should find some means to finish the uncompleted task or there would be a vacancy for a senior captain in the Hussars of Conflans.

I passed unquestioned down the broad boulevard, which I have already described, until I came to the great stone convent which formed the outwork of the defence. It was built in a square with a garden in the centre. In this garden some hundreds of men were assembled, all armed and ready, for it was known, of course, within the town that this was the point against which the French attack was likely to be made. Up to this time our fighting all over Europe had always been done between one army and another. It was only here in Spain that we learned how terrible a thing it is to fight against a people. On the one hand there is no glory, for what glory could be gained by defeating this rabble of elderly shopkeepers, ignorant peasants, fanatical priests, excited women and all the other creatures who made up the garrison? On the other hand there were extreme discomfort and danger, for these people would give you no rest, would observe no rules of war and were desperately earnest in their desire by hook or by crook to do you an injury. I began to realize how odious was our task as I looked upon the motley but ferocious groups who were gathered round the watch fires in the garden of the Convent of the Madonna. It was not for us soldiers to think about politics, but from the beginning there always seemed to be a curse upon this war in Spain.

However, at the moment I had no time to brood over such matters as these. There was, as I have said, no difficulty in getting as far as the convent garden, but to pass inside the convent unquestioned was not so easy. The first thing which I did was to walk round the garden, and I was soon able to pick out one large stained-glass window which must belong to the chapel. I had understood from Hubert that the Mother Superior's room in which the powder was stored was near to this, and that the train had been laid through a hole in the wall from some neighbouring cell. I must at all costs get into the convent. There was a guard at the door, and how could

I get in without explanations? But a sudden inspiration showed me how the thing might be done. In the garden was a well, and beside the well were a number of empty buckets. I filled two of these and approached the door. The errand of a man who carries a bucket of water in each hand does not need to be explained. The guard opened to let me through. I found myself in a long stone-flagged corridor lit with lanterns, with the cells of the nuns leading out from one side of it. Now at last I was on the high road to success. I walked on without hesitation, for I knew by my observations in the garden which way to go for the chapel.

A number of Spanish soldiers were lounging and smoking in the corridor, several of whom addressed me as I passed. I fancy it was for my blessing that they asked, and my '*Ora pro nobis*' seemed to entirely satisfy them. Soon I had got as far as the chapel, and it was easy to see that the cell next door was used as a magazine, for the floor was all black with powder in front of it. The door was shut, and two fierce-looking fellows stood on guard outside it, one of them with a key stuck in his belt. Had we been alone it would not have been long before it would have been in my hand, but with his comrade there it was impossible for me to hope to take it by force. The cell next door to the magazine on the far side from the chapel must be the one which belonged to Sister Angela. It was half open. I took my courage in both hands, and leaving my buckets in the corridor, I walked unchallenged into the room.

I was prepared to find half a dozen fierce Spanish desperadoes within, but what actually met my eyes was even more embarrassing. The room had apparently been set aside for the use of some of the nuns, who for some reason had refused to quit their home. Three of them were within, one an elderly, stern-faced dame who was evidently the Mother Superior, the other young ladies of charming appearance. They were seated together at the far side of the room, and I saw with some amazement, by their manner and expressions, that my coming was both welcome and expected. In a moment my presence of mind had returned, and I saw exactly how the matter lay. Naturally, since an attack was about to be made upon the convent, these sisters had been expecting to be directed to some place of safety. Probably they were under vow not to quit the walls, and they had been told to remain in this cell until they had received further orders. In any case I adapted my conduct to this supposition, since it was clear that I must get them out of the room, and this would give me a ready excuse to do so. I first cast a glance at the door and observed that the key was within. I then made a gesture to the nuns to follow me. The Mother Superior asked me some question, but I shook my head impatiently and beckoned to her again. She hesitated, but I stamped my foot and called them forth in so imperious a manner that they came at once. They would be safer in the chapel, and thither I led them, placing them at the end which was farthest from the magazine. As the three nuns took their places before the altar my heart bounded with joy and pride within me, for I felt that the last obstacle had been lifted from my path.

And yet how often have I not found that this is the very moment of danger? I took a last glance at the Mother Superior, and to my dismay I saw that her piercing dark eyes were fixed, with an expression in which surprise was deepening into suspicion, upon my right hand. There were two points which might well have attracted her attention. One was that it was red with the blood of the sentinel whom I had stabbed in the tree. That alone might count for little, as the knife is as familiar as the breviary to the monks of Saragossa. But on my forefinger I wore a heavy gold ring – the gift of a German baroness whose name I may not mention. It shone brightly in the light of the altar lamp. Now, a ring upon a friar's hand is an impossibility, since they are vowed to absolute poverty. I turned quickly and made for the door of the chapel, but the mischief was done. As I glanced back I saw that the Mother Superior was already hurrying after me. I ran through the chapel door and along the corridor, but she called out some shrill warning to the two guards in front. Fortunately I had the presence of mind to call out also, and to point down the passage as if we were both pursuing the same object. Next instant I had dashed past them, sprang into the cell, slammed the heavy door, and fastened it upon the inside. With a bolt above and below and a huge lock in the centre it was a piece of timber that would take some forcing.

Even now if they had had the wit to put a barrel of gunpowder against the door I should have been ruined. It was their only chance, for I had come to the final stage of my adventure. Here at last, after such a string of dangers as few men have ever lived to talk of I was at one end of the powder train, with the Saragossa magazine at the other. They were howling like wolves out in the passage, and muskets were crashing against the door. I paid no heed to their clamour, but I looked eagerly round for that train of which Hubert had spoken. Of course, it must be at the side of the room next to the magazine. I crawled along it on my hands and knees, looking into every crevice, but no sign could I see. Two bullets flew through the door and flattened themselves against the wall. The thudding and smashing grew ever louder. I saw a grey pile in a corner, flew to it with a cry of joy, and found that it was only dust. Then I got back to the side of the door where no bullets could ever reach me – they were streaming freely into the room – and I tried to forget this fiendish howling in my ear and to think out where this train could be. It must have been carefully laid by Hubert lest these nuns should see it. I tried to imagine how I should myself have arranged it had I been in his place. My eye was attracted by a statue of St Joseph which stood in the corner. There was a wreath of leaves along the edge of the pedestal, with a lamp burning amidst them. I rushed across to it and tore the leaves aside. Yes, yes, there was a thin black line, which disappeared through a small hole in the wall. I tilted over the lamp, and threw myself on the ground. Next instant came a roar like thunder, the walls wavered and tottered around me, the ceiling clattered down from above, and over the yell of the terrified Spaniards was heard the terrific shout of the storming column of the Grenadiers. As in a dream – a happy dream – I heard it, and then I heard no more.

When I came to my senses two French soldiers were propping me up, and my head was singing like a kettle. I staggered to my feet and looked around me. The plaster had fallen, the furniture was scattered, and there were rents in the bricks, but no signs of a breach. In fact, the walls of the convent had been so solid that the explosion of the magazine had been insufficient to throw them down. On the other hand, it had caused such a panic among the defenders that our stormers had been able to carry the windows and throw open the doors almost without resistance. As I ran out into the corridor I found it full of troops, and I met Marshal Lannes himself, who was entering with his staff. He stopped and listened eagerly to my story.

'Splendid, Captain Gerard, splendid!' he cried. 'These facts will certainly be reported to the Emperor.'

'I would suggest to your Excellency,' said I, 'that I have only finished the work that was planned and carried out by Monsieur Hubert, who gave his life for the cause.'

'His services will not be forgotten,' said the Marshal. 'Meanwhile, Captain Gerard, it is half-past four, and you must be starving after such a night of exertion. My staff and I will breakfast inside the city. I assure you that you will be an honoured guest.'

'I will follow your Excellency,' said I. 'There is a small engagement which detains me.'

He opened his eyes.

'At this hour?'

'Yes, sir,' I answered. 'My fellow-officers, whom I never saw until last night, will not be content unless they catch another glimpse of me the first thing this morning.'

'*Au revoir*, then,' said Marshal Lannes, as he passed upon his way.

I hurried through the shattered door of the convent. When I reached the roofless house in which we had held the consultation the night before, I threw off my gown, and I put on the busby and sabre which I had left there. Then, a Hussar once more, I hurried onwards to the grove which was our rendezvous. My brain was still reeling from the concussion of the powder, and I was exhausted by the many emotions which had shaken me during that terrible night. It is like a dream, all that walk in the first dim grey light of dawn, with the smouldering camp-fires around me and the buzz of the waking army. Bugles and drums in every direction were mustering the infantry, for the explosion and the shouting had told their own tale. I strode onwards until, as I entered the little clump of cork oaks behind the horse lines, I saw my twelve comrades waiting in a group, their sabres at their sides. They looked at me curiously as I approached. Perhaps with my powder-blackened face and my blood-stained hands I seemed a different Gerard to the young captain whom they had made game of the night before.

'Good morning, gentlemen,' said I. 'I regret exceedingly if I have kept you waiting, but I have not been master of my own time.'

They said nothing, but they still scanned me with curious eyes. I can see them now, standing in a line before me, tall men and short men, stout men and thin men; Olivier, with his warlike moustache;

the thin, eager face of Pelletan; young Oudin, flushed by his first duel; Mortier, with the sword-cut across his wrinkled brow. I laid aside my busby and drew my sword.

'I have one favour to ask you, gentlemen,' said I. 'Marshal Lannes has invited me to breakfast, and I cannot keep him waiting.'

'What do you suggest?' asked Major Olivier.

'That you release me from my promise to give you five minutes each, and that you will permit me to attack you all together.' I stood upon my guard as I spoke.

But their answer was truly beautiful and truly French. With one impulse the twelve swords flew from their scabbards and were raised in salute. There they stood, the twelve of them, motionless, their heels together, each with his sword upright before his face.

I staggered back from them. I looked from one to the other. For an instant I could not believe my eyes. They were paying me homage, these, the men who had jeered me! Then I understood it all. I saw the effect that I had made upon them and their desire to make reparation. When a man is weak he can steel himself against danger, but not against emotion. 'Comrades,' I cried, 'comrades – !' but I could say no more. Something seemed to take me by the throat and choke me. And then in an instant Olivier's arms were round me, Pelletan had seized me by the right hand, Mortier by the left, some were patting me on the shoulder, some were clapping me on the back, on every side smiling faces were looking into mine; and so it was that I knew that I had won my footing in the Hussars of Conflans.

THE RAID
(A Volunteer's Story. 1852)

Count Leo Tolstoy

O N 12th July Captain Hlopov came in at the low door of my mud-hut, wearing his epaulettes and his sabre – a full uniform, in which I had not seen him since I had arrived in the Caucasus.

'I have come straight from the colonel,' he said in reply to the look of inquiry with which I met him; 'our battalion is marching tomorrow.'

'Where to?' I asked.

'To N –. That's where the troops are to concentrate.'

'From there they will advance into action, I suppose?'

'Most likely.'

'Where? What do you think?'

'I don't think. I am telling you what I know. A Tatar galloped up last night with instructions from the general – the battalion to set off, taking two days' rations of biscuits. But where, and what for, and for how long – that, my dear sir, we don't ask; we're told to go and that's enough.'

'If you're only taking biscuit for two days, though, the troops won't be detained longer than that.'

'Oh, well, that doesn't prove anything. . .'

'How's that?' I asked with surprise.

'Why, they marched to Dargi taking biscuit for a week and were nearly a month there.'

'And can I go with you?' I asked after a short silence.

'You can, of course, but my advice is, better not go. Why should you run any risk?'

'No, you must allow me not to follow your advice; I have been a whole month here simply on the chance of seeing an action, and you want me to miss it.'

'Go, if you will. Only, wouldn't it be better to stay here, really? You could wait here till we came back, you could have some shooting, while we would go, as God wills! And that would be first-rate!' he said in such a persuasive tone that I really did feel for the first minute that it would be first-rate. I answered firmly, however, that I would not stay behind for any consideration.

'And what is there you haven't seen in it?' the captain went on, trying to persuade me. 'If you want to know what battles are like, read Mihailosky-Danilevsky's *Description of War* – it's a fine book. It's all described in detail there – where every corps was stationed and how the battles were fought.'

'But that's just what doesn't interest me,' I answered.

'What is it then? You simply want to see how men are killed, it seems? . . . In 1832 there was a civilian here too, a Spaniard, I think he was. He went on two expeditions with us, wearing a blue cloak of some sort . . . they did for him just the same. You can't astonish anybody here, my dear sir.'

Though I felt sore at the captain's putting such a despicable construction on my intentions, I did not attempt to set him right.

'Was he a brave man?' I asked.

'How can I tell? He used to be always in the front; wherever there was firing, he was in it.'

'Then he must have been brave,' I said.

'No, it doesn't follow that a man's brave because he thrusts himself where he's not wanted.'

'What do you call being brave then?'

'Brave? brave?' repeated the captain, with the air of a man to whom such a question is presented for the first time. '*He's a brave man who behaves as he ought,*' he said after a moment's reflection.

I recalled Plato's definition of bravery – *the knowledge of what one need and what one need not fear,* and in spite of the vagueness and looseness of expression in the captain's definition, I thought that the fundamental idea of both was not so different as might be supposed, and that the captain's definition was, indeed, more correct than the Greek philosopher's, because if he could have expressed himself like

Plato, he would probably have said that the brave man is he who fears only *what he ought to fear*, and not *what he need not fear*.

I wanted to explain my idea to the captain.

'Yes,' I said, 'it seems to me that in every danger there is a choice, and the choice made, for instance, under the influence of a sense of duty is bravery, while the choice made under the influence of a low feeling is cowardice, because the man who risks his life from vanity, or curiosity, or greed of gain, can't be called brave; while, on the other hand, a man who refuses to face danger from an honourable feeling of duty to his family, or simply on conscientious grounds, can't be called a coward.'

The captain looked at me with rather an odd expression while I was talking.

'Well, I'm not equal to proving that,' he said, filling his pipe, 'but we have an ensign who is fond of philosophizing. You must talk to him. He writes verses even.'

I had only met the captain in the Caucasus, though I knew a great deal about him in Russia. His mother, Marya Ivanovna Hlopov, was living on her small estate a mile and a half from my home. Before I set off for the Caucasus, I went to see her. The old lady was delighted that I was going to see her Pashenka, as she called the grey-headed elderly captain, and that I could, like a living letter, tell him how she was getting on, and take him a parcel from home. After regailing me with a capital pie and salted game, Marya Ivanovna went into her bedroom and fetched from there a rather large black amulet, with a black silk ribbon sewn on it.

'This is our Holy Guardian, Mother of the Burning Bush,' she said, crossing herself, and kissing the image of the Mother of God, before putting it into my hand, 'be so kind, sir, as to give it to him. When he went to the *Caucasus*, you know, I had a service sung for him, and made a vow that if he were alive and unhurt I would have that image made of the Holy Mother. Now it's eighteen years that our Guardian Lady and the holy saints have had mercy on him. He has not once been wounded, and yet what battles he has been in! . . . When Mihailo, who was with him, told me about it, would you believe it, it made my hair stand on end. If I hear anything about him, it's only from other people, though; he, dear boy, never writes a word to me about his campaigns – he's afraid of frightening me.'

It was only in the Caucasus, and then not from the captain, that

I learned that he had been four times severely wounded, and, I need hardly say, had written no more to his mother about his wounds than about his campaigns.

'So let him wear this holy figure now,' she went on; 'I send him my blessing with it. The Most Holy Guardian Mother will protect him! Let him always have it on him, especially in battles. Tell him, please, that his mother bids him.'

I promised to carry out her instructions exactly.

'I am sure you will like my Pashenka,' the old lady went on, 'he's such a dear boy! Would you believe it, not a year goes by without his sending me money, and Annushka, my daughter, has had a great deal of help from him, too . . . and it's all out of nothing but his pay! I am ever truly thankful to God,' she concluded, with tears in her eyes, 'for giving me such a son.'

'Does he often write to you?' I asked.

'Not often; usually only once a year; when he sends money, he'll send a word or two, but not else. "If I don't write, mother," he says, "it means that I'm alive and well; if anything, which God forbid, should happen, they'll write to you for me." '

When I gave the captain his mother's present – it was in my hut – he asked for a piece of tissue-paper, wrapped it carefully up and put it away. I gave him a minute account of his mother's daily life; the captain did not speak. When I finished, he turned away and was rather a long time filling his pipe in the corner.

'Yes, she's a splendid old lady!' he said without turning, in a rather husky voice. 'Will God send me back to see her again, I wonder?'

A very great deal of love and sadness was expressed in those simple words.

'Why do you serve here?' I said.

'I have to,' he answered with conviction. 'The double pay for active service means a great deal for a poor man like me.'

The captain lived carefully; he did not play; seldom drank, and smoked a cheap tobacco, which for some unknown reason he used to call not shag, but *Sambrotalik*. I liked the captain from the first; he had one of those quiet, straightforward Russian faces, into whose eyes one finds it pleasant and easy to look straight. But after this conversation I felt a genuine respect for him.

★

At four o'clock next morning the captain came to fetch me. He was wearing a frayed old coat without epaulettes, full Caucasian breeches, a white astrakhan cap with the wool shabby and yellowish, and he had an inferior-looking Asiatic sabre slung over his shoulder. The white Caucasian pony, on which he was mounted, held its head down, moved with little ambling paces, and incessantly shook its thin tail. Though there was nothing martial nor fine-looking about the good captain's appearance, it showed such indifference to everything surrounding him that it inspired an involuntary feeling of respect.

I did not keep him waiting a minute, but got on my horse at once, and we rode out of the fortress gates together.

The battalion was already some six hundred yards ahead of us and looked like a dark, compact heavy mass. We could only tell that they were infantry because the bayonets were seen like a dense mass of long needles and from time to time we caught snatches of the soldiers' song, the drum, and the exquisite tenor voice of the leading singer of the sixth company, which I had heard with delight more than once in the fortress. The road ran down the midst of a deep and wide ravine, along the bank of a little stream, which was at that time 'in play', that is to say, overflowing its banks. Flocks of wild pigeons were hovering about it, settling on its stony bank and then wheeling in the air and flying up in swift circles out of sight. The sun was not yet visible, but the very top of the cliff on the right side began to show patches of sunlight. The grey and whitish stones, the yellow-green moss, the dense bushes of Christ's thorn, dog-berries and dwarf elm, stood out with extraordinary sharpness, in the limpid golden light of sunrise. But the hollow and the opposite side of the ravine were damp and dark with a thick mist that hung over them in rolling uneven masses like smoke, and through it dimly one caught an elusive medley of changing hues, pale lilac, almost black, dark green and white. Straight before us, against the dark blue of the horizon, rose with startling clearness the dazzling, dead-white of the snow mountains, with their fantastic shadows and outlines that were daintily beautiful to the minutest detail. Grasshoppers, crickets, and thousands of other insects were awake in the high grass and filling the air with their shrill, incessant sounds. An infinite multitude of tiny bells seemed to be ringing just in one's ears. The air was full of the smell of water and grass and mist, of the smell, in fact, of a fine morning in summer.

The captain struck a light and lit his pipe; the smell of the *Sambrotalik* tobacco and of the tinder were exceptionally pleasant to me.

We kept on the side of the road so as to overtake the infantry more quickly. The captain seemed more thoughtful than usual. He did not take his Daghestan pipe out of his mouth, and at every yard gave a shove with his feet to urge on his pony, who, swaying from side to side, left a scarcely visible dark green track in the wet, long grass. An old cock pheasant flew up from under its very hoofs, with the gurgling cry and the whir of wings that sets a sportman's heart beating, and slowly rose in the air. The captain did not take the slightest notice of it.

We were almost overtaking the battalion when we heard the hoofs of a galloping horse behind us, and in the same instant a very pretty and boyish youth, in the uniform of an officer, and a high white astrakhan cap, galloped up. As he passed us, he smiled, nodded, and waved his whip . . . I had only time to notice that he sat his horse and held his reins with a certain individual grace, and that he had beautiful black eyes, a delicate nose, and only the faintest trace of moustache. I was particularly charmed at his not being able to help smiling when he saw we were admiring him. From that smile alone one could have been sure that he was very young.

'And what is it he's galloping to?' the captain muttered with an air of vexation, not removing his pipe from his lips.

'Who is that?' I asked him.

'Ensign Alanin, a subaltern of my company . . . It's only a month since he joined from the military school.'

'I suppose it's the first time he's going into action,' I said.

'That's just why he's so happy about it!' answered the captain, shaking his head with an air of profundity. 'Ah, youth!'

'Well, how can he help being glad? I can understand that for a young officer it must be very interesting.'

The captain did not speak for a couple of minutes.

'That's just what I say; it's youth!' he resumed in his bass voice. 'What is there to be pleased about before one knows what it's like! When you have been out often, you're not pleased at it. We've now, let us say, twenty officers on the march; that somebody will be killed or wounded, that's certain. Today it's my turn, tomorrow his, and next day another man's. So what is there to be happy about?'

The bright sun had scarcely risen from behind the mountains and begun to shine on the valley along which we were marching, when the billowy clouds of mist parted, and it became hot. The soldiers, with their guns and knapsacks on their backs, walked slowly along the dusty road; from time to time I heard snatches of Little Russian talk and laughter in the ranks. A few old soldiers in white canvas tunics – for the most part sergeants or corporals – marched along on the side of the road, smoking their pipes and talking soberly. The wagons, drawn by three horses and piled high with baggage, moved forward at a walking pace, stirring up a thick, immovable cloud of dust. The officers rode in front; some of them were jigiting, as they say in the Caucasus, that is, whipping up their horses till they made them prance some four times, and then sharply pulling them up with their heads on one side. Others entertained themselves with the singers, who, in spite of the stifling heat, untiringly kept up one song after another. About three hundred yards in front of the infantry, on a big white horse surrounded by Tatar cavalry, rode an officer famous in the regiment for his reckless daring, and for being a man who would tell the truth to anyone's face. He was a tall, handsome man, dressed in Asiatic style, in a black tunic with embroidered borders, leggings to match, new, richly-embroidered, closely-fitting shoes, a yellow Circassian coat and a tall astrakhan cap tilted backwards on his head. Over his chest and back he had bands of silver embroidery in which his powder-horn was thrust in front and his pistol behind. A second pistol and a dagger in a silver sheath hung at his belt. Over all this was girt a sabre in a red morocco case edged with embroidery, and over his shoulder was slung a rifle in a black case. His costume, his manner of riding and holding himself, and every movement he made showed that he was trying to look like a Tatar. He even spoke to the Tatars riding with him in a language I did not know. But from the puzzled and sarcastic looks the latter gave one another, I fancied that they did not understand him either. This was a young lieutenant, one of the so-called jigit-gallants who model themselves on Marlinsky and Lermontov. These men cannot see the Caucasus except through the prism of the 'heroes of our times', of Mullah-Nur, etc., and in every gesture they are guided not by their own tastes but by the example of these paragons.

The lieutenant, for instance, was perhaps fond of the society of ladies and persons of importance – generals, colonels, adjutants – I feel sure, indeed, that he was very fond of such society because he was excessively vain. But he thought it his imperative duty to turn his rough side to all people of consequence, though his rudeness after all never amounted to very much. And whenever a lady made her appearance at the fortress he felt bound to pass by her window with his boon companions, wearing a red shirt and with nothing but slippers on his bare feet, and to shout and swear as loudly as possible. But all this was not so much from a desire to offend her as to show her what splendid white legs he had, and how easy it would be to fall in love with him, if he chose to wish it.

Often he would go out at night into the mountains with two or three peaceable Tatars to lie in ambush by the wayside so as to waylay and kill hostile Tatars who might pass by, and though he felt more than once in his heart that there was nothing very daring in this, he felt bound to make men suffer because he affected to be disappointed in them for some reason and so affected to hate and despise them. Two objects he never removed from his person; a large ikon on his neck and a dagger which he wore over his shirt, even when he went to bed. He genuinely believed that he had enemies. To persuade himself that he must be avenged on someone and wipe out some insult with blood was his greatest enjoyment. He was convinced that the feelings of hatred, revenge and disdain for the human race were the loftiest and most poetical sentiments. But his mistress, a Circassian, of course, with whom I happened to become acquainted later on, told me that he was the kindest and gentlest of men, and that every evening after jotting down his gloomy reflections he made up his accounts on ruled paper and knelt down to say his prayers. And what sufferings he underwent simply to appear to himself what he wanted to be! For his comrades and the soldiers were unable to regard him as he wanted them to. On one of his night expeditions with his companions he chanced to wound one of the hostile tribesmen in the foot with a bullet and took him prisoner. This man lived for seven weeks after this in the lieutenant's quarters, and the latter tended him and looked after him as though he had been his dearest friend, and when his wound was healed let him go loaded with presents. Later on, when on one of his expeditions the lieutenant was retreating in a line of scouts and firing to keep back the enemy, he heard one among them call him by his name and his wounded guest came forward and invited the lieutenant by signs to do the same. The latter went forward to meet his visitor and shook hands with him. The mountaineers kept their distance and did not fire at him; but as soon as the lieutenant turned his horse several shot at him, and one bullet grazed him below the spine.

Another incident I saw myself. There was a fire in the fortress one night, and two companies of soldiers were engaged in putting it out. Suddenly the tall figure of a man on a coal-black horse appeared in the midst of the crowd, lighted up by the red glow of the fire. The figure pushed through the crowd and rode straight to the fire. Riding right up to it the lieutenant leaped off his horse and ran into the house, one side of which was in flames. Five minutes later he came out with his hair singed and a burn on his elbow, carrying in his coat two pigeons which he had rescued from the fire.

His surname was Rosenkranz; but he often talked of his origin, somehow tracing his descent from the Varengians, and proving unmistakably that he and his fathers before him were of the purest Russian blood.

The sun had passed the zenith and was casting hot rays across the baked air upon the parched earth. The dark blue sky was perfectly clear; only at the foot of the snow mountains whitish lilac clouds were beginning to gather. The still air seemed to be filled with a sort of transparent dust. It had become unbearably hot. When we had come half-way we reached a little stream where the troops halted. The soldiers, stacking up their rifles, rushed to the stream; the officer in command of the battalion sat down on a drum in the shade, and expressing in every feature of his face the full dignity of his grade, disposed himself for a meal with his officers. The captain lay down on the grass under the company's baggage-wagon. Gallant Lieutenant Rosenkranz and a few other young officers, squatting on outspread cloaks, were preparing for a carouse, as might be seen from the bottles and flagons set out around them and from the peculiar animation of the singers, who stood in a semi-circle round them, playing and whistling a Caucasian dancing-song to the tune of the Lesginka:

> 'Shamil plotted a rebellion
> In the years gone by
> Tri-ri, ra-ta-ti
> In the years gone by.'

Among these officers was the youthful ensign who had overtaken us in the morning. He was very amusing; his eyes were shining, his tongue faltered a little from time to time; he was longing to kiss everyone and to tell them all how he loved them. . . . Poor boy! He had not learned yet that he might seem ridiculous in feeling so, that his frankness and the affectionateness with which he approached everybody might set other people jeering at him instead of giving him the affection he longed for so much. Nor did he know either that when he flung himself down on his cloak, and leaning on his arm tossed back his thick black hair, he was exceedingly charming.

Two officers were sitting under a wagon playing 'fools', with a barrel for a card-table.

I listened with curiosity to the talk of the soldiers and the officers, and watched the expression of their faces attentively. But not in a single one of them could I discover a trace of the uneasiness I was feeling myself. Jokes, laughter, stories – all expressed the general carelessness and indifference to the danger before them. It was as though no one could conceive that some of them were destined not to come back along that road

At seven o'clock in the evening, dusty and wary, we entered the fortified gates of the fortress of N –. The sun was setting and casting a slanting pink light on the picturesque batteries of the fortress and its gardens full of tall poplars, on the tilled yellow fields, and on the white clouds, which, huddling about the snow mountains as though in mimicry, formed a chain as fantastic as beautiful. The new crescent moon looked like a transparent cloud on the horizon. In the Tatar village near the fortress, a Tatar on the roof of a hut was calling all the faithful to prayer. Our singers, with fresh energy and vigour, broke out again.

After resting and tidying myself up a little, I went to see an adjutant of my acquaintance to ask him to inform the general of my intentions. On the way from the outlying part of the town where I was staying I observed things I had not expected to find in the fortress of N –. An elegant victoria, in which I saw a fashionable hat and heard chatter in French, overtook me. From the open window of the commander's house floated the strains of some 'Lizanka' or 'Katenka' polka, played on a piano that was wretchedly out of tune. In the tavern by which I passed I saw several clerks sitting over glasses of beer with cigarettes in their hands, and I overheard one of them saying to the other: 'Excuse me . . . but as regards politics, Marya Grigoryevna is our leading lady.' A Jew, with bent figure and a sickly-looking face, wearing a shabby coat, was dragging along a squeaky, broken barrel-organ, and the whole suburb was echoing with the last bars of 'Lucia'. Two women with rustling skirts, silk kerchiefs on their heads, and bright-coloured parasols in their hands, swam by me on the wooden footpath. Before a low-pitched little house two girls, one in a pink and the other in a blue dress, stood with bare heads, going off into shrill artificial giggles, evidently in the hope of attracting the attention of officers as they walked by. Officers in new coats, white gloves and dazzling epaulettes swaggered jauntily about the streets and the boulevard.

I found my acquaintance on the ground-floor of the general's house. I had only just had time to explain what I wanted, and he to reply that it could easily be managed, when an elegant carriage, which I had noticed at the entrance, rolled past the window at which we were sitting. A tall, well-built man, in an infantry uniform with the epaulettes of a major, got out of the carriage and went towards the general's.

'Ah, excuse me, please,' said the adjutant, getting up, 'I must go to tell the general.'

'Who has come?' I asked.

'The countess,' he answered, and buttoning up his uniform he ran upstairs.

A few minutes later a short but very handsome man, in a coat without epaulettes, with a white cross at his button-hole, came out on to the steps. Behind him came the major, the adjutant and two

other officers. In the carriage, in the voice and in every gesture of
the general one could see that he was a man well aware of his own
great consequence.

'Bon soir, madame la comtesse,' he said, putting his hand in at
the carriage window.

A hand in a kid glove pressed his hand, and a pretty, smiling little
face under a yellow hat appeared at the carriage window.

Of the conversation, which lasted several minutes, I only heard,
in passing, the general say with a smile:

'Vous savez que j'ai fait vœu de combattre les infidèles, prenez
donc garde de le devenir.'

There was laughter in the carriage.

'Adieu donc, cher général.'

'Non, à revoir,' said the general, as he mounted the steps, 'n'ou-
bliez pas que je m'invite pour la soirée de demain.'

The carriage rolled away.

'Here, again, is a man,' I mused as I went back home, 'who has
everything a Russian can desire; rank, wealth, distinction – and on
the eve of a battle which will end, God only knows how, this man
is jesting with a pretty woman and promising to drink tea with her
next day, just as though he were meeting her at a ball!'

I met there, at the adjutant's, a man who amazed me even more.
He was a lieutenant of the K. regiment, a young man of almost
womanish timidity and gentleness. He had come to the adjutant to
pour out his anger and indignation against the persons who had, he
said, intrigued against his receiving a command in the coming
action. He said it was disgusting to behave in such a way, that it
was unworthy of comrades, that he should not forget it, etc. Intently
as I watched the expression of his face and listened to the sound of
his voice, I could not help believing that he was in earnest, that he
was deeply hurt and disappointed at not being allowed to fire at
Circassians and to expose himself to their fire. He was as sore as a
child who has been unjustly whipped . . . I was utterly unable to
understand it all.

The troops were to set off at ten o'clock in the evening. At half-
past eight I mounted my horse and rode to the general's, but as I
thought both he and the adjutant would be engaged, I waited in the

street, tied my horse to the fence and sat down on a projecting part of the wall, meaning to overtake the general as soon as he rode out.

The heat and glare of the sun had by now given place to the coolness of the night and the dim light of the new moon, which was beginning to set in a pale half-circle of light against the dark blue of the starry sky. Lights had begun to shine in the windows of houses and through the chinks in the shutters of the mud huts. The graceful poplars in the garden looked taller and blacker than ever standing up on the horizon against the whitewashed huts with the moonlight on their thatched roofs. Long shadows of the houses, trees and fences lay picturesquely on the shining, light, dusty road . . . By the river the frogs kept up an unceasing noise;[1] in the streets I could hear hurried footsteps and talk, and the tramp of a horse; from the suburb floated the sounds of a barrel-organ, first, 'The Winds do Blow', then some 'Aurora Waltz'.

I will not describe my musings; in the first place, because I should be ashamed to confess the gloomy images which hovered in haunting succession before my heart, while I saw nothing but gaiety and cheerfulness around me; and secondly, because they do not come into my story. I was so absorbed in my thoughts that I did not even notice that the bell had struck eleven o'clock and that the general and his suite had ridden by me. The rearguard was already at the gates of the fortress. I had much ado to get over the bridge in the crush of cannon, caissons, baggage and officers loudly shouting instructions.

When I had ridden out of the gates, I trotted after the troops moving silently in the darkness and stretching over almost a verst of road, and overtook the general. Above the heavy artillery and horsemen drawn out in one long line, above, over the guns, the officers and men, like a jarring discord in a slow solemn harmony, rose a German voice, shouting:

'Antichrist, give me a linstock!' and a soldier hurriedly calling: 'Shevchenko! the lieutenant's asking for a light!'

A great part of the sky was covered with long, dark grey clouds; stars shone dimly here and there between them. The moon had already sunk behind the near horizon of black mountains, visible on the right, and shed a faint tremulous twilight on their peaks in sharp

---

[1]The frogs in the Caucasus make a noise that has no resemblance to the croaking of Russian frogs.

contrast with the impenetrable darkness wrapped about their base. The air was warm and so still that it seemed as though not one blade of grass, not one cloud was stirring. It was so dark that one could not distinguish objects quite near at hand; at the sides of the road I seemed to see rocks, animals and strange figures of men, and I only knew they were bushes when I heard their rustling and felt the freshness of the dew with which they were covered. Before me I saw a compact heaving black mass followed by a few moving blurs; it was the vanguard of the cavalry with the general and his suite. A similar black mass was moving in the midst of us, but it was lower than the first; this was the infantry. So complete a silence reigned in the whole detachment that one could hear distinctly all the mingling sounds of the night, full of mysterious charm. The distant mournful howl of the jackals, sometimes like a wail of despair, sometimes like a chuckle, the shrill monotonous notes of the grasshopper, of the frog, of the quail, a vague approaching murmur, the cause of which I could not explain, and all those faintly audible night-movements of Nature, impossible to interpret or define, blended into one full melodious sound which we call the silence of the night. That silence was broken by, or rather mingled with, the dull thud of horses' hoofs and the rustle of the high grass under the slowly-moving detachment.

Only from time to time the rumble of a heavy gun, the jingling of bayonets, subdued talk, or the snort of a horse, was heard in the ranks.

All Nature seemed filled with peace-giving power and beauty.

Is there not room enough for men to live in peace in this fair world under this infinite starry sky? How is it that wrath, vengeance, or the lust to kill their fellow men, can persist in the soul of man in the midst of this entrancing Nature? Everything evil in the heart of man ought, one would think, to vanish in contact with Nature, in which beauty and goodness find their most direct expression.

We had been marching more than two hours. I felt shivery and began to be sleepy. The same indistinct objects rose dimly in the darkness; at a little distance a wall of blackness with the same moving blurs; close beside me the haunches of a white horse which paced along switching its tail and straddling its hind legs; a black in a white Circassian coat against which a rifle in a black case and the white stock of a pistol in an embroidered cover showed up distinctly; the glow of a cigarette lighting up a flaxen moustache, a beaver collar and a hand in a wash-leather glove.

I was bending over my horse's neck, closing my eyes, and I kept losing myself for a few minutes, till suddenly the familiar rustle and thud would arouse me; I looked about me and it seemed as though I were standing still while the black wall facing me was moving upon me, or that that wall was standing still and I should ride against it in another moment. At one such instant of awakening that unaccountable continuous murmur, which seemed to come closer and closer, sounded more loudly than ever; it was the sound of water. We had entered a deep ravine and were close upon a mountain stream which was at the time overflowing its banks.[1] The murmur grew louder, the damp grass was thicker and higher, the bushes were closer, and the horizon narrower. Here and there, against the dark background of the mountains, bright fires flared up and died down again in an instant.

'Tell me, please, what are those lights?' I asked in a whisper of a Tatar riding beside me.

'Why, don't you know?' he answered.

'No, I don't.'

'That's the mountaineer has tied straw to a stake and will wave the fire about,' he said in broken Russian.

'What's that for?'

'That every man may know the Russian is coming. Now in the villages,' he added, laughing, 'aie, aie, there'll be a fine upset; everyone will be dragging his belongings into hiding.'

'What! Do they know already in the mountains that the detachment is coming?' I asked.

'Aie! aie! To be sure he knows! He always knows! Our folks are like that.'

'Is Shamil, too, preparing to fight then?' I asked.

'Nay,' he answered, shaking his head. 'Shamil is not going to come out to fight. Shamil will send his chiefs and look through a tube from up above.'

'And does he live far away?'

'No, not far. Yonder to the left it will be ten versts.'

[1]The rivers in the Caucasus overflow their banks in July.

'How do you know?' I asked him. 'Have you been there?'

'I have. All of us have been in the mountains.'

'And have you seen Shamil?'

'Pich! Shamil is not to be seen by us. A hundred, three hundred, a thousand guards are round him. Shamil will be in the middle!' he said with an expression of servile admiration.

Glancing upwards into the sky, which had grown clearer, one could already discern a light in the east, and the Pleiades were already sinking to the horizon; but in the ravine along which we were marching it was damp and dark.

Suddenly, a little in front of us, several little lights began to glimmer, and at the same instant bullets whizzed by us with a sharp ping, and in the stillness all around us we heard shots in the distance and a loud piercing shriek. It was the enemy's advance picket. The Tatars of whom it consisted halloed, fired at random, and scattered in all directions.

All was silent. The general summoned the interpreter. A Tatar in a white Circassian coat rode up to him and, gesticulating and whispering, talked to him about something for rather a long time.

'Colonel Hasanov, give the orders that the line of scouts move into more open formation,' said the general, in a quiet, drawling, but very distinct voice.

The detachment had reached the river. The black mountains of the ravine were left behind; it began to grow light. The sky, upon which the pale, dim stars were hardly visible, seemed to be higher; the red glow of dawn began gleaming in the east; a fresh penetrating breeze sprang up from the west, and a shimmering mist rose like steam over the noisy river.

The guide pointed out the ford; the vanguard of the cavalry and the general with his suite followed. The water rose breast-high about the horses and rushed with extraordinary force between the white stones, which, in some places, were visible at the surface, and formed swirling, foaming eddies round the horses' legs. The horses, startled by the noise of the water, threw up their heads and pricked up their ears, but stepped steadily and warily over the uneven bottom against the current. Their riders lifted up their legs and their guns. The infantry soldiers, wearing literally nothing but their shirts, held their muskets above the water with their clothes and their knapsacks slung upon them. The men linked themselves arm-in-arm in lines of twenty, and one could see, by the strained expression of their faces, the effort with which they withstood the current. The artillery riders, with a loud shout, urged their horses into the water at a trot. The cannon and the green caissons, over which the water splashed from time to time, rumbled over the stony bottom; but the sturdy Cossack horses, pulling all together, and churning the water into foam, with wet tails and manes struggled out on the other side.

As soon as the crossing was over the general's face suddenly showed a certain gravity and thoughtfulness. He turned his horse, and with the cavalry trotted across a wide glade, shut in by woods, which stretched before us. The Cossack cavalry scouts scattered along the edge of the wood. We caught sight of a man on foot, in the wood, wearing a Circassian coat and cap; then a second . . . and a third. One of the officers said: 'There are the Tatars.' Then there was a puff of smoke from behind a tree . . . a shot . . . and another. Our volleys drowned the sound of the enemy's firing. Only now and then a bullet whizzing by with a deliberate note like the sound of a bee showed that all the firing was not on our side. Then the infantry at a run, and the artillery at a quick trot, passed through the line of scouts. We heard the deep bass notes of the cannon, the metallic click of the ejected cartridges, the hissing of shells, the crack of the musketry. The cavalry, the infantry and artillery were to be seen on all sides of the glade. The smoke of the cannon, of the shells and of the muskets melted away in the greenness of the wood and mingled with the mist. Colonel Hasanov galloped up to the general and pulled his horse up sharply.

'Your Excellency,' he said, raising his hand to his Circassian cap, 'give the order for the cavalry to charge; there are the flags.' And he pointed with his whip to some Tatars on horseback, before whom two men were riding with red and blue rags on sticks.

'Very well, Ivan Mihailovitch,' said the general.

The colonel immediately wheeled his horse round, waved his sabre in the air and shouted:

'Hurrah!'

'Hurrah! Hurrah! Hurrah!' rang out in the ranks, and the cavalry flew after him.

Everybody watched eagerly; there was one flag, then another, a third, and a fourth . . .

The enemy did not await the attack; they vanished into the wood and opened fire from there. Bullets flew more thickly.

'Quel charmant coup d'œil!' said the general, rising lightly in the saddle, in the English fashion, on his black slender-legged horse.

'Charmant,' answered the major, rolling his rs, and flicking his horse with a whip he rode up to the general. 'C'est un vrai plaisir que la guerre dans un aussi beau pays,' he said.

'Et surtout en bonne compagnie,' added the general with an affable smile.

The major bowed.

At that moment, with a rapid unpleasant hiss, one of the enemy's balls flew by, and something was hit; the moan of a wounded man was heard in the rear. This moan impressed me so strangely that all the charm of the picturesque battle scene was instantly lost for me; but no one but me apparently noticed it; the major seemed to be laughing with greater zest than ever; another officer finished a sentence he was uttering with perfect composure; the general looked in the opposite direction and said something in French with the serenest of smiles.

'Do you command us to answer their fire?' the officer in command of the artillery inquired, galloping up to the general.

'Yes, scare them a bit,' the general assented carelessly, lighting a cigar.

The battery was drawn up and a cannonade began. The earth groaned at the sound; there was a continual flash of light, and the smoke, through which one could scarcely discern the moving figures of the gunners, blinded the eyes.

The Tatar village was shelled. Again Colonel Hasanov rode up, and at the command of the general dashed into the village. The battle-cry rang out again, and the cavalry disappeared in the cloud of dust which it raised.

The spectacle was truly magnificent. To me, taking no part in the action, and unaccustomed to such things, one thing spoilt the impression: the movement, the excitement and the shouting all seemed to me superfluous. I could not help thinking of a man swinging his axe and hewing at the empty air.

★

The Tartar village had been taken by our troops, and not one of the enemy was left in it, when the general with his suite, to which I had attached myself, entered it.

The long clean huts, with their flat mud roofs and picturesque chimneys, were built upon uneven rocky crags, among which flowed a little stream. Upon one side lay green gardens lighted up by the brilliant sunshine and filled with huge pear trees and plum trees; on the other side loomed strange shadows – the tall, perpendicular stones of the graveyard, and tall wooden posts, adorned at the top with balls and different coloured flags. (These were the tombs of the *jigits*.)

The troops stood drawn up in order by the gate. A minute later the dragoons, Cossacks and the infantry, with evident delight, scattered among the crooked by-ways and the empty village was instantly full of life again. Here a roof was being broken down; we heard the ring of an axe against hard wood as a door was smashed in; in another place a haystack was blazing, a fence and a hut were on fire and the smoke rose in dense clouds into the clear air. Here a Cossack was hauling along a sack of flour and a rug. A soldier with a gleeful face was pulling a tin pan and a rag of some sort out of a hut; another was trying with outstretched arms to capture two hens which were cackling loudly and fluttering against a fence; a third had found somewhere a huge pot of milk; he drank from it, and then with a loud laugh flung it on the ground.

The battalion with which I had come from Fort N – was also in the village. The captain was sitting on the roof of a hut and was puffing clouds of *Sambrotalik* tobacco smoke from a short pipe with such an unconcerned air that when I caught sight of him I forgot that I was in an enemy's village and felt as though I were quite at home.

'Ah, you are here, too!' he said, observing me.

The tall figure of Lieutenant Rosenkranz darted hither and thither about the village; he was incessantly shouting commands and had the air of a man extremely worried about something. I saw him come out of a hut with a triumphant air; two soldiers following him out, leading an old Tatar with his hands bound. The old man, whose whole attire consisted of a torn parti-coloured tunic and ragged breeches, was so decrepit that his bony arms, bound tightly behind his back, seemed to be coming off his shoulders, and his bare bent legs were scarcely able to move. His face, and even part of his shaven head, was deeply furrowed with wrinkles! his misshapen, toothless mouth surrounded by close-cropped grey moustaches and beard moved incessantly as though he were chewing something; but his red lashless eyes still had a gleam of fire and clearly expressed an old man's contempt of life.

Rosenkranz, through the interpreter, asked him why he had not gone away with the others.

'Where was I to go?' he said, looking calmly round him.

'Where the rest have gone,' answered somebody.

'The *jigits* have gone to fight the Russians, but I am an old man.'

'Why, aren't you afraid of the Russians?'

'What will the Russians do to me? I am an old man,' he said again, glancing carelessly at the ring which had formed around him.

On the way back I saw the same old man without a cap, with his arms bound, jolting behind the saddle of a Cossack of the Line, and with the same unconcerned expression gazing about him. He was needed for the exchange of prisoners.

I clambered on to the roof and settled myself beside the captain.

'It seems there were but few of the enemy,' I said to him, anxious to learn his opinion of what had just taken place.

'Enemy?' he repeated in surprise, 'why, there were none at all. Do you call these the enemy? Wait till the evening and see how we get away. You'll see how they'll escort us home; how they'll spring up!' he added, pointing with his pipe to the copse which we had passed through in the morning.

'What is this?' I asked, uneasily, interrupting the captain, pointing to a little group of Don Cossacks which had formed round something not far from us.

We heard in their midst something like a child's cry, and the words:

'Don't stab it! Stop . . . they'll see us . . . Have you a knife, Evstigneitch? Give us the knife.'

'They're sharing something, the rascals!' said the captain, coolly.

But at that very moment, with a hot, scared face, the pretty ensign ran round the corner, and waving his arms, rushed at the Cossacks.

'Don't touch it! Don't kill it!' he screamed in a childish voice.

Seeing an officer the Cossacks gave way and set free a little white kid. The young ensign was completely taken aback, he muttered something, and with a shamefaced expression stopped short before it.

Seeing the captain and me on the roof he flushed more than ever and ran lightly towards us.

'I thought they were going to kill a baby,' he said with a shy smile.

The general with the cavalry had gone on ahead. The battalion with which I had come from Fort N – formed the rearguard. The companies of Captain Hlopov and Lieutenant Rosenkranz were retreating together.

The captain's prediction was completely justified; as soon as we entered the copse of which he had spoken we were continually catching glimpses, on both sides of the road, of mountaineers on horse and on foot. They came so near that I could distinctly see some of them bending down, musket in hand, running from tree to tree. The captain took off his cap and reverently made the sign of the cross. Several of the elder soldiers did the same. We heard calls in the wood, and shouts of 'Iay, Giaour! Iay, Urus!' The short, dry musket-shots followed one another, and bullets came whizzing from both sides. Our men answered silently with a running fire; only from time to time one heard in the ranks exclamations such as: 'Where's *he*[1] firing from?' 'It's all right for *him* in the wood!' 'We ought to use the cannon!' – and so forth.

The cannon were brought into line, and after a few shots from them the enemy seemed to weaken; but a minute later, at every step the troops advanced, the firing and the shouts and halloos were more incessant.

We had not gone more than six hundred yards from the village when the enemy's cannon-balls began to whistle over our heads. I saw a soldier killed by one of them .... but why give the details of that awful scene when I would give a great deal to forget it myself?

Lieutenant Rosenkranz kept firing his own musket. He was not silent for a moment, and in a hoarse voice shouted to the soldiers, and kept galloping at full speed from one end of the line to the

[1] The pronoun 'he' is used by the Caucasian soldiers as the collective term for the enemy.

other. He was rather pale, which was extremely becoming to his martial countenance.

The pretty ensign was in ecstasy: his fine black eyes shone with daring; his lips wore a faint smile; he was continually riding up to the captain and asking his permission to dash into the wood.

'We shall beat them back,' he said persuasively; 'we shall, really!'

'No need to,' the captain answered briefly; 'we have to retreat.'

The captain's company took up their position at the edge of the wood, and, lying down, kept off the enemy with their fire. The captain, in his shabby coat and draggled cap, slackening the rein of his white horse, sat in silence, with his legs bent from the shortness of his stirrups. (The soldiers knew, and did their business so well that there was no need to give them instructions.) Only from time to time he raised his voice and called to men who had lifted up their heads. There was nothing martial about the captain's appearance; but there was so much genuineness and simplicity that it made an extraordinary impression upon me.

'That's true courage,' was the thought that rose instinctively within me.

He was exactly as I had always seen him, the same calm movements, the same quiet voice, the same guileless expression on his plain but open face; only in the unusual alertness of his glance could one detect the intentness of a man quietly absorbed in the work before him. It is easy to say 'the same as always', but how many shades of difference I have observed in other people; one tries to appear more composed than usual, another tries to be sterner, a third more cheerful; but one could see by the captain's face that he did not understand why one should try to appear anything.

The Frenchman who said at Waterloo, 'La garde meurt, mais ne se rend pas,' and other heroes, especially French ones, who have delivered themselves of memorable utterances, were brave, and their utterances really are worth remembering. But between their bravery and the bravery of the captain there was this difference: that if, on any occasion whatsoever, some grand saying had stirred in my hero's soul, I am convinced that he would not have uttered it, in the first place, because he would have been afraid that in uttering the great saying he would be spoiling the great deed; and secondly, that when a man feels that he has the strength for a great action no word whatever is needed. This, to my thinking, is the peculiar and noble characteristic of Russian courage, and, that being so, how can a Russian help a pang at the heart when he hears among our young officers hackneyed French phrases that aim at the imitation of obsolete French chivalry?

Suddenly, on the side where the pretty ensign had been standing, was heard a shout of 'hurrah!' neither loud nor unanimous. Looking in the direction of the shout I saw about thirty soldiers running laboriously over a ploughed field, with muskets in their hands and knapsacks on their backs. They kept stumbling, but still pushed on and shouted. In front of them the young ensign galloped, waving his sword.

They all vanished into the wood.

After a few minutes of shouting and musket fire a terrified horse ran out and soldiers appeared at the edge of the wood carrying the dead and the wounded; among the latter was the young ensign. Two soldiers were holding him up under the arms. He was as white as a handkerchief, and his pretty little head, on which only the faintest shadow of the martial elation of a moment before could be seen, seemed somehow fearfully sunk between his shoulders and drooping on his breast. Upon his white shirt, under his open coat, could be seen a small red spot.

'Oh, what a pity!' I said, instinctively turning away from this piteous sight.

'Of course it's a pity,' said an old soldier who was standing beside me with a morose face, leaning on his musket. 'He was afraid of nothing; how can anyone do so?' he added, looking intently at the wounded boy. 'Still young and foolish – and so he has paid for it.'

'Why, are you afraid then?' I asked.

'To be sure!'

Four soldiers were carrying the ensign on a stretcher. A soldier from the fortress followed them, leading a thin, broken-down horse laden with two green boxes containing the surgical requisites. They were waiting for the doctor. The officers rode to the stretchers and tried to encourage and comfort the wounded boy.

'Well, brother Alanin, it will be some time before we dance with the castagnettes again,' said Lieutenant Rosenkranz, going up to him with a smile.

He probably expected that these words would keep up the pretty ensign's courage; but as far as one could judge from the cold and mournful expression of the latter they did not produce the desired effect.

The captain, too, went up to him. He looked intently at the wounded boy and his usually unconcerned cool face expressed genuine sympathy.

'My dear Anatole Ivanovitch,' he said in a voice full of affectionate tenderness, which I should never have expected of him, 'it seems it was God's will.'

The wounded boy looked round; his pale face was lit up by a mournful smile.

'Yes; I didn't obey you.'

'Better say it was God's will,' repeated the captain.

The doctor, who had arrived, took from the assistant some bandages, a probe, and other things, and turning up his sleeves with an encouraging smile went up to the ensign.

'Well, it seems they've made a little hole in a sound place,' he said jokingly, in a careless tone; 'show me.'

The ensign obeyed; but in the expression with which he looked at the light-hearted doctor there was both wonder and reproach which the latter did not observe. He began to probe the wound and examine it from all sides; but, losing patience, the wounded boy, with a heavy groan, pushed away his hand.

'Let me be,' he said, in a voice scarcely audible. 'Anyway I shall die.'

With those words he sank upon his back, and five minutes later when I approached the group standing round him and asked a soldier how the ensign was, he answered me, 'He's passing away.'

It was late when the detachment, formed into a wide column, marched, singing, up to the fortress. The sun had set behind the ridge of snow-mountains, and was shedding its last rosy light on a long filmy cloud which lingered on the clear limpid horizon. The snow-mountains were beginning to be veiled by a purple mist; only their topmost outlines stood out with marvellous clearness against the red glow of the sunset. The transparent moon, which had long been up, was beginning to turn white against the dark blue of the sky. The green of the grass and the trees was turning black and was drenched with dew.

The troops moved in dark masses with steady tramp through the luxuriant meadow. Tambourines, drums and merry songs were to be heard on all sides. The singer of the sixth company was singing at the top of his voice, and the notes of his pure deep tenor, full of strength and feeling, floated far and wide in the limpid evening air.

THE AFFAIR AT COULTER'S NOTCH

Ambrose Bierce

'Do you think, colonel, that your brave Coulter would like to put one of his guns in here?' the general asked.

He was apparently not altogether serious; it certainly did not seem a place where any artillerist, however brave, would like to put a gun. The colonel thought that possibly his division commander meant good-humouredly to intimate that Captain Coulter's courage had been too highly extolled in a recent conversation between them.

'General,' he replied, warmly, 'Coulter would like to put a gun anywhere within reach of those people,' with a motion of his hand in the direction of the enemy.

'It is the only place,' said the general. He was serious, then.

The place was a depression, a 'notch', in the sharp crest of a hill. It was a pass, and through it ran a turnpike, which, reaching this highest point in its course by a sinuous ascent through a thin forest, made a similar, though less steep, descent toward the enemy. For a mile to the left and a mile to the right the ridge, though occupied by Federal infantry lying close behind the sharp crest, and appearing as if held in place by atmospheric pressure, was inaccessible to artillery. There was no place but the bottom of the notch, and that was barely wide enough for the roadbed. From the Confederate side this point was commanded by two batteries posted on a slightly lower elevation beyond a creek, and a half-mile away. All the guns but one were masked by the trees of an orchard; that one – it seemed a bit of impudence – was directly in front of a rather grandiose building, the planter's dwelling. The gun was safe enough in its exposure – but only because the Federal infantry had been forbidden to fire. Coulter's Notch – it came to be called so – was not, that pleasant summer afternoon, a place where one would 'like to put a gun'.

Three or four dead horses lay there, sprawling in the road, three or four dead men in a trim row at one side of it, and a little back, down the hill. All but one were cavalrymen belonging to the Federal advance. One was a quartermaster. The general commanding the division, and the colonel commanding the brigade, with their staffs and escorts, had ridden into the notch to have a look at the enemy's guns – which had straightway obscured themselves in towering clouds of smoke. It was hardly profitable to be curious about guns which had the trick of the cuttlefish, and the season of observation was brief. At its conclusion – a short remove backward from where it began – occurred the conversation already partly reported. 'It is the only place,' the general repeated thoughtfully, 'to get at them.'

The colonel looked at him gravely. 'There is room for but one gun, General – one against twelve.'

'That is true – for only one at a time,' said the commander with something like, yet not altogether like, a smile. 'But then, your brave Coulter – a whole battery in himself.'

The tone of irony was now unmistakable. It angered the colonel, but he did not know what to say. The spirit of military subordination is not favourable to retort, nor even deprecation. At this moment a young officer of artillery came riding slowly up the road attended by his bugler. It was Captain Coulter. He could not have been more than twenty-three years of age. He was of medium height, but very slender and lithe, sitting his horse with something of the air of a civilian. In face he was of a type singularly unlike the men about him; thin, high-nosed, grey-eyed, with a slight blond moustache, and long, rather straggling hair of the same colour. There was an apparent negligence in his attire. His cap was worn with the visor a trifle askew; his coat was buttoned only at the sword belt, showing a considerable expanse of white shirt, tolerably clean for that stage of the campaign. But the negligence was all in his dress and bearing; in his face was a look of intense interest in his surroundings. His grey eyes, which seemed occasionally to strike right and left across the landscape, like search-lights, were for the most part fixed upon the sky beyond the Notch; until he should arrive at the summit of the road, there was nothing else in that direction to see. As he came opposite his division and brigade commanders at the roadside he saluted mechanically and was about to pass on. Moved by a sudden impulse, the colonel signed him to halt.

'Captain Coulter,' he said, 'the enemy has twelve pieces over there on the next ridge. If I rightly understand the general, he directs that you bring up a gun and engage them.'

There was a blank silence; the general looked stolidly at a distant regiment swarming slowly up the hill through rough undergrowth, like a torn and draggled cloud of blue smoke; the captain appeared not to have observed him. Presently the captain spoke, slowly and with apparent effort :

'On the next ridge, did you say, sir? Are the guns near the house?'

'Ah, you have been over this road before! Directly at the house.'

'And it is – necessary – to engage them? The order is imperative?'

His voice was husky and broken. He was visibly paler. The colonel was astonished and mortified. He stole a glance at the commander. In that set, immobile face was no sign; it was as hard as bronze. A moment later the general rode away, followed by his staff and escort. The colonel, humiliated and indignant, was about to order Captain Coulter into arrest, when the latter spoke a few words in a low tone to his bugler, saluted, and rode straight forward into the Notch, where, presently, at the summit of the road, his field-glass at his eyes, he showed against the sky, he and his horse, sharply defined and motionless as an equestrian statue. The bugler had dashed down the road in the opposite direction at headlong speed and disappeared behind a wood. Presently his bugle was heard singing in the cedars, and in an incredibly short time a single gun with its caisson, each drawn by six horses and manned by its full complement of gunners, came bounding and banging up the grade in a storm of dust, unlimbered under cover, and was run forward by hand to the fatal crest among the dead horses. A gesture of the captain's arm, some strangely agile movements of the men in loading, and almost before the troops along the way had ceased to hear the rattle of the wheels, a great white cloud sprang forward down the slope, and with a deafening report the affair at Coulter's Notch had begun.

It is not intended to relate in detail the progress and incidents of that ghastly contest – a contest without vicissitudes, its alterations only different degrees of despair. Almost at the instant when Captain Coulter's gun blew its challenging cloud twelve answering clouds rolled upward from among the trees about the plantation house, a deep multiple report roared back like a broken echo, and thenceforth to the end the Federal cannoneers fought their hopeless battle in an atmosphere of living iron whose thoughts were lightnings and whose deeds were death.

Unwilling to see the efforts which he could not aid and the slaughter which he could not stay, the colonel had ascended the ridge at a point a quarter of a mile to the left, whence the Notch, itself invisible but pushing up successive masses of smoke, seemed the crater of a volcano in thundering eruption. With his glass he watched the enemy's guns, noting as he could the effects of Coulter's fire – if Coulter still lived to direct it. He saw that the Federal gunners, ignoring the enemy's pieces, whose position could be determined by their smoke only, gave their whole attention to the one which maintained its place in the open – the lawn in front of the house, with which it was accurately in line. Over and about that hardy piece the shells exploded at intervals of a few seconds. Some exploded in the house, as could be seen by thin ascensions of smoke from the breached roof. Figures of prostrate men and horses were plainly visible.

'If our fellows are doing such good work with a single gun,' said the colonel to an aide who happened to be nearest, 'they must be suffering like the devil from twelve. Go down and present the commander of that piece with my congratulations on the accuracy of his fire.'

Turning to his adjutant-general he said, 'Did you observe Coulter's damned reluctance to obey orders?'

'Yes, sir, I did.'

'Well, say nothing about it, please. I don't think the general will care to make any accusations. He will probably have enough to do in explaining his own connection with this uncommon way of amusing the rear guard of a retreating enemy.'

A young officer approached from below, climbing breathless up the acclivity. Almost before he had saluted he gasped out :

'Colonel, I am directed by Colonel Harmon to say that the enemy's guns are within easy reach of our rifles, and most of them visible from various points along the ridge.'

The brigade commander looked at him without a trace of interest in his expression. 'I know it,' he said quietly.

The young adjutant was visibly embarrassed. 'Colonel Harmon would like to have permission to silence those guns,' he stammered.

'So should I,' the colonel said in the same tone. 'Present my compliments to Colonel Harmon and say to him that the general's orders not to fire are still in force.'

The adjutant saluted and retired. The colonel ground his heel into the earth and turned to look again at the enemy's guns.

'Colonel,' said the adjutant-general, 'I don't know that I ought to say anything, but there is something wrong in all this. Do you happen to know that Captain Coulter is from the South?'

'No; *was* he, indeed?'

'I heard that last summer the division which the general then commanded was in the vicinity of Coulter's home – camped there for weeks, and –'

'Listen!' said the colonel, interrupting with an upward gesture. 'Do you hear *that*?'

'That' was the silence of the Federal gun. The staff, the orderlies, the lines of infantry behind the crest – all had 'heard', and were looking curiously in the direction of the crater, whence no smoke now ascended except desultory cloudlets from the enemy's shells. Then came the blare of a bugle, a faint rattle of wheels; a minute later the sharp reports recommenced with double activity. The demolished gun had been replaced with a sound one.

'Yes,' said the adjutant-general, resuming his narrative, 'the general made the acquaintance of Coulter's family. There was trouble – I don't know the exact nature of it – something about Coulter's wife. She is a red-hot Seccesionist, as they all are, except Coulter himself, but she is a good wife and high-bred lady. There was a complaint to army headquarters. The general was transferred to this division. It is odd that Coulter's battery should afterward have been assigned to it.'

The colonel had risen from the rock upon which they had been sitting. His eyes were blazing with a generous indignation.

'See here, Morrison,' said he, looking his gossiping staff officer straight in the face, 'did you get that story from a gentleman or a liar?'

'I don't want to say how I got it, Colonel, unless it is necessary'

– he was blushing a trifle – 'but I'll stake my life upon its truth in the main.'

The colonel turned toward a small knot of officers some distance away. 'Lieutenant Williams!' he shouted.

One of the officers detached himself from the group, and, coming forward, saluted, saying: 'Pardon me, Colonel, I thought you had been informed. Williams is dead down there by the gun. What can I do, sir?'

Lieutenant Williams was the aide who had had the pleasure of conveying to the officer in charge of the gun his brigade commander's congratulations.

'Go,' said the colonel, 'and direct the withdrawal of that gun instantly. Hold! I'll go myself.'

He strode down the declivity toward the rear of the Notch at a break-neck pace, over the rocks and through brambles, followed by his little retinue in tumultuous disorder. At the foot of the declivity they mounted their waiting animals and took to the road at a lively trot, round a bend and into the Notch. The spectacle which they encountered there was appalling.

Within the defile, barely broad enough for a single gun, were piled the wrecks of no fewer than four. They had noted the silencing of only the last one disabled – there had been a lack of men to replace it quickly. The débris lay on both sides of the road; the men had managed to keep an open way between, through which the fifth piece was now firing. The men? – they looked like demons of the pit! All were hatless, all stripped to the waist, their reeking skins black with blotches of powder and spattered with gouts of blood. They worked like madmen, with rammer and cartridge, lever and lanyard. They set their swollen shoulders and bleeding hands against the wheels at each recoil and heaved the heavy gun back to its place. There were no commands; in that awful environment of whooping shot, exploding shells, shrieking fragments of iron, and flying splinters of wood, none could have been heard. Officers, if officers there were, were indistinguishable; all worked together – each while he lasted – governed by the eye. When the gun was sponged, it was loaded; when loaded, aimed and fired. The colonel observed something new to his military experience – something horrible and unnatural: the gun was bleeding at the mouth! In temporary default of water, the man sponging had dipped his spoon in a pool of his comrades' blood. In all this work there was no clashing; the duty of the instant was obvious. When one fell, another, looking a trifle cleaner, seemed to rise from the earth in the dead man's tracks, to fall in his turn.

With the ruined guns lay the ruined men – alongside the wreckage, under it and atop of it; and back down the road – a ghastly procession! – crept on hands and knees such of the wounded as were able to move. The colonel – he had compassionately sent his cavalcade to the right about – had to ride over those who were entirely dead in order not to crush those who were partly alive. Into that hell he tranquilly held his way, rode up alongside the gun, and, in the obscurity of the last discharge, tapped upon the cheek the man holding the rammer, who straightway fell, thinking himself killed. A fiend seven times damned sprang out of the smoke to take his place, but paused and gazed up at the mounted officer with an unearthly regard, his teeth flashing between his black lips, his eyes, fierce and expanded, burning like coals beneath his bloody brow. The colonel made an authoritative gesture and pointed to the rear. The fiend bowed in token of obedience. It was Captain Coulter.

Simultaneously with the colonel's arresting sign, silence fell upon the whole field of action. The procession of missiles no longer streamed into that defile of death; the enemy also had ceased firing. His army had been gone for hours, and the commander of his rear guard, who had held his position perilously long in hope to silence the Federal fire, at that strange moment had silenced his own. 'I was not aware of the breadth of my authority,' thought the colonel, facetiously, riding forward to the crest to see what had really happened.

An hour later his brigade was in bivouac on the enemy's ground, and its idlers were examining, with something of awe, as the faithful inspect a saint's relics, a score of straddling dead horses and three disabled guns, all spiked. The fallen men had been carried away; their crushed and broken bodies would have given too great satisfaction.

Naturally, the colonel established himself and his military family in the plantation house. It was somewhat shattered, but it was better than the open air. The furniture was greatly deranged and broken. The walls and ceilings were knocked away here and there, and there was a lingering odour of powder smoke everywhere. The beds, the closets of women's clothing, the cupboards were not greatly damaged. The new tenants for a night made themselves comfortable, and the practical effacement of Coulter's battery supplied them with an interesting topic.

During supper that evening an orderly of the escort showed himself into the dining room and asked permission to speak to the colonel.

'What is it, Barbour?' said that officer pleasantly, having overheard the request.

'Colonel, there is something wrong in the cellar; I don't know what – somebody there. I was down there rummaging about.'

'I will go down and see,' said a staff officer, rising.

'So will I,' the colonel said; 'let the others remain. Lead on, orderly.'

They took a candle from the table and descended the cellar stairs, the orderly in visible trepidation. The candle made but a feeble light, but presently, as they advanced, its narrow circle of illumination revealed a human figure seated on the ground against the black stone wall which they were skirting, its knees elevated, its head bowed sharply forward. The face, which should have been seen in profile, was invisible, for the man was bent so far forward that his long hair concealed it; and, strange to relate, the beard, of a much darker hue, fell in a great tangled mass and lay along the ground at his feet. They involuntarily paused; then the colonel, taking the candle from the orderly's shaking hand, approached the man and attentively considered him. The long dark beard was the hair of a woman – dead. The dead woman clasped in her arms a dead babe. Both were clasped in the arms of the man, pressed against his breast, against his lips. There was blood in the hair of the woman; there was blood in the hair of the man. A yard away lay an infant's foot. It was near an irregular depression in the beaten earth which formed the cellar's floor – a fresh excavation with a convex bit of iron, having jagged edges, visible in one of the sides. The colonel held the light as high as he could. The floor of the room above was broken through, the splinters pointing at all angles downward. 'This casemate is not bomb-proof,' said the colonel gravely; it did not occur to him that his summing up of the matter had any levity in it.

They stood about the group awhile in silence; the staff officer was thinking of his unfinished supper, the orderly of what might possibly be in one of the casks on the other side of the cellar. Suddenly the man, whom they had thought dead, raised his head and gazed tranquilly into their faces. His complexion was coal black; the cheeks were apparently tattooed in irregular sinuous lines from the eyes downward. The lips, too, were white, like those of a stage negro. There was blood upon his forehead.

The staff officer drew back a pace, the orderly two paces.

'What are you doing here, my man?' said the colonel, unmoved.

'This house belongs to me, sir,' was the reply, civilly delivered.

'To you? Ah, I see! And these?'

'My wife and child. I am Captain Coulter.'

WITH THE MAIN GUARD

Rudyard Kipling

Der jungere Uhlanen
Sit round mit open mouth
While Breitmann tell dem sdories
Of fightin' in the South;
Und gif dem moral lessons,
How before der battle pops,
Take a little prayer to Himmel
Und a goot long drink of Schnapps.

C.G. Leland

'MARY, Mother av Mercy, fwhat the divil possist us to take an' kape this melancolious counthry? Answer me that, sorr.'

It was Mulvaney who was speaking. The time was one o'clock of a stifling June night, and the place was the main gate of Fort Amara, most desolate and least desirable of all fortresses in India. What I was doing there at that hour is a question which only concerns M'Grath the Sergeant of the Guard, and the men on the gate.

'Slape,' said Mulvaney, 'is a shuparfluous necessity. This yard'll shtay lively till relieved.' He himself was stripped to the waist; Learoyd on the next bedstead was dripping from the skinful of water which Ortheris, clad only in white trousers, had just sluiced over his shoulders; and a fourth private was muttering uneasily as he dozed open-mouthed in the glare of the great guard-lantern. The heat under the bricked archway was terrifying.

'The worrst night that iver I remimber. Eyah! Is all Hell loose this tide?' said Mulvaney. A puff of burning wind lashed through the wicket-gate like a wave of the sea, and Ortheris swore.

'Are ye more heasy, Jock?' he said to Learoyd. 'Put yer 'ead between your legs. It'll go orf in a minute.'

'Ah doan't care. Ah would not care, but ma heart is plaayin' tivvy-tivvy on ma ribs. Let ma die! Oh, leave ma die!' groaned the huge Yorkshireman, who was feeling the heat acutely, being of fleshy build.

The sleeper under the lantern roused for a moment and raised himself on his elbow. 'Die and be damned then!' he said. '*I'm* damned and I can't die!'

'Who's that?' I whispered, for the voice was new to me.

'Gentleman born,' said Mulvaney; 'Corp'ril wan year, Sargint nex'. Red-hot on his C'mission, but dhrinks like a fish. He'll be gone before the cowld weather's here. So!'

He slipped his boot, and with the naked toe just touched the trigger of his Martini. Ortheris misunderstood the movement, and the next instant the Irishman's rifle was dashed aside, while Ortheris stood before him, his eyes blazing with reproof.

'You!' said Ortheris. 'My Gawd, *you*! If it was you, wot would *we* do?'

'Kape quiet, little man,' said Mulvaney, putting him aside, but very gently; ''tis not me, nor will ut be me whoile Dinah Shadd's here. I was but showin' somethin'.'

Learoyd, bowed on his bedstead, groaned, and the gentleman-ranker sighed in his sleep. Ortheris took Mulvaney's tendered pouch, and we three smoked gravely for a space while the dust-devils danced on the glacis and scoured the red-hot plain.

'Pop?' said Ortheris, wiping his forehead.

'Don't tantalize wid talkin' av dhrink, or I'll shtuff you into your own breech-block an' – fire you off!' grunted Mulvaney.

Ortheris chuckled, and from a niche in the veranda produced six bottles of gingerade.

'Where did ye get ut, ye Machiavel?' said Mulvaney. ''Tis no bazar pop.'

''Ow do *I* know wot the orf'cers drink?' answered Ortheris. 'Arst the mess-man.'

'Ye'll have a Disthrict Coort-Martail settin' on ye yet, me son,' said Mulvaney, 'but' – he opened a bottle – 'I will not report ye this time. Fwhat's in the mess-kid is mint for the belly, as they say, 'specially whin that mate is dhrink. Here's luck! A bloody war or a – no, we've got the sickly season. War, thin!' – he waved the innocent 'pop' to the four quarters of heaven. 'Bloody war! North, East, South, an' West! Jock, ye quakin' hayrick, come an' dhrink.'

But Learoyd, half mad with the fear of death presaged in the swelling veins of his neck, was begging his Maker to strike him dead, and fighting for more air between his prayers. A second time Ortheris drenched the quivering body with water, and the giant revived.

'An' Ah divn't see thot a mon is i' fettle for gooin' on to live; an' Ah divn't see thot there is owt for t' livin' for. Hear now, lads! Ah'm tired – tired. There's nobbut watter i' ma bones. Leave ma die!'

The hollow of the arch gave back Learoyd's broken whisper in a bass boom. Mulvaney looked at me hopelessly, but I remembered how the madness of despair had once fallen upon Ortheris, that weary, weary afternoon on the banks of the Khemi River, and how it had been exorcised by the skilful magician Mulvaney.

'Talk, Terence!' I said, 'or we shall have Learoyd slinging loose, and he'll be worse than Ortheris was. Talk! He'll answer to your voice.'

Almost before Ortheris had deftly thrown all the rifles of the guard on Mulvaney's bedstead, the Irishman's voice was uplifted as that of one in the middle of a story, and, turning to me, he said:

'In barracks or out av it, as *you* say, sorr, an Irish rig'mint is the divil an' more. 'Tis only fit for a young man wid eddicated fisteses. Oh, the crame av disrupshin is an Irish rig'mint, an' rippin', tearin', ragin' scattherers in the field av war! My first rig'mint was Irish – Faynians an' rebils to the heart av their marrow was they, an' *so* they fought for the Widdy betther than most, bein' contrary – Irish. They was the Black Tyrone. You've heard av thim, sorr?'

Heard of them! I knew the Black Tyrone for the choicest collection of unmitigated blackguards, dog-stealers, robbers of hen-roosts, assaulters of innocent citizens, and recklessly daring heroes in the Army List. Half Europe and half Asia has had cause to know the Black Tyrone – good luck be with their tattered Colours as Glory has ever been!

'They *was* hot pickils an' ginger! I cut a man's head tu deep wid me belt in the days av me youth, an', afther some circumstances which I will oblitherate, I came to the Ould Rig'mint, bearin' the character av a man wid hands an' feet. But, as I was goin' to tell you, I fell acrost the Black Tyrone agin wan day whin we wanted thim powerful bad. Orth'ris, me son, fwhat was the name av that place where they sint wan comp'ny av us an' wan av the Tyrone roun' a hill an' down agin, all for to tache the Paythans something they'd niver learned before? Afther Ghuzni 'twas.'

'Don't know what the bloomin' Paythans called it. We called it Silver's Theayter. You know that, sure!'

'Silver's Theatre – so 'twas. A gut betwix' two hills, as black as a bucket, an' as thin as a gurl's waist. There was over-many Paythans for our convaynience in the gut, an' begad they called thimsilves a Reserve – bein' impident by natur'! Our Scotchies an' lashin's av Gurkys was poundin' into some Paythan rig'mints, I think 'twas. Scotchies an' Gurkys are twins bekaze they're so onlike, an' they get dhrunk together whin God plazes. As I was sayin', they sint wan comp'ny av the Ould an' wan av the Tyrone to double up the hill an' clane out the Paythan Reserve. Orf'cers was scarce in thim days, fwhat wid dysint'ry an' not takin' care av thimsilves, an' we was sint out wid only wan orf'cer for the comp'ny; but he was a Man that had his feet beneath him an' all his teeth in their sockuts.'

'Who was he?' I asked.

'Captain O'Neil – Old Crook – Cruik-na-bulleen – him that I tould ye that tale av whin he was in Burma.[1] Hah! He was a Man. The Tyrone tuk a little orf'cer bhoy, but divil a bit was he in command, as I'll dimonsthrate prisintly. We an' they came over the brow av the hill, wan on each side av the gut, an' there was that ondacint Reserve waitin' down below like rats in a pit.

' "Howld on, men," sez Crook, who tuk a mother's care av us always. "Rowl some rocks on thim by way av visitin'-kyards." We hadn't rowled more than twinty bowlders, an' the Paythans was beginnin' to swear tremenjus, whin the little orf'cer bhoy av the Tyrone shqueaks out acrost the valley: "Fwhat the divil an' all are

---

[1] Now first of the foemen of Boh Da Thone
Was Captain O'Neil of the Black Tyrone.
The Ballad of Boh Da Thone

you doin', shpoilin' the fun for my men? Do ye not see they'll stand?"

' "Faith, that's a rare pluckt wan!" sez Crook. "Niver mind the rocks, men. Come along down an' take tay wid thim!"

' "There's damned little sugar in ut!" sez my rear-rank man; but Crook heard.

' "Have ye not all got spoons?" he sez, laughin', an' down we wint as fast as we cud. Learoyd bein' sick at the Base, he, av coorse, was not there.'

'Thot's a lie!' said Learoyd, dragging his bedstead nearer. 'Ah gotten *thot* theer, an' you knaw it, Mulvaaney.' He threw up his arms, and from the right armpit ran, diagonally through the fell of his chest, a thin white line terminating near the fourth left rib.

'My mind's goin',' said Mulvaney, the unabashed. 'Ye were there. Fwhat was I thinkin' av? 'Twas another man, av coorse. Well, you'll remember thin, Jock, how we an' the Tyrone met wid a bang at the bottom an' got jammed past all movin' among the Paythans?'

'Ow! It *was* a tight 'ole. I was squeezed till I thought I'd bloomin' well bust,' said Ortheris, rubbing his stomach meditatively.

''Twas no place for a little man, but *wan* little man' – Mulvaney put his hand on Ortheris's shoulder – 'saved the life av me. There we shtuck, for divil a bit did the Paythans flinch, an' divil a bit dare we; our business bein' to clear 'em out. An' the most exthryordinar' thing av all was that we an' they just rushed into each other's arrums, an' there was no firin' for a long time. Nothin' but knife an' bay'nit when we cud get our hands free: an' that was not often. We was breast-on to thim, an' the Tyrone was yelpin' behind av us in a way I didn't see the lean av at first. But I knew later, an' so did the Paythans.

' "Knee to knee!" sings out Crook, wid a laugh whin the rush av our comin' into the gut shtopped, an' he was huggin' a hairy great Paythan, neither bein' able to do anything to the other, tho' both was wishful.

' "Breast to breast!" he sez, as the Tyrone was pushin' us forward closer an' closer.

' "An' hand over back! sez a Sargint that was behin'. I saw a sword lick out past Crook's ear, an' the Paythan was tuk in the apple av his throat like a pig at Dromeen Fair.

' "Thank ye, Brother Inner Guard," sez Crook, cool as a cucumber widout salt. "I wanted that room." An' he wint forward by the thickness av a man's body, havin' turned the Paythan undher him. The man bit the heel off Crook's boot in his death-bite.

' "Push, men!" sez Crook. "Push, ye paper-backed beggars!" he sez. "Am *I* to pull ye through?" So we pushed, an' we kicked, an' we swung, an' we swore, an' the grass bein' slippery, our heels wudn't bite, an' God help the front-rank man that wint down that day!'

"Ave you ever bin in the Pit hentrance o' the Vic. on a thick night?' interrupted Ortheris. 'It was worse nor that, for they was goin' one way, an' we wouldn't 'ave it. Leastaways, I 'adn't much to say.'

'Faith, me son, ye said ut, thin. I kep' this little man betune my knees as long as I cud, but he was pokin' roun' wid his bay'nit, blindin' an' stiffin' feroshus. The divil of a man is Orth'ris in a ruction – aren't ye?' said Mulvaney.

'Don't make game!' said the Cockney. 'I knowed I wasn't no good then, but I guv 'em compot from the lef' flank when we opened out. No!' he said, bringing down his hand with a thump on the bedstead, 'a bay'nit ain't no good to a little man – might as well 'ave a bloomin' fishin'-rod! I 'ate a clawin', maulin' mess, but gimme a breech that's wore out a bit an' hamminition one year in store, to let the powder kiss the bullet, an' put me somewheres where I ain't trod on by 'ulking swine like you, an' s'elp me Gawd, I could bowl you over five times outer seven at height 'undred. Would yer try, you lumberin' Hirishman?'

'No, ye wasp. I've seen ye do ut. I say there's nothin' better than the bay'nit, wid a long reach, a double twist av ye can, an' a slow recover.'

'Dom the bay'nit,' said Learoyd, who had been listening intently. 'Look a-here!' He picked up a rifle an inch below the foresight with an underhanded action, and used it exactly as a man would use a dagger.

'Sitha,' said he softly, 'thot's better than owt, for a mon can bash t' faace wi' thot, an', if he divn't, he can breeak t' forearm o' t' guaard. 'Tis nut i' t' books, though. Gie me t' butt.'

'Each does ut his own way, like makin' love,' said Mulvaney quietly; 'the butt or the bay'nit or the bullet accordin' to the natur' av the man. Well, as I was sayin', we shtuck there breathin' in each other's faces an' swearin' powerful; Orth'ris cursin' the mother that bore him bekaze he was not three inches taller.

'Prisintly he sez: "Duck, ye lump, an' I can get a man over your shoulther!"

' "You'll blow me head off," I sez, throwin' my arrum clear; "go through under my arrumpit, ye bloodthirsty little scutt," sez I, "but don't shtick me or I'll wring your ears round."

'Fwhat was ut ye gave the Paythan man forninst me, him that cut at me whin I cudn't move hand or foot? Hot or cowld was ut?'

'Cold,' said Ortheris, 'up an' under the ribjints. 'E come down flat. Best for you 'e did.'

'Thrue, me son! This jam thing that I'm talkin' about lasted for five minut's good, an' thin we got our arrums clear an' wint in. I misremimber exactly fwhat I did, but I didn't want Dinah to be a widdy at the depôt. Thin, afther some a promishcuous hackin' we shtuck agin, an' the Tyrone behin' was callin' us dogs an' cowards an' all manner av names; we barrin' their way.

' "Fwhat ails the Tyrone?" thinks I. "They've the makin's av a most convanient fight here."

'A man behind me sez beseechful an' in a whisper: "Let me get at thim! For the love av Mary, give me room beside ye, ye tall man!"

' "An' who are you that's so anxious to be kilt?" sez I, widout turnin' my head, for the long knives was dancin' in front like the sun on Donegal Bay whin ut's rough.

' "We've seen our dead," he sez, squeezin' into me; "our dead that was men two days gone! An' me that was his cousin by blood cud not bring Tim Coulan off! Let me get on," he sez, "let me get to thim or I'll run ye through the back!"

' "My troth," thinks I, "if the Tyrone have seen their dead, God help the Paythans this day!" An' thin I knew why the Tyrone was ragin' behind us as they was.

'I gave room to the man, an' he ran forward wid the Haymakers' Lift on his bay'nit an' swung a Paythan clear off his feet by the belly-band av the brute, an' the iron bruk at the lockin'-ring.

' "Tim Coulan 'll slape aisy to-night," sez he wid a grin; an' the next minut' his head was in two halves and he wint down grinnin' by sections.

'The Tyrone was pushin' an' pushin' in, an' our men was swearin' at thim, an' Crook was workin' away in front av us all, his sword-arrum swingin' like a pump-handle an' his revolver spittin' like a cat. But the strange thing av ut was the quiet that lay upon. 'Twas like a fight in a drame – excipt for thim that was dead.

'Whin I gave room to the Irishman I was expinded an' forlorn in my inside. 'Tis a way I have, savin' your presince, sorr, in action. "Let me out, bhoys," sez I, backin' in among thim. "I'm goin' to be onwell!" Faith they gave me room at the wurrud, though they wud not ha' given room for all Hell wid the chill off. When I got clear, I was, savin' your presince, sorr, outrajis sick bekaze I had dhrunk heavy that day.

'Well an' far out av harm was a Sargint av the Tyrone sittin' on the little orf'cer bhoy who had stopped Crook from rowlin' the rocks. Oh, he was a beautiful bhoy, an' the long black curses was slidin' out av his innocint mouth like mornin'-jew from a rose!

' "Fwhat have you got there?" sez I to the Sargint.

' "Wan av Her Majesty's bantams wid his spurs up," sez he. "He's goin' to Coort-Martial me."

' "Let me go!" sez the little orf'cer bhoy. "Let me go and command me men!" manin' thereby the Black Tyrone which was beyond any command – even av they had made the Divil Field-Orf'cer.

' "His father howlds my mother's cow-feed in Clonmel," sez the man that was sittin' on him. "Will I go back to *his* mother an' tell her that I've let him throw himsilf away? Lie still, ye little pinch of dynamite, an' Coort-Martial me aftherwards."

' "Good," sez I; "'tis the likes av him makes the likes av the Commandher-in-Chief, but we must presarve thim. Fwhat d'you want to do, sorr?" sez I, very politeful.

' "Kill the beggars – kill the beggars!" he shqueaks, his big blue eyes brimmin' wid tears.

' "An' how'll ye do that?" sez I. "You've shquibbed off your revolver like a child wid a cracker; you can make no play wid that fine large sword av yours; an' your hand's shakin' like an asp on a leaf. Lie still and grow," sez I.

' "Get back to your comp'ny," sez he; "you're insolint!"

' "All in good time," sez I, "but I'll have a dhrink first."

'Just thin Crook comes up, blue an' white all over where he wasn't red.

' "Wather!" sez he; "I'm dead wid drouth! Oh, but it's a gran' day!"

'He dhrank half a skinful, and the rest he tilts into his chest, an' it fair hissed on the hairy hide av him. He sees the little orf'cer bhoy undher the Sargint.

' "Fwhat's yonder?" sez he.

' "Mutiny, sorr," sez the Sargint, an' the orf'cer bhoy begins pleadin' pitiful to Crook to be let go; but divil a bit wud Crook budge.

' "Kape him there," he sez; "tis no child's work this day. By the same token," sez he, "I'll confishcate that iligant nickel-plated scent-sprinkler av yours, for my own has been vomitin' dishgraceful!"

'The fork av his hand was black wid the back-spit av the machine. So he tuk the orf'cer bhoy's revolver. Ye may look, sorr, but, by my faith, *there's a dale more done in the field than iver gets into Field Ordhers!*

' "Come on, Mulvaney," sez Crook; "is this a Coort-Martial?" The two av us wint back together into the mess an' the Paythans was still standin' up. They was not *too* impart'nint though, for the Tyrone was callin' wan to another to remimber Tim Coulan.

'Crook holted outside av the strife an' looked anxious, his eyes rowlin' roun'.

' "Fwhat is ut, sorr? sez I; "can I get ye anything?"

' "Where's a bugler?" sez he.

'I wint into the crowd – our men was dhrawin' breath behin' the Tyrone, who was fightin' like sowls in tormint – an' prisintly I came acrost little Frehan, our bugler bhoy, pokin' roun' among the best wid a rifle an' bay'nit.

' "Is amusin' yoursilf fwhat you're paid for, ye limb?" sez I, catchin' him by the scruff. "Come out av that an' attind to your jooty," I sez; but the bhoy was not plazed.

' "I've got wan," sez he, grinnin', "big as you, Mulvaney, an' fair half as ugly. Let me go get another."

'I was dishplazed at the personability av that remark, so I tucks him under my arrum an' carries him to Crook, who was watchin' how the fight wint. Crook cuffs him till the bhoy cries, an' thin sez nothin' for a whoile.

'The Paythans began to flicker onaisy, an' our men roared. "Opin

ordher! Double!" sez Crook. "Blow, child, blow for the honour av
the British Arrmy!"

'That bhoy blew like a typhoon, an' the Tyrone an' we opind out
as the Paythans bruk, an' I saw that fwhat had gone before wud be
kissin' an huggin' to fwhat was to come. We'd dhruv thim into a
broad part av the gut whin they gave, an' thin we opind out an'
fair danced down the valley, dhrivin' thim before us. Oh, 'twas
lovely, an' stiddy, too! There was the Sargints on the flanks av what
was left av us, kapin' touch, an' the fire was runnin' from flank to
flank, an' the Paythans was dhroppin'. We opind out wid the wid-
enin' av the valley, an' whin the valley narrowed we closed agin
like the shticks on a lady's fan, an' at the far ind av the gut where
they thried to stand, we fair blew them off their feet, for we had
expinded very little ammunition by reason av the knife-work.'

'*I* used thirty rounds goin' down that valley,' said Ortheris, 'an'
it was gentleman's work. Might 'a' done it in a white 'andkerchief
an' pink silk stockin's, that part. *Hi* was on in that piece.'

'You cud ha' heard the Tyrone yellin' a mile away,' said Mulvaney, 'an' 'twas all their Sargints cud do to get thim off. They was
mad – mad – mad! Crook sits down in the quiet that fell whin we
had gone down the valley, an' covers his face wid his hands. Prisintly
we all came back agin accordin' to our natur's and disposishins, for
they, mark you, show through the hide av a man in that hour.

' "Bhoys! bhoys!" sez Crook to himsilf. "I misdoubt we cud ha'
engaged at long range an' saved betther men than me." He looked
at our dead an' said no more.

' "Captain dear," sez a man ave the Tyrone, comin' up wid his
mouth bigger than iver his mother kissed ut, spittin' blood like a
whale; "Captain dear," sez he, "if wan or two in the shtalls have
been dishcommoded, the gallery have enjoyed the performinces av
a Roshus."

'Thin I knew that man for the Dublin dock-rat he was – wan av
the boys that made the lessee av Silver's Theatre grey before his
time wid tearin' out the bowils av the benches an' throwin' thim
into the pit. So I passed the wurrud that I knew whin I was in the
Tyrone an' we lay in Dublin. "I don't know who 'twas," I whish-
pers, "an' I don't care, but anyways I'll knock the face av you, Tim
Kelly."

' "Eyah!" sez the man, "was you there too? We'll call ut Silver's

Theatre." Half the Tyrone, knowin' the ould place, tuk ut up: so we called ut Silver's Theatre.

'The little orf'cer bhoy av the Tyrone was thremblin' an' cryin'. He had no heart for the Coort-Martials that he talked so big upon. "Ye'll do well later," sez Crook, very quiet, "for not bein' allowed to kill yoursilf for amusemint."

' "I'm a dishgraced man!" sez the little orf'cer bhoy.

' "Put me undher arrst, sorr, if you will, but, by my sowl, I'd do ut agin sooner than face your mother wid you dead," sez the Sargint that had sat on his head, standin' to attenshin an' salutin'. But the young wan only cried as tho' his little heart was breakin'.

'Thin another man av the Tyrone came up, wid the fog av fightin' on him.'

'The what, Mulvaney?'

'Fog av fightin'. You know, sorr, that, like makin' love, ut takes each man diff'rint. Now, I can't help bein' powerful sick whin I'm in action. Orth'ris, here, niver stops swearin' from ind to ind, an' the only time that Learoyd opins his mouth to sing is whin he is messin' wid other people's heads; for he's a dhirty fighter is Jock. Recruities sometime cry, an' sometime they don't know fwhat they do, an' sometime they are all for cuttin' throats an' such-like dhirtiness; but some men get heavy-dead-dhrunk on the fightin'. This man was. He was staggerin', an' his eyes were half shut, an' we cud hear him dhraw breath twinty yards away. He sees the little orf'cer bhoy, talkin' thick an' drowsy to himsilf. "Blood the young whelp!" he sez; "Blood the young whelp"; an' wid that he threw up his arrums, shpun roun', an' dropped at our feet, dead as a Paythan, an' there was niver sign or scratch on him. They said 'twas his heart was rotten, but oh, 'twas a quare thing to see!

'Thin we wint to bury our dead, for we wud not lave thim to the Paythans, an' in movin' among the haythen we nearly lost that little orf'cer bhoy. He was for givin' wan divil wather and layin' him aisy against a rock. "Be careful, sorr," sez I; "a wounded Paythan's worse than a live wan." My troth, before the words was out av me mouth, the man on the ground fires at the orf'cer bhoy lanin' over him, an' I saw the helmit fly. I dropped the butt on the face av the man an' tuk his pistol. The little orf'cer bhoy turned very white, for the hair av half his head was singed away.

' "I tould you so, sorr!" sez I; an', afther that, whin he wanted to help a Paythan I stud wid the muzzle contagious to the ear. They dared not do anythin' but curse. The Tyrone was growlin' like dogs over a bone that has been taken away too soon, for they had seen their dead an' they wanted to kill ivry sowl on the ground. Crook tould thim that he'd blow the hide off any man that misconducted himsilf; but, seeing that ut was the first time the Tyrone had iver seen their dead, I do not wondher they was on the sharp. 'Tis a shameful sight! Whin I first saw ut I wud niver ha' given quarter to any man north of the Khyber – no, nor woman either, for the wimmen used to come out afther dhark – Auggrh!

'Well, evenshually we buried our dead an' tuk away our wounded, an' come over the brow av the hills to see the Scotchies an' the Gurkys takin' tay with the Paythans in bucketsfuls. We were a gang av dissolute ruffians, for the blood had caked the dust, an' the sweat had cut the cake, an' our bay'nits was hangin' like butchers' steels betune our legs, an' most av us was marked one way or another.

'A Staff Orf'cer man, clane as a new rifle, rides up an' sez: "What damned scarecrows are you?"

' "A comp'ny av Her Majesty's Black Tyrone an' wan av the Ould Rig'mint," sez Crook very quiet, givin' our visitors the flure as 'twas.

' "Oh!" sez the Staff Orf'cer. "Did you dislodge that Reserve?"

' "No!" sez Crook, an' the Tyrone laughed.

' "Thin fwhat the divil have ye done?"

' "Disthroyed ut," sez Crook, an' he took us on, but not before Toomey that was in the Tyrone sez aloud, his voice somewhere in his stummick: "Fwhat in the name av misfortune does this parrit widout a tail mane by shtoppin' the road av his betthers?"

'The Staff Orf'cer wint blue, an' Toomey makes him pink by changin' to the voice av a minowdherin' woman an' sayin': "Come an' kiss me, Major dear, for me husband's at the wars an' I'm all alone at the depôt."

'The Staff Orf'cer wint away, an' I cud see Crook's shoulthers shakin'.

'His Corp'ril checks Toomey. "Lave me alone," sez Toomey, widout a wink. "I was his batman before he was married an' he knows fwhat I mane, av you don't. There's nothin' like livin' in the hoight av society." D'you remember that, Orth'ris?'

'Yuss. Toomey, 'e died in 'orspital, next week it was, 'cause I bought 'arf his kit; an' I remember after that –'

'GUARRD, TURN OUT!'

The Relief had come; it was four o'clock. 'I'll catch a kyart for yo, sorr,' said Mulvaney, diving hastily into his accoutrements. 'Come up to the top av the Fort an' we'll pershue our invistigations into M'Grath's shtable.' The relieved guard strolled round the main bastion on its way to the swimming-bath, and Learoyd grew almost talkative. Ortheris looked into the Fort Ditch and across the plain. 'Ho! it's weary waitin' for Ma-ary!' he hummed; 'but I'd like to kill some more bloomin' Paythans before my time's up. War! Bloody war! North, East, South, and West.'

'Amen,' said Learoyd slowly.

'Fwhat's here?' said Mulvaney, checking at a blur of white by the foot of the old sentry-box. He stooped and touched it. 'It's Norah – Norah M'Taggart! Why, Nonie darlin', fwhat are ye doin' out av your mother's bed at this time?'

The two-year-old child of Sergeant M'Taggart must have wandered for a breath of cool air to the very verge of the parapet of the Fort Ditch. Her tiny nightshift was gathered into a wisp round her neck and she moaned in her sleep. 'See there!' said Mulvaney; 'poor lamb! Look at the heatrash on the innocint shkin av her. 'Tis hard – crool hard even for us. Fwhat must it be for these? Wake up, Nonie, your mother will be woild about you. Begad, the child might ha' fallen into the Ditch!'

He picked her up in the growing light, and set her on his shoulder, and her fair curls touched the grizzled stubble of his temples. Ortheris and Learoyd followed snapping their fingers, while Norah smiled at them a sleepy smile. Then carolled Mulvaney, clear as a lark, dancing the baby on his arm:

> 'If any young man should marry you,
>   Say nothin' about the joke;
> That iver ye slep' in a sinthry-box,
>   Wrapped up in a soldier's cloak.'

'Though, on my sowl, Nonie,' he said gravely, 'there was not much cloak about you. Niver mind, you won't dhress like this ten years to come. Kiss your frinds an' run along to your mother.'

Nonie, set down close to the Married Quarters, nodded with the quiet obedience of the soldier's child, but, ere she pattered off over the flagged path, held up her lips to be kissed by the Three Musketeers. Ortheris wiped his mouth with the back of his hand and swore sentimentally! Learoyd turned pink; and the two walked away together. The Yorkshireman lifted up his voice and gave in thunder the chorus of *The Sentry-Box*, while Ortheris piped at his side.

'Bin to a bloomin' sing-song, you two?' said the Artilleryman, who was taking his cartridge down to the Morning Gun. 'You're over merry for these dashed days.'

> 'I bid ye take care o' the brat, said he,
>   For it comes of a noble race,'

Learoyd bellowed. The voices died out in the swimming-bath.

'Oh, Terence!' I said, dropping into Mulvaney's speech, when we were alone, 'it's you that have the Tongue!'

He looked at me wearily; his eyes were sunk in his head, and his face was drawn and white. 'Eyah!' said he; 'I've blandandhered thim through the night somehow, but can thim that helps others help thimsilves? Answer me that, sorr!'

And over the bastions of Fort Amara broke the pitiless day.

THE GILDED STAFF
(A Tale of the Old Contemptibles)

Boyd Cable

BROADLY speaking, the average regimental officer and man of the fighting units is firmly convinced beyond all argument that a 'Staff job' is an absolutely safe and completely *cushy* one, that the Staff-wallah always has the best of food and drink, a good roof over him, and a soft bed to lie on, nothing to do except maybe sign his name to a few papers when he feels so inclined, and perhaps in a casual and comfortable chat after a good dinner decide on a tactical move, a strafe of some sort, issue the orders in a sort of brief 'Take Hill 999' or 'retire by Dead Cow Corner to Two Tree Trench' style, and leave the regiments concerned to carry on. Briefly, the opinion of the firing line might be summed up in a short Credo:

'I believe the Staff is No Good.

'I believe the Staff has the cushiest of cushy jobs.

'I believe the Staff never hears a bullet whistle or sees a shell burst except through a telescope.

'I believe the Staff exists solely to find soft jobs for the wealthy and useless portion of the aristocracy.

'I believe the Staff does nothing except wear a supercilious manner and red tabs and trimmings.

'I believe the Staff is No Good.'

As to the average of correctness in this Credo I say nothing, but I can at least show that these things are not always thus.

The Staff had been having what the General's youthful and irrepressibly cheerful aide-de-camp called 'a hectic three days'. The Headquarters signallers had been going hard night and day until one of them was driven to remark bitterly as he straightened his bent back from over his instrument and waggled his stiffened fingers that had been tapping the 'buzzer' for hours on end, 'I'm developin' a permanent hump on my back like a dog scrapin' a pot, an' if my fingers isn't to be wore off by inches I'll have to get the farrier to put a set of shoes on 'em.' But the signallers had some advantages that the Staff hadn't, and one was that they could arrange spells of duty and at least have a certain time off for rest and sleep. The Staff Captain would have given a good deal for that privilege by about the third night. The worst of his job was that he had no time when he could be sure of a clear ten minutes' rest. He had messages brought to him as he devoured scratch meals; he was roused from such short sleeps as he could snatch lying fully dressed on a camp bed, by telephone and telegraph messages, or, still worse, by horrible scrawls badly written in faint pencillings that his weary eyes could barely decipher as he sat up on his bed with a pocket electric glaring on the paper; once he even had to abandon an attempt to shave, wipe the lather from his face, and hustle to impart some information to a waiting General. A very hot fight was raging along that portion of front, and almost every report from the firing line contained many map references which necessitated so many huntings of obscure points on the maps that the mere reading and understanding of a message might take a full five or ten minutes; and in the same way the finding of regiments' positions for the General's information or the sending of orders added ten-fold to the map-hunting.

The third day was about the most 'hectic' of all. For the Captain it began before daybreak with a call to the telephone which came just two hours after he had shuffled and shaken together the papers he had been working on without a break through the night, pulled off his boots, blown out his lamp, and dropped with a sigh of relief on his bed in a corner of the room. It was an urgent and personal call, and the first dozen words effectually drove the lingering sleep from the Captain's eyes and brain. 'Yes, yes, "heavily attacked," I got that; go on . . . no, I don't think I need to refer to the map; I very nearly know the beastly thing by heart now . . . yes . . . yes . . . Who? . . . killed outright . . . that's bad . . . Who's in command now then . . . right. The Dee and Don Trenches – wait a minute, which are they? Oh yes, I remember, south from the Pigsty and across to Stink Farm . . . right. I'll pass it on at once and let you know in five minutes . . . just repeat map references so I can make a note . . . yes . . . yes . . . yes . . . right . . .'Bye.'

The urgency of the message, which told of a heavy and partially successful attack on the Divisional Front, wiped out any hope the Captain might have had of a return to his broken sleep. For the next two hours his mind was kept at full stretch reducing to elaborated details the comprehensive commands of the General, locating reserves and supports and Battalion H.Q.s, exchanging long messages with the Artillery, collecting figures of ammunition states, available strengths, casualty returns, collating and sifting them out, reshuffling them and offering them up to the Brigade Major or the General, absorbing or distributing messages from and to concrete personalities or nebulous authorities known widely if vaguely as the D.A.A.G., D.A.Q.M.G., D.A.D.O.S., A.D.M.S., C.D.S., and T., and other strings of jumbled initials.

He washed in the sparing dimensions of a canvas wash-stand, Field Service, x Pattern, deliberately taking off his coat and rolling up his shirt-sleeves, and firmly turning a deaf and soap-filled ear to the orderly who placed a ruled telephone message form on his table and announced it urgent. Afterwards he attended to the message, and talked into the telephone while his servant cleared one side of his table and served plentiful bacon, and eggs of an unknown period. Immediately after this a concentrated bombardment suddenly developed on a ruined château some three or four hundred yards from the H.Q. farm. To the youthful aide-de-camp who had arrived from the outer dampness dripping water from every angle of a streaming mackintosh he remarked wrathfully on the prospect of having to move once again in the middle of such beastly waterfall weather. The aide stood at the brown-paper patched window, chuckling and watching the shells rewreck the already wrecked château. 'Looks as if their spies had sold 'em a pup this time,' he said gleefully. 'I believe they must have been told we were in that old ruin instead of here. Or they were told this place and mistook it on the map for the château. Rather a lark – what!'

'Confound the larks,' said the Captain bitterly, 'especially if they come any nearer this way. This place is quite leaky and draughty enough now without it getting any more shrap or splinter holes punched in it.'

Here the Captain had a short break from his inside job, leaving another officer to look after that and accompanying the General on horseback to a conference with various Brigadiers, Colonels, and Commanding Officers. The ride was too wet to be pleasant, and at no time could a better pace than a jog trot be made because on the road there was too much horse, foot, and wheeled traffic, and off the road in the swimming fields it took the horses all their time to keep their feet.

The conference was held under the remaining quarter-roof of a shell-smashed farm, and the Captain listened and made notes in a damp book, afterwards accompanying the General on a ride round to where something could be seen of the position, and back to H.Q. Here, under the General's direction in consultation with the Brigade Major, he elaborated and extended his notes, drafted detailed directions for a number of minor moves next day, and translated them into terms of map-reference language, and a multitude of details of roads to be followed by different units, billeting areas, rationing, and refilling points, and so on.

He made a hasty, tinned lunch, and at the General's request set out to find one of the Battalion Headquarters and there meet some C.O.s and make clear to them certain points of the dispositions arranged. He went in a motor, sped on his way by the cheerful information of the aide that the town through which he must pass had been under 'a deuce of hot fire' all day, had its streets full of Jack Johnson holes, and was in a continual state of blowing up, falling down, or being burnt out. 'I was through there this morning,' said the aide, 'and I tell you it was warmish. Sentry outside on the road wanted to stop me at first; said he'd orders to warn everybody it wasn't safe. Wasn't safe,' repeated the youth, chuckling, 'Lord, after I'd been through there I'd have given that sentry any sort of a certificate of truthfulness. It was *not* safe.'

The Captain went off with his motor skating from ditch to ditch down the greasy road. The guns were rumbling and banging up in front, and as the car bumped and slithered nearer to the town the Captain could hear the long yelling whistle and the deep rolling crashes of heavy shells falling somewhere in it. He too was stopped at the outskirts by a sentry who held up his hand to the driver, and then came and parleyed with the Captain through the window. The Captain impatiently cut his warnings shorts. There was no other road that would take him near the point he desired to reach; he must go through the town; he must ride since he could not spare time to walk. He climbed out and mounted beside the driver, with some instinctive and vaguely formed ideas in his mind that if the driver were hit he might have to take the wheel, that the car might be upset and pin him underneath, that he might be able to assist in picking a course through rubbish and shell-holes, to jump out and clear any slight obstruction from in front of the wheels. The car ran on slowly into the town. Decidedly the aide had been right, except that 'warmish' was a mild word for the state of affairs. The Germans were flinging shells into the town as if they meant to destroy it utterly. The main street through was littered with bricks and tiles and broken furniture; dead horses were sprawled in it, some limp and new killed with the blood still running from their wounds, others with their four legs sticking out post-stiff in the air; in several places there were broken-down carts, in one place a regular mass of them piled up and locked in a confused tangle of broken wheels, splintered shafts, cut harness, and smashed woodwork, their contents spilled out anyhow and mixed up inextricably with the wreckage.

There was not much traffic in the main street, and such as was there was evidently, like the Captain himself, only there because no other road offered. There were half a dozen artillery ammunition waggons, a few infantry transport carts, several Army Service Corps vehicles. All of them were moving at a trot, the waggons rumbling and lumbering heavily and noisily over the cobble-stones, the drivers stooped forward and peering out anxiously to pick a way between the obstacles in their path. The shells were coming over continuously, moaning and howling and yelling, falling with tearing crashes amongst the houses, blowing them wall from wall, slicing corners off or cutting a complete top or end away, breaking them down in rattling cascades of tiles and bricks, bursting them open and flinging them high and far upwards and outwards in flying fragments. As the car crawled cautiously through the débris that littered the street, pieces of brick and mortar, whole or broken slates, chips of wood and stone, pattered and rapped constantly down about and on the car; the wheels crunched and ground on splintered glass from the gaping windows. A shell roared down on the street ahead of them, burst thunderously in a vivid sheet of flame and spurting black cloud of smoke, an appalling crash that rolled and reverberated loud and long up and down the narrow street. 'Go easy,' cautioned the Captain as the black blinding reek came swirling down to meet them, 'or you'll run into the hole that fellow made.' The driver's face was set and white, and his hands gripped tight on the wheel; the Captain had a sudden compunction that he had brought him, that he had not left the car outside the town and walked through. They edged carefully past the yawning shell-crater with the smoke still clinging and curling up from its edges, and, free of the smoke again, saw a fairly clear stretch ahead of them. The Captain heard the thin but rising whistle of another heavy shell approaching, and 'Open her out,' he said quickly, 'and let her rip.' The driver, he noticed, for all his white face had his nerves well under control, and steadily caught the change of gear on the proper instant, speeded up sharply but quite smoothly. The car swooped down the clear stretch, the roar of the shell growing louder and closer, and just as they reached and crammed the brakes on to take the corner, they heard the shell crash down behind them. The Captain leaned out and looked back, and had a momentary glimpse of a house on the street spouting black smoke, dissolving and cascading down and out across the road in a torrent of bricks and wreckage. In another two minutes they shot out clear of the town. A mile farther on a soldier warned them that the cross-roads were practically impassable, the roadway being broken and churned up by the heavy shells that all afternoon had been and were still at intervals falling upon it. So the Captain left the car and went on a-foot. He was nearly caught at the cross-roads, a shell fragment ripping a huge rent in his mackintosh just over his ribs. Before he reached the communication trenches too he had a highly uncomfortable minute with light high-explosive shells bursting round him while he crouched low in a muddly shell-crater. He reached the meeting-place at last, and spent an hour talking over plans and movements, and by the time he was ready to start back it was rapidly growing dark. It was completely dark before he found his way back to the road again, stumbling over the shell-holed ground, slipping and floundering through the mud, tripping once and falling heavily over some strands of barbed wire. When he found the car again he was so dirty and draggled and dishevelled and ragged – the barbed wire had taken the cap from his head and dropped it in a mud puddle, and left another tear or two in his mackintosh – so smeared and plastered with mud, that his driver at first failed to recognize him. In the town he found parties of the Sappers filling up the worst of the shell-holes and clearing away the débris that blocked the road where he had seen the house blown down, while the shells still screamed up and burst clattering over and amongst the houses, and bullets and splinters whistled and sang overhead, clashed and rattled on the causeway.

He slept snatchily through the rest of the journey, waking many times as the car bumped badly, and once, when it dropped heavily into a shell-hole and bounced out again, flinging him bodily upwards until his head and shoulder banged solidly against the roof, taking half a minute to regain his scattered wits and dissipate a wild dream that the car had been fairly hit by a shell.

And when at last he reached H.Q., crawled wearily out of the car, and staggered, half asleep and utterly worn out, into his room, he found there the other officer he had left to handle his work and the youthful aide humped over the table copying out reports.

'Hullo,' said the senior, 'you're late. I say, you do look tucked up.'

The Captain grunted. 'Not more'n I feel,' he said, blinking at the light. 'Thank the Lord my job's over and everything fixed and ready so far's this end goes.'

'You've heard, I suppose?' said the other. 'No? Baddish news. Our left has cracked and the Germ has a slice of their trenches. It upsets all our plans, and we've got 'em all to make over again.'

The Captain stared blankly at him. 'All to make . . . that means all today's work to begin and go through again. All today's work – well, I'm . . .'

The aide had been eyeing the mud-bedaubed figure with water dripping from the torn coat, the sopping cap dangling in the dirty hand, the blue unshaven chin and red-rimmed eyes. He giggled suddenly. 'I say, you know what the troops call the Staff?' He spluttered laughter. 'The Gilded Staff,' he said, pointing at the Captain. 'Behold – oh, my aunt – behold the *Gilded Staff*.'

THE SURVIVOR

Bartimeus

'. . . And regrets to report only one survivor.'
Admiralty Announcement.

THE glass dropped another point, and the captain of the cruiser glanced for the hundredth time from the lowering sky to the two destroyers labouring stubbornly in the teeth of the gale on either beam. Then he gave an order to the yeoman of signals, who barked its repetition to the shelter-deck where the little group of signalmen stamped their feet and blew on their numbed fingers in the lee of the flag-lockers. Two of the group scuffled round the bright-coloured bunting: the clips of the halliards snapped a hoist together, and vivid against the grey sky the signal went bellying and fluttering to the masthead.

The figures on the bridges of the destroyers wiped the stinging spray from their swollen eyelids and read the message of comfort.

'Return to base. Weather conditions threatening.'

They surveyed their battered bridges and forecastles, their stripped, streaming decks and guns' crews; they thought of hot food, warm bunks, dry clothing, and all the sordid creature comforts for which soul and body yearn so imperiously after three years of North Sea warfare. Their answering pendants fluttered acknowledgement, and they swung round on the path for home, praising Allah who had planted in the brain of the cruiser captain a consideration for the welfare of his destroyer screen.

'If this is what they call "threatening",' observed the senior officer of the two boats, as his command clove shuddering through the jade-green belly of a mountainous sea, flinging the white entrails broadcast, 'if this is merely threatening I reckon it's about time someone said "Home, James!" '

His first lieutenant said nothing. He had spent three winters in these grey wastes, and he knew the significance of that unearthly clear visibility and the inky clouds banked ahead to the westward. But presently he looked up from the chart and nodded towards the menace in the western sky. 'That's snow,' he said. 'It ought to catch us about the time we shall make Scaw Dhu light.'

'We'll hear the fog buoy all right,' said the captain.

'If the pipes ain't frozen,' was the reply. 'It's perishing cold.' He ran a gauntletted hand along the rail and extended a handful of frozen spray. 'That's salt – *and* frozen . . .'

The snow came as he had predicted, but rather sooner. It started with great whirling flakes like feathers about a gull's nesting-place, a soundless ethereal vanguard of the storm, growing momentarily denser. The wind, from a temporary lull, reawakened with a roar. The air became a vast witch's cauldron of white and brown specks, seething before the vision in a veritable Bacchanal of Atoms. Sight became a lost sense: time, space, and feeling were overwhelmed by that shrieking fury of snow and frozen spray thrashing pitilessly about the homing grey hulls and the bowed heads of the men who clung to the reeling bridges.

The grey, white-crested seas raced hissing alongside and, as the engine-room telegraphs rang again and again for reduced speed, overtook and passed them. Out of the welter of snow and spray the voices of the leadsmen chanting soundings reached the ears of those inboard as the voice of a doctor reaches a patient in delirium, fruitlessly reassuring . . .

Number Three of the midship gun on board the leading destroyer turned for the comfort of his soul from the contemplation of the pursuing seas to the forebridge, but snow-flakes blotted it from view. Providence, as he was accustomed to visualize it in the guise of a red-cheeked lieutenant-commander, had vanished from his ken. Number Three drew his hands from his pockets, and raising them to his mouth leaned towards the gunlayer. The gunlayer was also staring forward as if his vision had pierced that whirling grey curtain and was contemplating something beyond it, infinitely remote . . . There was a concentrated intensity in his expression not unlike that of a dog when he raises his head from his paws and looks towards a closed door.

''Ere,' bawled Number Three, seeking comradeship in an oppressive, indefinable loneliness. ''Ow about it – eh? . . .' The wind snatched at the meaningless words and beat them back between his chattering teeth.

The wind backed momentarily, sundering the veil of whirling obscurity. Through this rent towered a wall of rock, streaked all about with driven snow, at the foot of which breakers beat themselves into a smoking yeast of fury. Gulls were wailing overhead. Beneath their feet the engine room gongs clanged madly.

Then they struck.

The foremost destroyer checked on the shoulder of a great roller as if incredulous: shuddered: struck again and lurched over. A mountainous sea engulfed her stern and broke thundering against the after-funnel. Steam began to pour in dense hissing clouds from the engine-room hatchways and exhausts. Her consort swept past with screeching syren, helpless in the grip of the backwash for all her thrashing propellers that strove to check her headlong way. She too struck and recoiled: sagged in the trough of two stupendous seas, and plunged forward again . . . Number Three, clinging to the greasy breech-block of his gun, clenched his teeth at the sound of that pitiless grinding which seemed as if it would never end . . .

Of the ensuing horror he missed nothing, yet saw it all with a wondering detachment. A wave swept him off his feet against a funnel-stay, and receding, left him clinging to it like a twist of waterlogged straw. Hand over hand he crawled higher, and finally hung dangling six feet above the highest wave, legs and arms round about the wire stay. He saw the forecastle break off like a stick of canteen chocolate and vanish into the smother. The other destroyer had disappeared. Beneath him, waist deep in boiling eddies, he saw men labouring about a raft, and had a vision of their upturned faces as they were swept away. The thunder of the surf on the beaches close at hand drowned the few shouts and cries that sounded. The wire from which he dangled jarred and twanged like a banjo-string, as the triumphant seas beat the soul out of the wreck beneath him.

A funnel-stay parted, and amid clouds of smoke and steam the funnel slowly began to list over the side. Number Three of the midship gun clung swaying like a wind-tossed branch above the maelstrom of seething water till a wave drove over the already-unrecognizable hull of the destroyer, leaped hungrily at the dangling human figure and tore him from his hold.

Bitterly cold water and a suffocating darkness engulfed him. Something clawed at his face and fastened on to his shoulder; he wrenched himself free from the nerveless clutch without ruth or understanding; his booted heel struck a yielding object as he struggled surfaceward, kicking wildly like a swimming frog . . . the blackness became streaked with grey light and pinpoints of fire. Number Three had a conviction that unless the next few strokes brought him to the surface it would be too late. Then abruptly the clamour of the wind and sea, and the shriek of the circling gulls smote his ears again. He was back on the surface once more, gulping greedy lungfuls of air.

A wave caught him and hurled him forward on its crest, spread-eagled, feebly continuing the motions of a swimmer. It spent itself, and to husband his strength the man turned on his back, moving his head from side to side to take in his surroundings.

He was afloat (he found it surprisingly easy to keep afloat) inside a narrow bay. On both sides the black cliffs rose, all streaked with snow, out of a thunderous welter of foam. The tide sobbed and lamented in the hollows of unseen caverns, or sluiced the length of a ledge to plash in cascades down the face of the cliff.

The snow had abated, and in the gathering dusk the broken water showed ghostly white. To seaward the gale drove the smoking rollers in successive onslaughts against the reef where the battered remains of the two destroyers lay. All about the distorted plating and tangle of twisted stanchions the surf broke as if in a fury of rapine and destruction . . .

Another wave gripped him and rushed him shoreward again. The thunder of the surf redoubled. 'Hi! hi! hi! hi!' screeched the storm-tossed gulls. Number Three of the midship gun abandoned his efforts to swim and covered his face with his soggy sleeve. It was well not to look ahead. The wave seemed to be carrying him towards the cliffs at the speed of an express train. He wondered if the rocks would hurt much, beating out his life . . . He tried desperately to remember a prayer, but all he could recall was a sermon he had once listened to on the quarter-deck, one drowsy summer morning

at Malta . . . About coming to Jesus on the face of the waters . . .
'And Jesus said "come" . . .' Fair whizzing along, he was . . .

Again the wave spent itself, and the man 'was caught in the
backwash, drawn under, rolled over and over, spun round and
round, gathered up in the watery embrace of another roller and
flung up on all fours on a shelving beach. Furiously he clawed at
the retreating pebbles, lurched to his feet, staggered forward a couple
of paces, and fell on hands and knees on the fringe of a snow-drift.
There he lay awhile, panting for breath.

He was conscious of an immense amazement, and, mingled with
it, an inexplicable pride. He was still alive! It was an astounding
achievement, being the solitary survivor of all those officers and
men. But he had always considered himself a bit out of the
ordinary . . . Once he had entered for a race at the annual sports at
the Naval Barracks, Devonport. He had never run a race before in
his life, and he won. It seemed absurdly easy. 'Bang!' went the
pistol: off they went, helter-skelter, teeth clenched, fists clenched,
hearts pounding, spectators a blur, roaring encouragement . . .

He won, and experienced the identical astonished gratification
that he felt now.

'You runs like a adjective 'are, Bill,' his chum had admitted,
plying the hero with beer at the little pub halfway up the cobbled
hill by the dockyard.

Then he remembered other chums, shipmates, and one in particular called Nobby. He rose into a sitting position, staring seaward.
Through the gloom the tumult of the seas, breaking over the reef
on which they had foundered, glimmered white. The man rose
unsteadily to his feet; he was alone on the beach of a tiny cove with
his back to forbidding cliffs. Save where his own footsteps showed
black, the snow was unmarked, stretching in an unbroken arc from
one side of the cove to the other. The solitary figure limped to the
edge of the surf and peered through the stinging scud. Then, raising
his hands to his mouth, he began to call for his lost mate.

'Nobby!' he shouted, and again and again, 'Nobby! Nobby! . . .
Nob-bee-e!' . . .

'Nobby,' echoed the cliffs behind, disinterestedly.

'Hi! Hi! Hi!' mocked the gulls.

The survivor waded knee-deep into the froth of an incoming sea.

'Ahoy!' he bawled to the driving snow-flakes and spindrift. His voice sounded cracked and feeble. He tried to shout again, but the thunder of the waves beat the sound to nothing.

He retraced his steps and paused to look round at the implacable face of the cliff, at the burden of snow that seemed to overhang the summit, then stared again to seaward. A wave broke hissing about his feet: the tide was coming in.

Up to that moment fear had passed him by. He had been in turn bewildered, incredulous, cold, sick, bruised, but sustained throughout by the furious animal energy which the body summons in a fight for life. Now, however, with the realization of his loneliness in the gathering darkness, fear smote him. In fear he was as purely animal as he had been in his moments of blind courage. He turned from the darkling sea that had claimed chum and shipmates, and floundered through the snow-drifts to the base of the cliff. Then, numbed with cold, and well-nigh spent, he began frantically to scale the shelving surfaces of the rock.

Barnacles tore the flesh from his hands and the nails from his finger-tips as he clawed desperately at the crevices for a hold. Inch by inch, foot by foot he fought his way upwards from the threatening clutch of the hungry tide, leaving a crimson stain at every niche where the snow had gathered. Thrice he slipped and slithered downwards, bruised and torn, to renew his frantic efforts afresh. Finally he reached a broad shelf of rock, halfway up the surface of the cliff, and there rested awhile, whimpering softly to himself at the pain of his flayed hands.

Presently he rose again and continued the dizzy ascent. None but a sailor or an experienced rock-climber would have dreamed of attempting such a feat single-handed, well-nigh in the dark. Even had he reached the top he could not have walked three yards in the dense snow-drifts that had gathered all along the edge of the cliffs. But the climber knew nothing about that; he was in search of *terra firma*, something that was not slippery rock or shifting pebbles, somewhere out of reach of the sea.

He was within six feet of the summit when he lost a foothold, slipped, grabbed at a projecting knob of rock, slipped again, and so slipping and bumping and fighting for every inch, he slid heavily down on to his ledge again.

He lay bruised and breathless where he fell. That tumble came near to finishing matters; it winded him – knocked the fight out of him. But a wave, last and highest of the tide, sluiced over the ledge and immersed his shivering body once more in icy water; the unreasoning terror of the pursuing tide that had driven him up the face of the cliff whipped him to his feet again.

He backed against the rock, staring out through the driving spindrift into the menace of the darkness. There ought to be another wave any moment: then there would be another: and after that perhaps another. The next one then would get him. He was too weak to climb again . . .

The seconds passed and merged into minutes. The wind came at him out of the darkness like invisible knives thrown to pin him to a wall. The cold numbed his intelligence, numbed even his fear. He heard the waves breaking all about him in a wild pandemonium of sound, but it was a long time before he realized that no more had invaded his ledge, and a couple of hours before it struck him that the tide had turned . . .

Towards midnight he crawled down from his ledge and followed the retreating tide across the slippery shale, pausing every few minutes to listen to the uproar of sea and wind. An illusion of hearing human voices calling out of the gale mocked him with strange persistence. Once or twice he stumbled over a dark mass of weed stranded by the retreating tide, and each time bent down to finger it apprehensively.

Dawn found him back in the shelter of his cleft, scraping limpets from their shells for a breakfast. The day came slowly over a grey sea, streaked and smeared like the face of an old woman after a night of weeping. Of the two destroyers nothing broke the surface. It was nearly high water, and whatever remained of their battered hulls was covered by a tumultuous sea. They were swallowed. The sea had taken them – them and a hundred-odd officers and men, old shipmates, messmates, townies, raggies – just swallowed the lot . . . He still owed last month's mess-bill to the caterer of his mess . . . He put his torn hands before his eyes and strove to shut out the awful grey desolation of that hungry sea.

During the forenoon a flotilla of destroyers passed well out to seaward. They were searching the coast for signs of the wrecks, and the spray blotted them intermittently from sight as they wallowed at slow speed through the grey seas.

The survivor watched them and waved his jumper tied to a piece of drift-wood; but they were too far off to see him against the dark rocks. They passed round a headland, and the wan figure, half frozen and famished, crawled back into his cleft like a stricken animal, dumb with cold and suffering. It was not until the succeeding low water, when the twisted ironwork was showing black above the broken water on the reef, that another destroyer hove in sight. She too was searching for her lost sisters, and the castaway watched her alter course and nose cautiously towards the cove. Then she stopped and went astern.

The survivor brandished his extemporized signal of distress and emitted a dull croaking sound between his cracked lips. A puff of white steam appeared above the destroyer's bridge, and a second later the reassuring hoot of a siren floated in from the offing. They had seen him.

A sudden reaction seized his faculties. Almost apathetically he watched a sea-boat being lowered, saw it turn and come towards him, rising and falling on the heavy seas, but always coming nearer . . . he didn't care much whether they came or not – he was that cold. The very marrow of his bones seemed to be frozen. They'd have to come and fetch him if they wanted him. He was too cold to move out of his cleft.

The boat was very near. It was a whaler, and the bowman had boated his oar, and was crouching in the bows with a heaving-line round his forearm. The boat was plunging wildly, and spray was flying from under her. The cliffs threw back the orders of the officer at the tiller as he peered ahead from under his tarpaulin sou'wester with anxiety written on every line of his weatherbeaten face. He didn't fancy the job, that much was plain; and indeed, small blame to him. It was no light undertaking, nursing a small boat close in to a dead lee shore, with the aftermath of such a gale still running.

They came still closer, and the heaving line hissed through the air to fall at the castaway's feet.

'Tie it round your middle,' shouted the lieutenant. 'You'll have to jump for it – we'll pull you inboard all right.'

The survivor obeyed dully, reeled to the edge of his ledge and slid once more into the bitterly cold water.

Half a dozen hands seemed to grasp him simultaneously, and he was hauled over the gunwale of the boat almost before he realized he had left his ledge. A flask was crammed between his chattering teeth; someone wound fold upon fold of blanket round him.

'Any more of you, mate?' said a voice anxiously; and then, 'Strike me blind if it ain't old Bill!'

The survivor opened his eyes and saw the face of the bowman contemplating him above his cork lifebelt. It was a vaguely familiar face. They had been shipmates somewhere once. Barracks, Devonport, p'raps it was. He blinked the tears out of his eyes and coughed as the raw spirit ran down his throat.

'Any more of you, Bill, ole lad?'

The survivor shook his head.

'There's no one,' he said, ''cept me. I'm the only one what's lef' outer two ships' companies.' Again the lost feeling of bewildered pride crept back.

'You always was a one, Bill!' said the bowman in the old familiar accent of hero-worship.

The survivor nodded confirmation. 'Not 'arf I ain't,' he said appreciatively. 'Sole survivor I am!' And held out his hand again for the flask. 'Christ! look at my 'ands!'

THE FIRST BLOOD SWEEP

C. E. Montague

And giddy Fortune's furious, fickle wheel:
That goddess blind
That stands upon the rolling, restless stone.
Ancient Pistol

WHAT happened that day put me off, and the place was not quite the same to me afterwards. It was the only good dug-out I knew – I was a full corporal then – in the jerry-built front east of Bully Grenay. 'If it isn't the snug little howl,' McGuffin would say, 'get me one.' It came up to the notions I had, when a boy, of the great times a marmot must have in winter. For one thing, it hadn't been cursed with a bolt-hole – a second way out – to give you your death with the draught. That was why a Brass Hat on the prowl had once called it a death-trap. The Germans, he said, had nothing to do but to bung up the open front door with a shell-cast of earth, in order to put us to death, cheaply. Brass Hats *have* to be talking. We called the place Old Death ever after. It made one more joke against the Hats. Besides, as McGuffin said, 'it's the wife ye're right fond of that ye'd be for callin' "Y'owld toad." '

To get in, you certainly had to be handy. You slung yourself in through a square, timbered hole, like the frame of a picture, set in the back wall of the trench. The bottom of this wooden hatch was clear above high-water mark, at any rate in good weather. Then down a dozen steps cut in the chalk. There was no need to fall down these stairs the way people did. At the foot of the stairs you did not turn right, nor yet left, as in most of the drains that passed for dug-outs in those parts. You went straight on, into the heart of the land. First came a bit of clean darkness, say thirty feet long. Then a belt, thirty or forty feet thick, of the smoke that had missed the chimney-pipe over our brazier. This barrage had to be crossed. As soon as it thinned you began to get visions of lights round an altar, burning straight up and quiet. Then you were there.

That nest was right out of the world. It had the warmth and scent of the fire, and all the air there was only just tinted a dreamy blue with the smoke. We knew we had a good thing, and we kept it up well. Two waterproof sheets were always hung neatly, spread under the roof, to catch the drippings of water, and milked into tins as soon as they bellied. We had a piece of board for a larder, hanging by strings in mid-air, to diddle the rats. We always brought up from billets a little clean straw, to lay on the floor, and we were so far from the door that most of the yellow mud and white chalk had rubbed off our boots before we had crossed the smoke belt. We had saved from the outer wall of a wrecked house at Grenay a twelve-foot length of iron pipe, a down-comer, and coaxed it through the earth above the brazier. It made a grand chimney – the one that was missed, as I said, by some of the smoke. But not by too much. You could do with a frowst, in reason, whenever you came in wet from the trench.

It was a good time, too, when this trouble began. I had just whacked the rations out for the day, and the jam was strawberry. Quite half of the bully had come out Maconochie of the prime. Price, our Q.M.S. (God reward him!), had thrown in a bit of cold ham. The two men, of our lot, who were officers' servants had failed to come round, up to time, for their cigarette ration, so this was a little bonus thrown in for the rest. We were all smoking. The fire was burning all right. The post had come in half an hour ago.

It was the post, so to speak, that began it. Ince, that we used to call Coom-fra-Wigan, had started reading a paper that was all creases and curves from coming by post. I had been watching his lips working, shaping the words as he read to himself. And then he let the paper fall on his legs – of course, he was sitting down on the floor like everyone else, with his back to the wall.

'Fair puts lid on, thot do,' he said in the flat, draggy way of speaking that some of them have in the north.

'Wot O?' Lance-Corporal Mason chirped up. Mason was always great on 'keeping up the *moral* o' my men,' as he said.

'Ah see in paaper,' Ince went trailing on, ''s 'ow foalks at whoam 'as got agaate o' stoppin' futball. Noa raacin'! Noa bowlin'! No whoamin' birds! An' it's noa futball noo!' he went on mourning.

Then Tommy Tween must cut in. Tommy would almost take the word out of your mouth. 'Ow, gow it! Turn 'em all dahn! Never mind us. 'Ow, naow! Wot'd we wawnt wiv a little bit of int'rest in life? Not likely!'

Ince went on from where he had stopped. 'Ah b'lieve it's these paapers done it.' He took a savage grip of the sample he had there on his thighs. 'Doan't like a bit o' spoort, paapers doan't. Costs 'em mooney.'

'Thet's it,' Tween interrupted, as if Ince had been stealing a story of his. 'The pipers done it. Want to get aht o' pyin' a fair wige to a taht for 'angin' abaht Noomawket 'Eath. It tikes a man o' skill to watch a maw'nin' gallop. Not like war correspondin'. Naow use feedin' backers a bag of emowshnal bilge abaht 'eroes an' cheery wounded an' any ol' muck. A taht must know 'is job. Ah, an' 'e's got to be there. An' wiges accordin'. You tike it from me, Wigan, it's orl a do, got up be the pipers.'

Ince still gripped his paper, so to speak, by the scruff of its neck. He shook it a little. 'They taalk a lot in the paaper,' he droned along, 'aboot "evils o' gamblin' ".'

'Lummy!' Tween cried out. 'Wot are we fightin' for? Libbety, yn't it? An' wot's backin' your ahn judgement? Libbety!'

'They sa-ay,' Coom-fra-Wigan went on, ''s 'ow it taakes men's minds orf o' their work.'

Tween was started now. 'Puts 'em on to it, more like. Wot mide th' Austrylians tike Polygon Wood? Down't orl the worl' know they was after the ricecourse?'

'Thot's reet,' Ince certified fairly.

'Sime wi' th' 'ole o' mankin',' said Tween, quite excited. It is not only that which comes in at a man's mouth that can go to his head, but that which goes out of it too. 'A Chink'll put a bit on anyfink – 'orses, cocks, dogs – nuffink comes wrong to 'im. Two Chinks 'll meet in the rowd an' each tike a louse aht of 'is tunic – proper 'oppers they 'ave, sime as ours – an' 'ev a match, ricin' 'em. Ah, an' stop there all dye! An' if one of 'em finds 'e's got 'old of a flyer, 'e'll put 'im back where 'e come from. Ullow! Ullow! Not time, shorely?'

None of these orators likes interruption. And now the interrupting old world was too much with us again. First, a plash of trench water lipping over our door-step, a hundred feet off, and slopping its way down the stairs, as somebody up in the trench waded nearer and nearer, kicking the waters before him. Then the voice of the platoon-sergeant, Gort, came smashing in at the door. 'Blunt and Gubbins! Get on guard.'

It always seemed to me like an adventure to have my name shouted by Gort. The harsh ring in his voice strung you up, the way some kinds of cold winds do. Blunt and Gubbins were buckling their belts in a second – unbuckling your belts was all the undressing allowed you in trenches. But Gort's voice came again like a box on the ear before they were out through the smoke: 'Why the hell don't you get a move on?'

Tween whispered: 'Bit stuffy, the sawjint.' But I could never have enough of the clang of Gort's voice. It made me feel what a lot of fine, rousing things there must be in the world that I had not thought of.

In five minutes more we heard the cascade splashing again on the stairs, and a little more than the usual swearing from somebody having the usual fight to get dry through the door. Then a few clod-hopping steps, and two men clumped in through the smoke. They were the two just relieved – he that had sworn such a lot, and another.

The other was Hanney, an eager, white boy with a thoroughbred face, just out on a draft. He had been with us three days. He had been in the army three weeks and had seen a deal of life in the time. The first ten days, not knowing his drill, he had spoilt the good looks of a section at home. Then a sage sergeant-major had ended the bother by getting Hanney put on to the next draft for the front, where there was no smartness needed. Hanney was charmed with this bit of policy. Still, it had its drawbacks. He had not learnt the soldierly knack of letting harm miss him. His first day with us he had seen a shell fall, but not burst, on the far side of the square by the café at Bully Grenay. With the God-given thirst of a wise child for knowledge, Hanney had rushed across to examine. The shell, on second thoughts, had gone off, and there cannot have been many vacant spaces, big enough to hold Hanney, between the flying bits of metal and paving-stone and other bad solids. But he was in one of the spaces, every bit of him. This business filled him with shame. Next day he had gone on a fatigue with a score of our tin water-bottles hung on his back, to fill at the cart. By one of the flukes that do happen, a flake of a shell had sheared right through the whole of this outfit of tin-ware, turning it all into silvery ribbons and rags. It had not touched the boy. This elated the boy, for he was not to blame. Still, he was rather apologetic about the interest he took in these little occurrences. All of us, he pretty clearly thought, must have had more stirring experiences daily. So we tried to be rather nice too, and allowed the Kid had powlert up and down a bit and had two rattling days. Today was his third. We did not know, really, whether to think that nothing could kill him ever, or that, at the rate he was going, he'd not last a week.

Tween had still a little bit left from his old rush of words to the mouth. 'Wot ow!' he said to the Kid. 'Is't you been gettin' aht the sawjint's shirt?'

Hanney laughed at the notion. 'Shirty! He's great. I could do a lot of work for Gort and not feel tired. You didn't hear, did you, just now?' He paused for a moment. 'Of course, it wasn't anything out of the way, but the old Boche put it across us a bit, just for a little. And then Gort was up and down the trench every minute, looking after us all. I'd hear him asking, before he came round the corner, "Hanney all right there?" "Hanney not hit?" All the time.'

'Wot! Downcher knaow?' Tween almost hooted.

'I know he's all right,' Hanney said sturdily. 'Regular father he is to his men.' You see, Hanney was young.

It made Tween roar. 'Ya silly baa-lamb! Downcher knaow Gort drew you in the sweep?'

I do say this for Tween – nobody could have thought that the Kid would mind it so much. Of course, the rest of us had long been used to the thought that whichever of us was first to be killed, each time we came into the line, would bring in a good two-pound-ten, or anything up to three pounds, to whoever had drawn the name of the deceased out of a tin hat. The queer part of it was that the Kid's joy fell right in like a soufflé.

'Was that,' he said, 'what we were drawing, just after I joined?'

'*You* knaow,' said Tween, in a firm, encouraging manner of

speaking, like someone awaking a sleeping man for his good. 'Tanner a time – 'ole comp'ny in – pye aht fust pawst the paowst. Fair awticles! Wotcher draw, 'Anney, yerself?'

'Never looked,' said the Kid; 'I suppose I drew something.'

The way he spoke gave an evident shock to Tween's mind. The Kid seemed not to have a sense of the value of money. 'Gordelpus, 'unt yer pockets, 'Anney!' said Tween, in distress. 'Yer mye 'ave got on to a winner.' Tommy Tween was perplexed – was the Kid a lost mind? Or had he the wind up? Wind, Tween seemed to conclude. ''S orl right, Kiddie,' he said; 'it down't do yer naow 'urt. S'pose yer do cop it fust – 's on'y like 'avin a bit to leave in yer will.'

But the Kid was off on some line of thought of his own. 'You said Gort was sick?' he asked us at large.

Ince admitted: 'Aye – seemed a bit stooffy-liike.'

'At my getting off?' Hanney said, with a bit of a made laugh.

'Well, ya knaow, ya *do* 'ang on to life a bit,' Tommy mildly reminded him.

Hanney turned with a snap on McGuffin as if Mac had taken his watch. 'What were you saying today – about that post I was in – did you say "hottest shop in the sector"?'

McGuffin tried to bluster it off. 'Ach! Hwat sort of talk are ye havin' out of ye at all, thinkin' bad of the sergeant?'

No good. The Kid had his nose well down to the scent. 'It's Gort,' he said, 'is it, that fixes the post for each man?'

He was a stout-hearted kid, and he needed it, having no strength in his body at all. We could see him now, out, as it were, in the twilight, wrestling with a sizable demon. 'Ah, then!' McGuffin fairly wailed in dismay, 'Gort never meant it a-purpose. He's not at all the description of schamer of David, the crook in the Bible, the King of the Jews.'

Ince tried to help. 'A mon may be streight,' he went so far as to say, 'though 'e do 'ave 'is feelin's.'

Then Tommy Tween launched out: ''Anney, you tike it from me – w'erever there's any bettin' people's 'earts is right. I seen it tested. Pretty 'igh too. In the trine it was, comin' back from 'Urst Pawk, an' twelve in the kerrij. Standin' up meself, an' proper tired. When we was gettin' on for Vaux'all – plice they useter tike the tickets then – a blowk gets orf 'is seat an' 'e says to me, '"Ev a seat, wowncher?"

' "Garn!" says I, "set where y'are." Didn' seem 'ardly worth tikin' a fyvour then, nex' door to Worterloo.

"E was 'ot on it, though. "Fac' is, I'm compelled," 'e says, "to mike an arryngement," 'e says, "with me creditors," an' then 'e crep' under the seat an' stretched down to it, fur in as 'e could.

'I 'adn' 'ardly set dahn in 'is plice when a man gives a shaht from the fur end of the kerrij: "Evens on, the c'llector nabs 'im! Evens on the c'llector!"

' "Gahn 'ome, ya silly swindle," says somebody else. "Mike it a livin' price. We're not givin' money awye."

'Then another blowk stawts in: "I'll bet the dead-'ead pulls it 'orf. I'll back the dead-'ead. 'Oo'll give three to one agen the dead-'ead?"

'Then the mawket begun to brike. "Three to two on the c'llector," a little quiet man stawts.

'The first man looks aht o' windy. "Lummy!" 'e says, "Vaux'all a'ready! 'Ere," 'e says, "I've 'ad a good dye. I wown't be 'ard on yer. Two to one on the c'llector! Twos on the c'llector! I'll back the c'llector!"

'A fair price, tike it all rahnd. We 'adn't 'ardly got our money on 'fore the c'llector come in. And now, I arst yer, Kiddie, solemn. Think 'ow easy it was for any man there, that 'ad backed the c'llector, to give that unfort'nate trav'ller awye – a lift o' the legs, a kick in th' eye to mike 'im 'oller, anyfink. Naow! They was as fytheful to 'im as 'is backers. Kep' their 'ocks strite. Gev all the cover they knew. Naow winkin'! Naow grinnin'! Naow nawrsty tricks to rise suspicion! Own'y think of it, 'Anney. 'Yn't you reelly sifer in th' 'ands of a 'ot sport as stands to win a bit if you're done in than wot you'd be in th' 'ands of 'most anyone else? 'Struth. You think it owver, Kiddie, 'fore you gaow on guard agen. You got three hour.'

'One,' said the Kid. He looked at a pretty wrist watch that he had. 'No. Thirty-five minutes.'

''Ullow!' said Tween, sharply. ''Ow's thet?'

'I swopped a turn with Banks.'

'Sawjint senction it?' Tween asked, sharply again. You see, Tween was really a fool. He had just worked like a good one, telling the tale, to keep up Hanney's heart, and now he would undo all the good, as likely as not, by a word let slip in a hurry, putting the Kid up to notions again. We could see it act on Hanney directly; he turned sharp on Tween, as if to pick something out of his face. That made us feel awkward; so there was a bit of a silence.

When you don't talk you can listen. One of the good points of Old Death was that the sound of shells would come to you there a deal bigger than life, and yet muted, as if every burst were a marvel, and yet far away, and nothing to us, like a wonderful thing in a book. We could hear it the way a child hears the big waves when he is in bed in a room on the land side of a house by the sea. At each burst the earth round us thudded softly; it did not seem to feel much of a shock – only a muffled, dreamy sort of heaving, as if it were not sleeping well. But there was always a kind of pulse, slow or fast, in this rumbly noise, and now it was rising.

'Un'ealthy weather, up top,' said Tween, as if that could do any good.

And then Pratt, that had not been minding our talk, but deep in one of his endless snarly games of cards with Barnard, away in a corner, broke in like an idiot with 'Sawjint Gort aht fancy snipin' agen, drawin' enemy fire?'

Hanney stared at him too. 'More evidence – eh?' – he didn't say that, but the thought was plain in the eyes of the Kid. McGuffin saw it there, too, for he charged in to give a lift with the job where Tommy had left it. You see what we were at. We were out to make the Kid fancy that human nature was lovely.

'That's a pow'rful case that ye've cited, Tommy,' McGuffin began, 'but here now is one that beats all. I know, for I see ut meself, in Gallip'li. Hot summer it was at the time, an' manny dead Turks a long time in the open, the way they'd be swelled beyant your belief, like the dead transport horses below be the road. So what'd we do, to be passin' the time, but each adopt a Turk for his own an' call him Hassan or Achmet or divvil knows hwat an' back him to burst before annyone else's. Apt we'd ha' been, but for that wan diversion, to die wi' th' ongwee of bein' definselessly et be the flies. Now, there wasn' a night but wan or more of ourselves 'd be goin' out wirin' or bombin' or only collectin' a good souvenir. An' never a case – mind ye, never as much as wan case – of a man attemptin' to mek himself rich be deflatin' the Turk he'd fancied! Not an offer at it! If it had been a matter of wanglin' a share of efficiency pay out of th' army we'd all have been out afther dark, puncthurin' every balloon in the lan'scape. 'Twas th' instinc' of sport kep' us straght. Men that had nothin' at all between them an' consid'rable wealth but givin' the touch of a bay'net in passin' ud dash the cup of joy down from their lips, the aquals of suff'rin' saints.'

The feast of beauty was spread, and we all looking to Hanney to fall to and eat and be comforted. But he hardly touched it at all; and that little, I think, for civility only. The Kid was always polite about anyone's yarn. I thought of how Isaac may have behaved when he saw what his father was up to, and how the boy looked while the old man was laying the fire. The pulse of the rumble around us was going on rising.

All we could do was just to get on with the little collection we had been making for Hanney. But I had no yarn about me, to put in the hat. Ince had none either, and yet he tried to put a mite in. 'Thot's reet,' he piped up like a man, 'Saame all worl' oaver. 'Indoos, coons, Chinks, all t'saame – nobbut fair do's anywhere, come to spoort. Tha's 'eard 'ow a Chink's buried, 'Anney? Noa? Dropped fair into t'graave, any'ow, saame as toss wi' cricket-bat, an' if 'e pitches faace oop it's kingdom coom. An', faace down, 'e's booked t'other gaate. Soa Chinks saay.'

'Thet's right. Thet's religion, thet is,' Tween corroborated.

'Eh, but think wot it ud be' – Ince ground it out, very slow and serious – 'if it were all lef' to religion. Ma woord, ye'd 'ave a proper ramp soa's ye couldn't 'ave noa confidence – priests and oondertaakers queerin' toss every tiime, to maake a bit from t'relaa-tions, 'cordin' t'wheer they'd liike t'felly to goa. Saaved by spoort, thot's wot 'tis. Every Chink in paarish 'as a bit on too, so's if paarson did t'dirty on 'em 'e'd be tore to bits by t'losers. Keeps t'clairgy streight, do thot.'

'One for the dad, that!' the Kid said to me, low, when he had heard Ince out to the end, very politely. I had not known the Kid's dad was a parson. Then he got busy again on those thoughts of his own. 'What did you say?' he said, 'is the name of this hole?' and I had to tell him 'Old Death', or 'The Death Trap'. That did him no good, I could see. And then Barnard, the rough of the place, must come butting into our talk.

Why couldn't Barnard have just carried on with his growling at

Pratt and spitting about all over the floor? It was temper, I think.
He always spat brown the first two days in the trenches, and when
he spat white, about the third day, we knew what his temper would
be until we came out of the line and he got at the beer. 'Paasons,'
he came creaking in, 'is t'worst soart. Ah seen a bit o' paasons – ah,
an' Chinks too – 's well as you. 'Ad charge of a gang o' Chinks, ah
'ave. Maakin' a dam. Ah' Scowfiel', the ganger nex' sector to me,
'ad been a church paason. They'd give 'im the go for likin' 'is beer.
Soa, when a Chink died, in 'is gang or mine, we'd 'ave a bit on,
saame's you was tellin'. One daay 'e come roun' to me. "Bung
Wun," 'e says, "is gone west. 'Ave ye any sort of a fancy about
'im?"

'Says I, "'E was a laad. The first time I seen 'im, Bung 'ad took
a good 'old o' both a friend's 'ands in 'is teeth an' was poonchin'
'is friend's two ears, fair an' easy. A gradely feighter! 'E'll be for
glory."

' "I doubt it," says Scowfiel'. "Bung 'ad the craf' an' subtlety of
the Devil, swingin' the lead himself an' teachin' that sin to the young
till the doctor'd not know were they shammin' illness at all or had
they some wil' disease out of Asia he hadn't got down in his books.
Nowt lef' for the doc but to ration 'em two days o' sickness a
month, every man, an' pay stopped at t'first word of a tummy-ache
over the ration. An' then Bung did 'im down, by formin' a comp'ny
for underwritin' losses of pay. Bung's for 'Ell, take my word, if
there's any moral rule over t'universe."

' "Ye'd bet that?" I asked. I liked my own opinion as well as
another's.

' "I would," says he. "A quid, level."

'I took 'im.

'Firs' thing's I saw at t'funer'l was 'ow t'bearers couldn't 'ardly
'ol' up under t'corpse. Nex' was 'ow t'corpse fleed through air into
t'graave soon as t'bearers let goa. Fair shook, t'earth did, when
Bung landed. Then ah looked into t'graave an' see Bung lie on's
faace an' bes' part of a 'oondredweight o' scrap iron busted oot
through t'front of his trousies. Scowfiel' thot was. Scowfiel' done
thot. E'd been a paason.'

Pratt had dealt out the cards. 'Eh, but they're poppin' 'em in, oop
top,' Barnard said, as he took up his hand. Little he cared. He was
the man due to turn out for guard in twelve minutes with Hanney.

But he was the kind of ox that will crop the weed grass in the butcher's yard. The rest of us listened, or felt the Kid listen. All through the earth round us the long, blunt rollers of sound were undulating and heaving more and more swiftly. They had been rather like distant thunder heard across plains; now they were more like thunder heard among mountains, where each peal lasts on into the next.

Hanney took the look at his wrist that he would not take while Barnard was pitching his tale. It made us want to darn the hole Barnard had ripped in the web we had been trying to weave, as you might say, across the Kid's eyes. Before we could think how to do it five minutes had gone, two hands of cards had been played; Barnard was prodding on Pratt to another deal. 'Dish 'em oot, mon! Gawd's saake, dish 'em oot! Owceans o' tiime!'

Pratt dealt, Barnard keeping a savage look-out on Pratt's hands for a foul, and marking time with a grouse or two at the bursts that were quickening outside. "Ark at 'em!' he snarled, and, again, 'An' we settin' 'ere in our misery!' Barnard said it the way you may hear a buck beggar practise a whine. He had no love or fear of man or God, death or dishonour; he was a kind of brave cur, base and fearless, that all soldiers know.

Ince was still fumbling about for some way to give a good turn to the talk. 'An' what did t'Chinks saay,' he asked, 'to your Scowfiel'?'

'Chinks!' Barnard jeered. 'The silly swine. They was 'eartbroaken. 'Twasn't t'mooney. Moast all of 'em was winners. But they was 'eartbroken. They'd thowt as Englishmen were sports an' not like Japs as oughter all be warned off toorf, ex-offishyer, saame daay as they're born. Fair broaken-'earted, t'Chinks was. The silly sof's!'

'Playin' the game is playin' the game, all the world over,' Corporal Mason put in. He would have made a great curate.

Nobody minded him, any more than if he were really a preacher. Hanney's face, I thought, was getting still greener. Pratt had dealt, and was looking very old at his cards. They must have been bad. 'Serve the Chinks bloody well right, an' you too,' he said to Barnard nastily. 'Didn't this Scahfiel' o' yourn tike 'is chawnce o' you plyin' orf the ballast on 'im, in the seat o' Wun's slacks 'stead o' their front? 'Yn't you to tike a bit o' risk as well as 'im? 'Yn't 'e to show a bit o' talent? Ah, would yer?'

Pratt had spat out the last three words like the swear of a cat. He must have thought Barnard was trying it on. Perhaps he was. The two of them held their tongues for a minute, and minded their job, while Tween tried to pick up an odd bit of good out of the mess they had made. 'O' course,' he began, 'yer mye get a Scahfiel' or two in any ol' country.'

Pratt had lost, by this time, both money and temper. 'Country!' he squealed. 'Gordelpyer! In any ol' sawjints' mess yer'll get 'arf a dozen. Wot abaht Sawjint Grice – gev Patsy Dunne a quid to lose the fight wi' Nobby? Wot abaht the sawjint-mijor – kep' a pub at Barnes afore the war, an' 'ad two scullers ricin owver the chempionship course for two 'undred a side, an' he findin' both o' their stikes an' pyin' both men's trynin' expenses, an' then gev 'em th' orfice w'ich man 'e'd 'ave win, as soon as 'e'd got all 'is money put on? Come to thet, wot abaht this Sawjint Gort yer 'avin' all the jaw abaht?'

'Well, wot abaht 'im?' Tween's voice was bold, but I guessed he had no sort of hope and was only calling Pratt's bluff on the chance, and that chance an off one. I looked at the Kid. The mask that he had kept all the time on his face was all right, except for the colour, but he was working his hands, unrolling and rolling up into a ball a bit of white paper. I think he had hooked it out of one of his pockets, to give his fingers something to do.

Pratt didn't mind going on. ''Ere's a bit abaht, 'im,' he said. 'Ow, a tysty bit! Did 'is own side dahn. Remember 'ow the Koylies beat us, dahn at Bulford Kemp. One gowl to nuffink, an' we plyin' agen three parts of a gile o' wind orl the first 'arf, an' then the wind droppin' dahn dead soon as we'd crossed? Yuss?'

We all remembered that blow. 'Lorst on the toss!' Pratt yelped triumphantly. 'Lorst by a swizzle, an' Gort done it on us. 'E was ahr skipper. Ah think 'e might 'a been fytheful.' Whenever Pratt tried to do the sob-story stunt I always thought his whimper was worse than his squeal. ''E torsed, an' the Koylies' skipper said 'Eads! It was a shillin'.'

'Thot's reet,' Barnard confirmed. 'Ah was theer, plaayin'.'

'There y'are!' Pratt's voice shrilled up into an argumentative treble. 'A shillin'!'

Somehow we all felt that this identification made things rather black. I don't know why.

'T'shillin' fell on edge,' Barnard further deposed, 'an' rowled under taable, reet oot o' siight.'

'Wot did I sye?' Pratt crowed over us all, as if this had made out his case. And I can't deny that we felt there was a lot of evidence knocking about, whatever it all came to. The little vitriol-squirt went on with it, exulting. 'Ol' man Gort dived under the tible, an' come up with the shillin'. '"Eads, all right," 'e says. "You got us." '

'Wot ow!' Tween piped up, in joy. ''Ow's that for strite? Good ol' iron!'

The Kid's face had begun to light too. It was strange the small things that worked on that boy. His hands had stopped their quick fretting; they were unrolling slowly the white bit of paper.

'Strite!' Pratt squeaked. 'You wite a mo. I says to 'im arter the match, "Ya silly mug," I says – 'e was a private then – "w'y cawn't yer tike a chawnce when yer got it?" "Wot chawnce, boy?" says 'e. "W'y," says I, "at the torse. W'y didn't yer sye it was tiles?" "It *was* tiles," says Gort. I fair let a shriek: "Gordelpus! W'y th'ell didn't yer sye so?" "Because," 'e says, narsty an' shawt, "if I 'ad I might 'a been tiken for you." 'E'll 'ave sol' thet match. 'Ullow! an' there 'e is agen!'

We could hear the splash coming near in the trench, and the drip on the stairs. But we could only just hear, for the earth all round was fairly booming now with the muffled beat of drum-fire. The Kid leapt up and buckled his belt. The green was not out of his face yet, so quick was the change, but the living joy had come back. We had all tried to cheer him, and only made matters worse, and now that gutter-sparrow had tried to make matters worse, and had cheered him. 'Now ye'll 'ear 'is yngel voice a-callin',' Pratt sneered.

Gort's voice did come. What a voice! It had always had a gallant clang, as I told you. To hear it would brace any nerve you had got. But now it was more than all that. Something had happened to it – what happens to wine when the sparkle gets in; it was bubbling with some kind of stir that had come to the man, though the words were nothing themselves – 'Pay attention, in there!'

Pratt jibed, in a whisper, ''Ark at 'im, 'Anney. '"Anney, 'Anney, come aht and be slortered. Yer keepin' me aht o' me money." '

Hanney laughed in Pratt's face, and then Gort blew the orders on that bugle voice that he had: 'Barnard, on guard! Hanney, stand by!'

Hanney stand by? What the deuce –? 'Oollo! 'Oollo! Wot's this?'

muttered Barnard. He was befogged. He did not care a curse that, while he went up into trouble, Hanney should stay, for the moment, in cover. But he had lost hold. His world was not working according to plan. Gort was not taking a chance when he got it. 'Coomin', sergeant,' he shouted, and then grumbled low again: 'Wot gaame can 'e 'ave got on?'

'Noan!' Ince's voice rushed up like a rocket. ''E's streight!'

'Gwan, y' 'oly Juggins!' said Pratt. 'Gort's sold the Kid. Thet'll be it. An' nah 'e's doin' a bit o' the dirty on 'oever's bought 'im – keepin' the Kid in aht o' the rine.'

Hanney did not look at Pratt. 'I'll stand by,' he whispered to me, 'in the trench.'

'You will not,' said I, being in charge. But he slipped me before I could grab him. The next I heard was Gort heading him back, with a jovial rant in his voice: 'You're not paid to choose the time you'll be shot, my boy. Off with you, back!'

Tween chuckled at that. 'Gowan, Bawnard,' he taunted cheerfully. ''Opit, Bawnard! Aht of it! Gow aht, Bawnard, an' git put to deaf.'

Barnard was dawdling to snarl; 'Wojjerbet that – ' when one of the finest wild blasts of Gort's voice came blowing along to me: 'Corporal Head, are you shifting that loafer?' I hustled out Barnard, mumbling of bets and half-dollars, as Hanney came back through the smoke. He still held by a corner that old slip of paper. But he had forgotten it.

'Down't gow an' lose yer benk-nowt,' said Tween, just to say something.

The Kid's mind was somewhere away. 'What?' he said. 'This?' When he saw what was meant he let the thing fall.

'Al'ays do to light a cig,' said Tween, who was always short of a match. He picked up the paper and smoothed it, to fashion a spill. The next thing, he let a yell: 'Chrahyst! if 'e yn't drawn the sawjint!'

Hanney stared at the noise. He did not take in, for a moment, that this was the slip he had drawn from a tin hat, as we all did, the morning he joined us, and had not even looked at.

Pratt helped him. Pratt's little dustbin of a mind was choke full of bits out of old movie plays, where everything works so that either one fellow has got to be killed or another. 'You or 'im, 'Anney,' he kept saying now. 'It's you or 'im.' Pratt was happy. A bit of real life seemed to be shaping at last like the trash that he enjoyed.

You could see the thing itself making its way in the mind of the Kid. You could almost feel his thoughts come, bit by bit – how he had been a beast ever to think of Gort's putting him up to be hit – and how Gort was probably wangling it now, to keep him alive – and how Gort himself had perhaps been killed by this time, and the blood-money gone not to Gort but to him, the Kid, who had whined in his heart. It all worked in him, clear to see, like the apple in some scraggy throat, till I jumped up and said, 'No, you don't!' and just got a hold upon him before he could make a break for the open again.

I was getting him tame when Gort's call of 'Corporal Head!' came ringing again.

I shouted back, 'Sergeant?'

'Double out here,' he called.

'Corporal Mason, take charge,' I sang out, and I doubled off through the smoke.

It was noon on a bleak clear day, clear without any sun, and the light seemed naked and pale and aghast, like a fainting face, after the warm, yellow gloom in Old Death. All the raw chalk in the open looked chilly and haggard, and wicked little whimpering winds were leaping about as they do just before the cruel bald dawns that you get in black frosts. When my tin hat went through our old hatch of a door it was tinkling at once with the little bits of metals and earth and stone and the like that kept falling. The Germans were doing it well. All round us, above, the level ground was jumping and splashing up everywhere, just as a puddle does in a rainstorm.

But Gort's face took me most. It had changed more than his voice. It had always seemed to me to be screwed up a bit, as if he were holding it tight in some shape that he thought was the best. It had gone easy now. He was like someone well rid of all sorts of anxiety. '*Trop de tintamarre!*' he said, with the first smile I had ever seen on him. '*Trop de brouilliamini!*'

I had not known he knew Molière, or anything else except 'Infantry Training, 1914'. *That* he knew like 'Our Father which art'. Just a grand sergeant the man had seemed to me till now; nothing else in the world.

'Not real drum-fire yet,' he said, like a collector rejecting a piece that is not quite the thing. 'A little *pas d'intimidation* only. Gad, but he's getting on to the Jocks, though. O the men! The dear men!' Where we stood was the right flank of our sector, so we looked down the trench where the Gordons were, on our right, and Gort had just seen a great shot with an enemy trench-mortar bomb.

It had plumped, at that moment, as fairly into the trench as a golf-ball prettily lofted over a stymie. There it had thrown up a great mound of chalk, damming the trench and rising a good yard above the parapet level. Out of the top of this mound a pair of legs, properly booted and putteed, were now sticking straight up in the air, from half way up the shin. I could have sworn they were just moving a little. Down in the mud of the trench, on our side of the dam, a kilted man, with his buttocks blown away and his body half-naked, was twisting like a cut worm and screaming for someone to put a bullet through his head. In an instant a little Jock private had rushed up on to the mound, in sight of enemy and friend, and begun to tear with his hands at the earth round the two legs, like a terrier when it gets frantic with trying to dig out a rat. In his frenzy of clawing his fingers looked long and hooked, like some great savage bird's. It was no good, of course. For a marvel he lived it out for a second or two hoisted up there like a target, and then a hulking Jock sergeant scrambled up to him and grabbed his collar and flung him down, like a kitten, into the shelter below, and dived after him, safe.

As they say, it put me in mind of my end. But there was work to do, luckily. 'You'll take charge of the sector,' said Gort. 'I'm shirking till this little trouble is over.'

The sergeant could say things like that. We knew him – at least, a bit of him – not all that I knew by now. For now I had found out the kind he was. I had suddenly slipped into knowing it, just as your heel will slip suddenly into a boot. I had seen a man like him before, when I was a boy – one that was always glum and sticky and not at his ease till a sailing-boat had sunk with three of us on her in winter, a good mile from shore. He was a wit and a happy man for an hour, until we got through. And then he had gone dull again. I suppose he was born about a wreck below par, and it took a pretty thick danger to give him the run of all the great stuff he had in him. The sergeant was like that.

'I've posted the sentries,' he said to me.

'Bar one,' said I, 'sergeant.'

'Oh, Hanney?' he said. 'He can wait. I've a use for that post. Carry on, you, patrolling. And, for the love of God, don't let the young uns get their heads free.' He was eager to get me away.

I went along to our left. It was a miracle. Not a man had been hurt, above a small scratch. Gort was a wonder at keeping down losses. He used to coach and practise the new men in judging the enemy's trench-mortar bombs, like catches at long-on in cricket, and jumping round corners of trench to put solid earth between them and the burst – and also in not trying, ever, to judge the rifle-grenades, but just lying low till the thin hiss or spit of the flight had finished up in the nasty metallic rip of the little beast's bursting. Every man that we had was trench wise, thanks to Gort, bar the Kid, who had not had time to learn anything yet.

I came back by degrees to our right, stopping at each post to buck up the sentry there with some chat. When I came to the mouth of the little curved sap running out to the post where Hanney had been I thought I would give a look in. It was on the near lip of a big mine crater, the enemy holding the opposite lip, with a few yards of air between their rifles' muzzles and ours. Gort was there, stooping to peer through the steel crack of a loop-hole. His back was a sight – like a cat's when she quivers and wags her haunches with joy, crouching and watching a bird.

While I was reporting all well, a fat T.M. bomb started waddling across through the air, with its timber tail waving. 'Resist not evil,' Gort said, with his new happy smile, 'with your head.' We judged the ball, called 'Left!' together, and jumped round an angle of earth in good time. It was near, though. I like them a bit farther off, but Gort's eyes were shining. They had a wild glee like a boy's when he hides in a bush, at some game, and the other side come close and don't see, but go on. Just to be chased and not caught, shot at and not hit – that's what one kind of man wants; it's his little nip of strong drink, and, wherever it's going, he'll never keep off it.

'Sergeant,' I said, 'do you know, this is very in-and-out running.' Of course it was cheek, and the more so as he had been always, to me, of the you-be-damned sort that will blast your eyes out of your head at the start of a talk and not go back very much on it afterwards. Still, I felt it would go. He was clean off the earth, I could see, he had lifted right clear of all fear and fuss and the pride of his rank, and all the whole boiling of little mean things.

He cocked an eye at me lightly, not angry a bit. 'Hullo,' he said, 'these be hard words.'

'You know,' I said, 'what you drew in the sweep?'

'Sweep?' he said. 'For the Derby?'

'The first-blooder,' said I, 'for this tour in trenches.'

'God knows,' he said; 'I fancy I looked, at the time. Anyhow, I've forgotten.'

He had. That was certain. 'Well, sergeant,' said I, 'is it time I got Hanney?'

He gave a look round, with a flicking look on his face, like a dog scenting. 'The muck's blowing over,' he said. I could have sworn his face fell. I could not have said, myself, yet, that the firing was less. 'Go the round again now,' he went on, 'and see are all fit.'

'And send Hanney along?' I said quickly. I felt it was urgent – I couldn't tell why. It was as if something, I couldn't tell what, had just begun to go on, and had to be stopped on the nail, like a fire.

He looked round and listened, again, sizing up the enemy's fire. He had been right about it, first time. A bombardment is just like a lot of notes played on a keyboard with changes of pace. I could tell now, it was slowing. Gort seemed to think for a moment, not minding. 'Sting in the wine of being,' I think he said to himself; 'salt in the feast.' And then to me, 'Send him along.'

I almost ran to the Trap. The storm was fast dropping into a calm. But you know how storms drop: with savage little returns, now and then, of their old pelting fury. Looking back as I went, I saw that nearly all of these last spurts seemed to fall near the crater. The dead calm was elsewhere.

I yelled to Hanney through the hatch, and he came bolting out like a whippet dog released to its master. Just at the moment he burst through the hatch I had a queer feeling that all the hurry was off. It was as if something too tight had gone snap. The urgency of the business seemed suddenly gone. As we started along the trench a little haystack of smoke, with the flame just put out in its heart, was drifting away from the crater. The sound of the burst, long after all others, came like the last dropping bark a dog gives at the end of a great bout of temper. Not another thing fell.

I had my job to do, urgent or not. It did not take us long to reach the post on the lip of the crater. It was not much shattered. Rifle-grenades make no earthquakes like shells, but they can dissect pretty small. Nothing that you could have called a dead sergeant was left. There are walking cases and stretcher cases, and there is the groundsheet case that only needs search and collection.

The boy, who had been in the leash half an hour, began to cry now and said he was shamed and had let the man die for him. But I bade him look to his front and I got the place cleaned.

The babble of voices there was in the Trap that evening! – and I with some sort of a letter to write to Gort's wife. Each talking after his kind, man or beast or creeping thing, as God had created him. Mason had to be saying, every few minutes, that it's an ill wind that blows nobody good. Barnard had drawn Tommy Tween in the sweep, and now he was sticking it out that Gort's death was not formally proved. 'Is 'e identified?' 'Show me t'body.' 'Wot's a near forefoot to go by?' When he was not saying one of these things he was saying another. Pratt was sucking up to the winner already: 'Wot abaht it, 'Anney? A little 'arf pint, 'long o' me, fust dye arter we're aht, jus' to wet the good luck?'

'O yes, if you like,' Hanney said, to be rid of him. Hanney had been writing too. He came across to me presently with his letter. 'Shall we send them together?' he said. I guessed where his letter was for, but I wondered how he knew about mine.

THE DIVING TANK

Boyd Cable

His Majesty's land-ship Hotstuff was busy rebunkering and refilling ammunition in a nicely secluded spot under the lee of a cluster of jagged stumps that had once been trees, while her Skipper walked round her and made a careful examination of her skin. She bore, on her blunt bows especially, the marks of many bullet splashes and stars and scars, and on her starboard gun turret a couple of blackened patches of blistered paint where a persistent Hun had tried his ineffectual best to bomb the good ship at close quarters, without any further result than the burnt paint and a series of bullet holes in the bomber.

As the Skipper finished his examination, finding neither crack, dent, nor damage to anything deeper than the paintwork, 'All complete' was reported to him, and he and his crew proceeded to dine off bully beef, biscuits, and uncooked prunes. The meal was interrupted by a motor-cyclist, who had to leave his cycle on the roadside and plough on foot through the sticky mud to the Hotstuff's anchorage, with a written message. The Skipper read the message, initialled the envelope as a receipt, and, meditatively chewing on a dry prune, carefully consulted a squared map criss-crossed and wriggled over by a maze of heavy red lines that marked the German trenches, and pricked off a course to where a closer-packed maze of lines was named as a Redoubt.

The Signals dispatch-rider had approached the crew with an enormous curiosity and a deep desire to improve his mind and his knowledge on the subject of 'Tanks'. But although the copybook maxims have always encouraged the improvement of one's mind, the crew of the Hotstuff preferred to remember another copybook dictum, 'Silence is golden,' and with the warnings of many months soaked into their very marrows, and with a cautious secrecy that by now had become second, if not first, nature to them, returned answers more baffling in their fullness than the deepest silence would have been.

'Is it true that them things will turn a point-blank bullet?' asked the dispatch-rider.

'Turn them is just the right word, Signals,' said the spokesman. 'The armour plating doesn't stop 'em, you see. They go through, and then by an *in*-genious arrangement of slanted steel venetian shutters just inside the skin, the bullets are turned, rico up'ard on to another set o' shutters, deflect again out'ards an' away. So every bullet that hits us returns to the shooters, with slightly decreased velocity nat'rally, but sufficient penetratin' power to kill at *con*-siderable range.'

Signals stared at him suspiciously, but he was so utterly solemn and there was such an entire absence of a twinkling eye or ghostly smile amongst the biscuit-munchers that he was puzzled.

'An' I hear they can go over almost anythin' – trenches, an' barbed wire, an' shell-holes, an' such-like?' he said interrogatively.

'*Almost* anything,' repeated the spokesman, with just a shade of indignation in his tone. 'She's built to go over anything without any almost about it. Why, this mornin',' he turned to the crew, 'what was the name o' that place wi' the twelve-foot solid stone wall round it? You know, about eleven miles behind the German lines.'

'Eleven miles?' said the Signaller in accents struggling between doubt and incredulity.

'About that, accordin' to the map,' said the other. 'That's about our average cruise.'

'But – but,' objected the Signaller, 'how wasn't you cut off – surrounded – er – '

'Cut off,' said the Hotstuff cheerfully, 'why, of course, we was surrounded, *and* cut off. But what good was that to 'em? You've seen some of us walkin' up an' over their front lines, and them shootin' shells an' rifles an' Maxims at us. But they didn't stop us, did they? So how d'you suppose they stop us comin' back? But about that wall,' he went on, having reduced the Signaller to pondering silence. 'We tried to butt through it an' couldn't, so we coupled on the grapplin'-hook bands, an' walked straight up one side an' down the other.'

'Yes,' put in one of the other Hotstuffs, 'an' doin' it the boxful o' tea an' sugar that was up in the front locker fell away when she upended and tumbled down to the other end. Spilt every blessed grain we had. I don't hold wi' that straight-up-and-down manoover myself.'

'Oh, well,' said the first man, 'I don't know as it was worse than when we was bein' towed across the Channel. She makes a rotten bad sea boat, I must confess.'

'Towed across?' said the startled Signaller. 'You don't mean to say she floats?'

'Why, of course,' said the Hotstuff simply. 'Though, mind you, we're not designed for long voyages under our own power. The whole hull is a watertight tank – wi' longtitoodinal an' transverse bulkheads, an' we've an adjustable screw propeller. I dunno as I ought to be talkin' about that, though,' and he sank his voice and glanced cautiously round at the Skipper folding up his map. 'Don't breathe a word o' it to a soul, or I might get into trouble. It's a little surprise,' he concluded hurriedly, as he saw the Skipper rise, 'that we're savin' up for the Hun when we gets to the Rhine. He reckons the Rhine is goin' to hold us up, don't he? Wait till he sees the Tanks swim it an' walk up the cliffs on the other side.'

The Skipper gave a few quiet orders and the crew vanished, crawling, and one by one, into a little man-hole. The Signaller's informant found time for a last word to him in passing. 'I b'lieve we're takin' a turn down across the river an' canal,' he said. 'If you follow us you'll most likely see us do a practice swim or two.'

'Well, I've met some dandy liars in my time,' the Signaller murmured to himself, 'but that chap's about IT.'

But he stayed to watch the Tank get under way, and after watching her performance and course for a few hundred yards he returned to his motor-bike with struggling doubts in his own mind as to how and in which direction he was likely to be the bigger fool – in believing or in refusing to believe.

The Hotstuff snorted once or twice, shook herself, and rumbled internally; her wheelbands made a slow revolution or two, churning out a barrowload or so of soft mud, and bit through the loose upper soil into the firmer ground; she jerk-jerked convulsively two or three times, crawled out of the deep wheel-ruts she had dug, turned, nosing a cautious way between the bigger shell craters, and then ploughed off on a straight course towards the road across the sticky mud – mud which the dispatch-rider had utterly failed to negotiate, and which, being impassable to him, he had, out of the knowledge born of long experience, concluded impassable to anything, light or heavy, that ran on wheels. A wide ditch lay between the field and the road, but the Hotstuff steered straight for it and crawled tranquilly across. The dispatch-rider watched the progress across the mud with great interest, whistled softly as he saw the Tank breast the ditch and reach out for the far bank, with her fore-end and nearly half her length hanging clear out over the water, gasped as the bows dipped and fell downward, her fore-feet clutching at and resting on the further bank, her bows and under-body – the descriptive terms are rather mixed, but then, so is the name and make-up of a Land Ship – hitting the water with a mighty splash. And then, in spite of himself, he broke from wide grins into open laughter as the Hotstuff got a grip of the far bank, pushed with her hind and pulled with her fore legs and dragged herself across. If ever you have seen a fat caterpillar perched on a cabbage leaf's edge, straining and reaching out with its front feet to reach another leaf, touching it, catching hold, and letting go astern, to pull over the gap, you have a very fair idea of what the Hotstuff looked like crossing that ditch.

She wheeled on to the road, and as the dispatch-rider, with mingled awe, amazement, and admiration, watched her lumbering off down it he saw an oil-blackened hand poked out through a gun port and waggled triumphantly back at him. 'Damme,' he said, 'I believe she *can* swim, or stand on her head, or eat peas off a knife. She looks human-intelligent enough for anything.'

But the Hotstuff on that particular trip was to display little enough intelligence, but instead an almost human perversity, adding nothing to her battle honours but very much to her skipper's and crew's already overcrowded vocabulary of strong language. The engineer showed signs of uneasiness as she trundled down the road, cocking his head to one side and listening with a look of strained attention, stooping his ear to various parts of the engines, squinting along rods, touching his finger-tips to different bearings.

'What's wrong?' asked the Skipper. 'Isn't she behaving herself?'

The engineer shook his head. 'There's something not exactly right wi' her,' he said slowly. 'I doubt she's going to give trouble.'

He was right. She gave trouble for one slow mile, more trouble for another half-mile, and then most trouble of all at a spot where the road had degenerated into a sea of thin, porridgy mud. We will say nothing of the technical trouble, but it took four solid hours to get the Hotstuff under way again. The road where she halted was a main thoroughfare to the firing line, and the locality of her break-down, fortunately for the traffic, was where a horse watering trough stood a hundred yards back from the road, and there was ample room to deflect other vehicles past the Hotstuff obstacle, which lay right in the fair-way. All the four hours a procession of motor-cars and lorries, G.S. waggons, and troops of horses streamed by to right and left of the helpless Hotstuff. The cars squirted jets of liquid mud on her as they splashed past, the lorries flung it in great gouts at her, the waggons plastered her lower body liberally, and the horses going to and from water raised objections to her appearance and spattered a quite astonishing amount of mud over her as high as her roof.

When finally she got her engines running and pulled out of the quagmire, it was too late to attempt to get her up into the action she had been called to, so her bows were turned back to her anchorage and she plodded off home. And by the luck of war, and his volunteering out of turn for the trip, the same dispatch-rider brought another message to her early next morning in her berth behind the line.

The crew's night had been spent on internal affairs, and, since there had been no time to attempt to remove any of the accumulation of mud that covered every visible inch of her, she looked like a gigantic wet clay antheap.

The dispatch-rider stared at her.

'Looks as if she wanted her face washed,' he remarked. 'What *has* she been up to? Thought you said she was going swimming. She don't look much as if she'd had a bath lately.'

His former glib informant slowly straightened a weary back, checked a tart reply, and instead spoke with an excellent simulation of cheeriness.

'Didn't you come an' watch us yesterday, then?' he said. 'Well, you missed a treat – brand-new dodge our Old Man has invented hisself. When we got 'er in the canal, we closed all ports, elevated our periscope an' new telescopic air-toob, submerged, and sank to the bottom. And she walked four measured miles under water along the bottom o' the canal. That' – and he waved his hand towards the mud-hidden Hotstuff – 'is where she got all the mud from.'

And to this day that dispatch-rider doesn't know whether he told a gorgeous truth or a still more gorgeous lie.

FIVE-FOUR-EIGHT

Jeffery E. Jeffery

RAIN! pitiless, incessant, drenching rain, that seemed to ooze and trickle and soak into every nook and cranny in the world, beat down upon the already sodden ground and formed great pools of water in every hollow. Fires blazed and flickered at intervals, revealing within the glowing circles of their light the huddled forms of weary soldiers; and all the myriad sounds of a huge camp blended imperceptibly with the raindrops' steady patter.

According to orders the 8th Division had concentrated upon the main army for the impending battle. At dawn that day its leading battalion had swung out of camp to face the storm and the mud; not until dusk had the last unit dropped exhausted into its bivouac. For fourteen hours the troops had groped their way along the boggy roads: and they had marched but one-and-twenty miles. Incredibly slow! incredibly wearisome! But they had effected the purpose of their chief. They had arrived in time.

The headquarters of the divisional artillery had been established in a ramshackle old barn at one corner of the field in which the batteries were camped. Within its shelter the General and his staff of three crouched over a small fire. The roof leaked, the floor was wet and indescribably filthy; their seats were saddles, and their only light a guttering candle. But to those four tired men, the little fire, the dirty barn, the thought of food and sleep, seemed Heaven.

Brigadier-General Maudeslay, known to his irreverent but affectionate subordinates as 'the Maud', was a fat little man of fifty, who owed his present rank largely to his steady adherence to principles of sound common-sense. For theoretical knowledge he depended, so he frankly declared, upon the two staff officers with whom he was supplied. Nevertheless, those who knew him well agreed that in quickness to grasp the salient points of any given situation and in accuracy of decision he had few superiors. It was his habit, when pondering on his line of action, to walk round in a circle, his hands behind his back, humming softly to himself. Then, swiftly and with conscious certainty, he would act. And he was seldom wrong.

At the moment, however, his thoughts were not concerned with tactics but with food. For some time he sat before the fire in silence, then suddenly exclaimed –

'Thank the Lord! I hear the baggage coming in. Go and hurry it up, Tony.'

Tony, whose rarely used surname was Quarme, was an artillery subaltern of seven years' service, attached to the General's staff as personal A.D.C. On him devolved the irksome task of catering for the headquarters mess. It was his principal, though not his only function: and, owing to scarcity of provisions, a daily change of camp, and a General who took considerable interest in the quality of his food, it was a duty which often taxed his temper and his ingenuity to the utmost.

He got up, wriggled himself into his clammy waterproof and splashed out into the mud and darkness.

'Tony,' observed the General to his Brigade-Major, 'is not such a failure at this job as you predicted.'

'He's astonished me so far, I must confess,' was the reply. 'I always thought him rather a lazy young gentleman, with no tastes for anything beyond horses and hunting.'

'My dear Hartley, he was lazy because he was bored.' The General, being devoted to hunting himself, spoke a little testily. 'Peace soldiering,' he went on, '*is* apt to bore sometimes. Tony is not what *you'd* call a professional soldier. His military interests are strictly confined to the reputation of his battery, and to his own ability to command two guns in action. Naturally he was pleased when I appointed him A.D.C. The part of the year's work which interested him, practice camp and so on, was over. In place of the tedium of manœuvres as a regimental subaltern, he foresaw a novel and more or less amusing occupation on my staff for the rest of the summer, and he knew that he would go back to his own station in the autumn in time for the hunting season. But he did not reckon on the possibility of war, and therefore he is now dissatisfied. I know it as well as if he'd told me so himself.'

'How do you mean, sir?'

'Oh! he doesn't dislike the job: I don't mean that. But he can't help feeling that he's been sold. I can almost hear him saying to himself, "Here have I struggled through seven years' soldierin' thinking always that some day I should be loosed upon a battlefield with a pair of guns and a good fat target of advancing infantry. And now that the time *has* come, I'm stuck with this rotten staff job." '

'By Jove!' said the other, 'I never thought of that.'

'No, Hartley, you wouldn't. In your case the "gunner" instinct has been obliterated by that of the staff officer. The guns have lost their fascination for you. Isn't that so?'

'In a way, yes.'

'Well, in some men – and Tony happens to be one of them – that fascination lasts as long as life itself. Often enough in ordinary times it lies dormant. But as soon as war comes it shows itself at once in the mad rush made by officers to get back to batteries – that is, to go on service *with the guns*. It is the curse of our regiment in some ways: many potential generals abandon their ambitions because of it. But it's also our salvation.'

He relapsed into silence, staring into the fire. Perhaps he, too, regretted for the moment that he was a general, and wished that, instead of thirteen batteries, he commanded only one.

Meanwhile the subject of their discussion had succeeded in finding the headquarters' baggage waggon. Ignoring the protests of infuriated transport officers who were endeavouring to direct more than two hundred vehicles to their destinations, he had lured it out of the chaos and guided it to its appointed place. As the waggon came to a standstill outside the barn the tarpaulin was raised at the back and the vast proportions of the gunner who combined the duties of servant to Tony and cook to the mess slowly emerged.

From his right hand dangled a shapeless flabby mass.

'What the devil have you got there, Tebbut?' demanded Tony.

'Ducks, sir,' was the unexpected reply. 'We was 'alted near a farm-'ouse today, so I took the chanst to buy some milk and butter. While the chap way away fetchin' the stuff, I pinched these 'ere ducks. Fat they are, too!'

He spoke in the matter-of-fact tones of one to whom the theft of a pair of ducks, and the feat of plucking them within the narrow confines of a packed G.S. waggon, was no uncommon experience.

'Well, look sharp and cook 'em. We're hungry,' said Tony.

He stayed until he saw that the dinner was well under way, and then floundered off through the mud to see his horses. Of these he was allowed by regulations three, but one, hastily purchased during the mobilization period by an almost distracted remount officer, had already succumbed to the effects of overwork and under-feeding. There remained the charger which he had had with his battery in peace time, and which he now used for all ordinary work – and Dignity.

The latter was well named. He was a big brown horse, very nearly thoroughbred – a perfect hunter and a perfect gentleman. Tony had bought him as a four-year-old at a price that was really far beyond his means, and had trained him himself. He used openly to boast that Dignity had taken to jumping as a duck takes to water, and that he had never been known to turn from a fence. In the course of four seasons, the fastest burst, the heaviest ground, the longest hunt had never been too much for him. Always he would gallop calmly on, apparently invincible. His owner almost worshipped him.

Horse rugs are not part of the field service equipment of an officer. But to the discerning (and unscrupulous) few there is a way round almost every regulation. Dignity had three rugs, and his legs were swathed in warm flannel bandages. As he stood there on the leeward side of a fence busily searching the bottom of his nose-bag for the last few oats of his meagre ration, he was probably the most comfortable animal of all the thousands in the camp.

Tony spent some time examining his own and the General's horses, and giving out the orders for the morning to the grooms. By the time he got back to the barn it was past ten, and Tebbut was just solemnly announcing 'dinner' as being served.

'The Maud' eyed the dish of steaming ducks with evident approval, but avoided asking questions. Loot had been very strictly forbidden.

'We ought by rights to have apple sauce with these,' he said, drawing his saddle close up to the low deal table and giving vent to a sigh of expectancy.

'Hi've got some 'ere, sir,' responded the resourceful Tebbut. 'There was a horchard near the road today.'

He produced, as he spoke, a battered tin which, from the

inscription on its label, had once contained 'selected peaches'. It was now more than half-full of a concoction which bore a passable resemblance to apple sauce.

For half an hour conversation languished. They had eaten nothing but a sandwich since early morning, and the demands of appetite were more exacting than their interest in the programme for the morrow.

But as soon as Tebbut, always a stickler for the usages of polite society, had brushed away the crumbs with a dirty dish-cloth and handed round pint mugs containing coffee, Hartley unrolled a map and, under instructions from the General, began to prepare the orders.

As a result of a reconnaissance in force that day the enemy's advanced troops had been driven in, and the extent of his real position more or less accurately defined. The decisive attack, of which the 8th Division was to form a part, was to be directed against the left. Barring the way on this flank, however, was a hill marked on the map as Point 548, which was situate about two miles in front of the main hostile position. The enemy had not yet been dislodged from this salient, but a brigade of infantry had been detailed to assault it that night. In the event of success a battery was to be sent forward to occupy it at dawn, after which the main attack would begin. General Maudeslay had been ordered to provide this battery.

'Don't put anything in orders about it, though, Hartley,' he said. 'It will have to be one from the 81st Brigade, which has suffered least so far. I'll send separate confidential instructions to the Colonel. Get an orderly, will you, Tony.'

'I'll take the message myself, sir, if I may,' suggested the A.D.C. 'It's my own brigade, and I'd like to look them up.'

'All right; only don't forget to come back,' said the General, smiling.

Tony pocketed the envelope and peered out into the night. The rain had ceased and the sky was clear. Far away to right and left the bivouac fires glimmered like reflections of the starry heavens. The troops, worn out with the hardships of the day, had fallen asleep and the camp was silent. Only the occasional whinny of a horse, the challenge of a sentry, or the distant rumbling of benighted transport broke the stillness.

Tony's way led through the lines of the various batteries. The horses stood in rows, tied by their heads to long ropes stretched between the ammunition waggons. Fetlock-deep in liquid mud, without rugs, wet and underfed, they hung their heads dejectedly – a silent protest against the tyranny of war.

'Poor old hairies,' thought Tony as he passed them, his mind picturing the spotless troop-stables and the shining coats that he had known so well in barracks, not a month ago.

He found the officers of his brigade assembled beneath a tarpaulin. Their baggage had been hours late, and though it was nearly eleven o'clock the evening meal was still in progress. He handed his message to the Adjutant and sat down to exchange greetings with his brother subalterns.

'Oh! there's bully beef for the batteries, but we've salmon all right on the staff,' he sang softly, after sniffing suspiciously at the unpleasant-looking mess on his neighbour's plate, which was, in fact, ration tinned beef boiled hurriedly in a camp kettle. The song, of which the words were his own, fitted neatly to a popular tune of the moment. It treated of the difference in comfort of life on the staff and that in the batteries, and gave a verdict distinctly in favour of the former. He had sung it with immense success about 3 A.M. on his last night at home with his own brigade.

'Now, Tony,' said someone, 'you're on the staff. What's going to happen tomorrow?'

'A big show – will last two or three days, they say. But,' he added, grinning, 'you poor devils stuck away behind the hill won't see much of it. I suppose I shall be sent on my usual message – to tell you that you're doing no dam' good and only wasting ammunition!'

But though he chaffed and joked his heart was heavy as he walked back an hour later. Somewhere out there in the mud was his own battery, which he worshipped as a god. And he was condemned to live away from it, to be absent when it dashed into action, when the breech-blocks rattled and the shells shrieked across the valleys.

He found the others still poring over the map. From the wallet on his saddle Tony pulled out a large travelling flask.

'I think that this is the time for the issue of my special emergency ration,' he announced.

'What is it, Tony?' asked 'the Maud'.

'Best old liqueur brandy from our mess in England,' he replied, pouring some into each of the four mugs.

Then he held up his own and added –

'Here's to the guns: may they be well served tomorrow.'

Over the enamelled rim the General's eyes met Tony's for a moment, and he smiled; for he understood the sentiment.

Tony crawled beneath his blankets and fell into a deep sleep, from which he roused himself with difficulty a few hours later as the first grey streaks of dawn were appearing in the sky.

The press of work at the headquarters of a division during operations comes in periods of intense activity, during which every member of the staff, from the general downwards, feels that he is being asked to do the work of three men in an impossibly short space of time. One of these periods, that in which the orders for the initial stages of the attack had been distributed, had just passed, and a comparative calm had succeeded. Even the operator of the 'buzzer' instrument, ensconced in a little triangular tent just large enough to hold one man in a prone position, had found time to smoke.

Divisional headquarters had been established at a point where five roads met, just below the crest of a low hill. A few yards away the horses clinked their bits and grazed. Occasionally the distant boom of a gun made them prick their ears and stare reflectively in the direction of the sound. The sun, with every promise of a fine day, was slowly dispelling the mist from the valley and woodlands below.

It was early: the battle had scarcely yet begun.

A huge map had been spread out on a triangular patch of grass at the road junction, its corners held down with stones. Staff officers lay around it talking eagerly. Above, on the top of the hill, General Maudeslay leant against a bank and gazed into the mist. The night attack, he knew, had been successful, and he was anxiously awaiting the appearance of the battery on Point 548.

Tony was stretched at full length on the grass below him. He was warm, he was dry and he was not hungry – a rare combination on service.

'This would be a grand cub-hunting morning, General,' he said.

Ordinarily 'the Maud' would have responded with enthusiasm,

for hounds and hunting were the passion of his life. But now his thoughts were occupied with other matters, and he made no reply.

Then suddenly, as though at the rising of a curtain at a play, things began to happen. The telephone operator lifted his head with a start as his instrument began to give out its nervous, jerky, zt-zzz-zt. There was a clatter of hoofs along the road, and the sliding scrape of a horse pulled up sharply as an orderly appeared and handed in a message. Rifle fire, up till then desultory and unnoticed, began to increase in volume. The mist had gone.

'The Maud', motionless against the bank, kept his glasses to his eyes for some minutes before lowering them, with a gesture of annoyance, and exclaimed –

'It's curious. That battery ought to be on 548 by now, but I can see no sign of it.'

'You can't see 548 from here, sir. It's hidden behind that wood,' said Tony, pointing as he spoke.

'What do you mean? There's 548,' said the General, also pointing, but to a hill much farther to their right.

'No, sir – at least not according to my map.'

'The Maud' snatched the map from Tony's hand. A second's glance was enough. On it Point 548 was marked as being farther to the left and considerably nearer to the enemy.

He turned on Tony like a flash.

'Good Lord! Why didn't you tell me that before?' he cried. 'There must be two different editions of this map. Which one had they in your brigade when you went over there last night – the right one or the wrong one?'

But Tony, unfortunately, had no idea. His interest in tactics, as we have seen, was small, and his visit had not involved him in a discussion of the plan of battle. He had not even looked at their maps.

'The Maud' walked round in one small circle while he hummed eight bars. Then he said –

'They must have started for the wrong hill, and in this mist they won't have realized their danger. That battery will be wiped out unless we can stop it.' He looked round quickly. 'Signallers – no – useless: and the telephone not yet through. Tony, you'll have to go. There's no direct road. Go straight across country and you may just do it.'

Tony was already half-way to the horses.

'Take up Dignity's stirrups two holes,' he called as he ran towards them. 'Quick, man, quick!'

It took perhaps twenty seconds, which seemed like as many minutes. He flung away belt and haversack, crammed his revolver into a side pocket and was thrown up into the saddle. 'The Maud' himself opened the gate off the road.

'Like hell, Tony, like hell!'

The General's words, shouted in his ear as he passed through on to the grass, seemed echoed in the steady beat of Dignity's hoofs as he went up to his bridle and settled into his long raking stride.

Tony leant out on his horse's neck, his reins crossed jockey fashion, his knees pressed close against the light hunting saddle. Before him a faded expanse of green stretched out for two miles to the white cottage on the hillside which he had chosen as his point. The rush of wind in his ears, the thud of iron-shod hoofs on sound old turf, the thrill that is born of speed, made him forget for a moment the war, the enemy, his mission. He was back in England on a good scenting morning in November. Hounds were away on a straight-necked fox, and he had got a perfect start. Almost could he see them beside him, 'close packed, eager, silent as a dream'.

This was not humdrum soldiering – cold and hunger, muddy roads and dreary marches. It was Life.

'Steady, old man.'

He leant back, a smile upon his lips, as a fence was flung behind them and the bottom of the valley came in sight.

'There's a brook: must chance it,' he muttered, and then, mechanically and with instinctive eye, he chose his place. He took a pull until he felt that Dignity was going well within himself, and then, fifty yards away, he touched him with his heels and let him out. The stream, swollen with the deluge of the previous day, had become a torrent of swirling muddy water, and it was by no means narrow. But Dignity knew his business. Gathering his powerful quarters under him in the last stride, he took off exactly right and fairly hurled himself into space.

They landed with about an inch to spare.

'Good for you!' cried Tony, standing in his stirrups and looking back as they breasted the slope beyond. From the top he had hoped to see the battery somewhere on the road, but he found that the wood obstructed his view, and he was still uncertain, therefore, as to whether he was in time or not.

'It's a race,' he said, and sat down in his saddle to ride a finish.

But half-way across the next field Dignity put a foreleg into a blind and narrow drain and turned completely over.

Tony was thrown straight forward on to his head and stunned.

A quarter of an hour later he had recovered consciousness and was staring about him stupidly. The air was filled with the din of battle, but apparently the only living thing near him was Dignity, quietly grazing. He noticed, at first without understanding, that the horse moved on three legs only. His off foreleg was swinging. Tony got up and limped stiffly towards him. He bent down to feel the leg and found that it was broken.

Slowly, reluctantly, he pulled out his revolver and put in a cartridge. It was, perhaps, the hardest thing he had ever had to do. He drew Dignity's head down towards the ground, placed the muzzle against his forehead and fired.

The horse swayed for a fraction of a second, then collapsed forward, lifeless, with a thud: and Tony felt as though his heart would break.

Gradually he began to remember what had happened, and he wondered vaguely how long he had lain unconscious. In front of him stretched the wood which he had seen before he started, hiding from his view not only the actual hill but the road which led to it. He knew that on foot, bruised and shaken as he was, he could never now arrive in time. He had failed and must return.

Then, as he stood sadly watching Dignity's fast glazing eyes, he heard the thunder of hundreds of galloping hoofs, and looked up quickly. Round the corner of the wood, in wild career, came, not a cavalry charge as he had half-expected, but teams – gun teams and limbers – but no guns. The battery had got into action on the hill, but a lucky hostile shell, wide of its mark, had dropped into the waggon line and stampeded the horses. A few drivers still remained, striving in vain to pull up. They might as well have tried to stop an avalanche.

Tony watched them flash past him to the rear. Still dazed with his fall, it was some seconds before the truth burst upon him.

He knew those horses.

'My God!' he cried aloud, 'it's my own battery that's up there!'

In a moment all thought of his obvious duty – to return and report – was banished from his mind. He forgot the staff and his connection with it. One idea, and one only, possessed him – somehow, anyhow, to get to the guns.

Dizzily he started off towards the hill. His progress was slow and laboured. His head throbbed as though there was a metal piston within beating time upon his brain. The hot sun caused the sweat to stream into his eyes. The ground was heavy, and his feet sank into it at every step. Twice he stopped to vomit.

At last he reached the road and followed the tracks of the gun-wheels up it until he came to the gap in the hedge through which the battery had evidently gone on its way into action. The slope was strewn with dead and dying horses: drivers were crushed beneath them; and an upended limber pointed its pole to the sky like the mast of a derelict ship. The ground was furrowed with the impress of many heavy wheels, and everywhere was ripped and scarred with the bullet marks of low-burst shrapnel. But ominously enough, amid all these signs of conflict no hostile fire seemed to come in his direction.

The hill rose sharply for a hundred yards or so, and then ran forward for some distance nearly flat. Tony therefore, crawling up, did not see the battery until he was quite close to it.

Panting, he stopped aghast and stared.

Four guns were in position with their waggons beside them. The remnants of the detachments crouched behind the shields. Piles of empty cartridge-cases and little mounds of turf behind the trails testified that these four guns, at least, had been well served. But the others! One was still limbered up: evidently a shell had burst immediately in front of it. Its men and horses were heaped up round it almost as though they were tin soldiers which a child had swept together on the floor. The remaining gun pointed backward down the hill, forlorn and desolate.

In the distance, for miles and miles, the noise of battle crashed and thundered in the air. But here it seemed some magic spell was cast, and everything was still and silent as the grave.

Sick at heart, Tony contemplated the scene of carnage and destruction for one brief moment. Then he made his way towards the only officer whom he could see, and from him learnt exactly what had happened.

The major commanding the battery, it appeared, deceived first by the map and then by the fog, had halted his whole battery where he imagined that it was hidden from view. But as soon as the mist had cleared away he found that it was exposed to the fire of the hostile artillery at a range of little more than a mile. The battery had been caught by a hail of shrapnel before it could get into action. Only this one officer remained, and there were but just enough men to work the four guns that were in position. Ammunition, too, was getting very short.

Tony looked at his watch. It was only eight o'clock. From his vague idea of the general plan of battle he knew that the decisive attack would eventually sweep forward over the hill on which he stood. But how soon?

At any moment the enemy might launch a counter-attack and engulf his battery. Its position could hardly have been worse. Owing to the flat top of the hill nothing could be seen from the guns except the three hundred yards immediately in front of them and the high ground a mile away on which the enemy's artillery was posted. The intervening space was hidden. Yet it was impossible to move. Any attempt to go forward to where they could see, or backward to where they would be safe, would be greeted, Tony knew well enough, with a burst of fire which would mean annihilation. Besides, he remembered the stampeding waggon line. The battery was without horses, immobile. To wait patiently for succour was its only hope.

Having ascertained that a man had been posted out in front to give warning of an attack, Tony sat down to await developments with philosophic calm. The fact that he had no right to be there at all, but that his place was with the General, did not concern him in the slightest. It had always been his ambition 'to fight a battery in the real thing', as he would himself have phrased it, and he foresaw that he was about to do so with a vengeance. He was distressed by the havoc that he saw, but in all other respects he was content.

For hours nothing happened. The enemy evidently considered that the battery was effectually silenced, and did not deign to waste further ammunition upon it. Then, when Tony had almost fallen asleep, the sentry at the forward crest semaphored in a message –

'Long thick line of infantry advancing: will reach foot of hill in about five minutes. Supports behind.' Almost at the same moment an orderly whom Tony recognized as belonging to his General's staff arrived from the rear. Tony seized upon him eagerly.

'Where have you come from?' he demanded.

'From the General, sir. 'E sent me to find you and to tell you to come back.'

'Did you pass any of our infantry on your way?'

'Yes, sir. There's a lot coming on. They'll be round the wood in a minute or two.'

'Well, go back to them and give *any* officer this message,' said Tony, writing rapidly in his note-book.

'Beg pardon, sir, but that will take me out of my way. I'm the last orderly the General 'as got left, and I was told to find out what 'ad 'appened 'ere, and then to come straight back.'

'I don't care a damn what you were told. You go with that message *now*.'

The man hurried off, and Tony walked along the line of guns, saw that they were laid on the crest line in front and that the fuses were set at zero. This would have the effect of bursting the shell at the muzzles, and so creating a death-zone of leaden bullets through which the attacking infantry would have to fight their way. Then he took up his post behind an ammunition waggon on the right of the battery and fixed his eyes on the signaller in front. He felt himself to be in the same state of tingling excitement as when he waited outside a good fox-covert expecting the welcome 'Gone away.'

Suddenly the signaller rose, and, crouching low, bolted back towards the guns. Just as he reached them a few isolated soldiers began to appear over the crest in front. As soon as they saw the guns they lay down waiting for support. They were the advanced scouts of a battalion.

A moment afterwards, a thick line of men came in sight. The sun gleamed on their bayonets. There was a shout, and they surged forward towards the battery.

'Three rounds gun fire,' Tony shouted. The four guns went off almost simultaneously, and at once the whole front was enveloped in thick white smoke from the bursting shell. In spite of diminished detachments the guns were quickly served. Again and once again they spoke within a second of each other.

The smoke cleared slowly, for there was scarcely a breath of wind. Meanwhile the assailants had taken cover and were beginning to use their rifles. Bullets, hundreds of them, tore the ground in front and clanged against the shields. Tony stepped back a few yards and looked down into the valley behind him. A thin line of skirmishers had almost reached the foot of the hill. His message had been delivered.

He came back to the cover of his waggon. The enemy began to come forward by rushes – a dozen men advancing twenty yards perhaps.

'Repeat,' said Tony.

Again the guns blazed and roared: again the pall of smoke obscured the view. A long trailing line of infantry began to climb the hill behind him. But the enemy was working round the flanks of the battery and preparing for the final rush. It was a question of whether friend or foe would reach him first. For the second time that day Tony muttered 'It's a race!'

Then, as he saw the whole line rise and charge straight at him –

'Gun fire,' he yelled above the din, knowing that by that order the ammunition would be expended to the last round.

He jumped to the gun nearest him, working the breech with mechanical precision, while the only gunner left in the detachment loaded and fired.

'Last round, sir,' came in a hoarse whisper, as Tony slammed the breech and leant back with left arm outstretched ready to swing it open again. In front they could see nothing: the smoke hung like a thick white blanket. Tony drew his revolver and stood up, peering over the shield, expecting every moment to see a line of bayonets emerge.

There was a roar behind. He heard the rush of feet and the rattle of equipment. He was conscious of the smell of sweating bodies and the sight of wild frenzied faces. Then the charge, arriving just in time, swept past him, a mad irresistible wave of humanity, driving the enemy before it and leaving the guns behind like rocks after the passage of a flood.

Tony fell back over the trail in a dead faint.

★

Long afterwards, when the tide of battle had rolled on towards the opposing heights, Tony, pale, grimy, but exultant, started back with the intention of rejoining his General. Half-way down the hill he met him riding up.

Tony turned and walked beside him.

'What's happened here, and where the devil have you been all day?' asked 'the Maud' angrily.

'I've been here, sir.'

'So it appears. I sent an orderly to find you, and all you did was to dispatch him on a message of your own, I understand. We were in urgent need of information as to what had happened up here. You failed to stop this battery, and it was your duty to come straight back and tell me so.'

Tony had never seen the placid Maud so angry. He glanced up at him as he sat there bolt upright on his horse looking straight to his front.

'It was my own battery,' said Tony. Then, after a pause, he added recklessly – 'Would you have come back, sir, if you'd been me?'

The Maud stared past him up the hill. He saw the guns, with the dead and wounded strewn around them, safe. He was a gunner first, a general only afterwards. He hummed a little tune.

'No,' he said, 'I wouldn't.'

THE BEGINNING OF THINGS

H. E. Bates

THE sudden arrival of M.E. 109s over the island in these early days was not pleasant. Even when they ran away they were good. They were very fast and after the Macchis they seemed very formidable and in the evenings there used to be long discussions in the Squadron on how to get them down.

McAlister was then about twenty: one of these people who are learning elementary physics one day, while a war is being planned by older men, who are wearing medals the next, by which time older men are already discussing what should happen when the war is over. The war is not over for McAlister by any means. The war and his life were the same thing: he did not want either to end. A D.F.C and bar and four Macchis and six dive-bombers down were only part of life: a few strips torn off, a wizard time, the beginning of things. He had been very scared most of the time, and at the same time very eager, very tense and very excited. He had a nice word for being scared, but it is not printable, and he had another for the war, but that is not printable either. Unfortunately I do not know what he thought of the men who made it, but no doubt that is unprintable too.

The spring weather was already hot on Malta when the first M.E.s began to appear. The young wheat was high and green in the fields and the sea very blue on the hot afternoons beyond the harbour. It was cool at night and on the nine o'clock watch in the mornings.

One morning the Hurricanes scrambled shortly after nine. Soon they were over Luca at twenty thousand. Far over Luca they were still climbing when the first M.E.s swooped down on them out of the sun. They swooped down very fast, screaming, and the Hurricanes split apart into a circle. This was as they had planned and McAlister took his place in the circle and looked about him. Just then the second M.E.s came down out of the sun, screaming like the first, trying to break the segment of the circle where McAlister was.

It all happened very quickly. McAlister turned back under the M.E.s and they overshot him. He looked round and there was nothing to see. And then he turned back and there in front of him was the M.E. he wanted. It was the M.E. he had wanted for a long time, the one they had all wanted. He felt that if he could shoot it down it would be more than a personal triumph. It would be perhaps even more than a Squadron triumph. It would be the first M.E. shot down over the island and it would be a victory for morale. He wanted it very badly. His hands were shaking and his blood was thumping very heavily in his throat and his mouth was sour as it watered. He was closing in very fast and he felt that nothing could stop him now.

The moment the crash came in his own cockpit he knew what an awful fool he had been. He had been much too excited to look in the mirror. And now he had made that utterly foolish, perhaps utterly fatal mistake. The cockpit was full of flying metal and the spray of blood. He went at once into a steep spiral dive. He was very angry with himself: very, very angry that he had been such a fool, that he had been beaten so easily, for the first time, at his own game.

When he came out of the dive he saw that his left arm was dripping with blood and when he tried to lift it it would not move. He did not know quite what else was happening. He afterwards remembered standing up in the cockpit. He remembered quite clearly, before that, how he opened the hood and disconnected his oxygen. He remembered breaking the R/T connections too. But between the moment of standing up and the moment of seeing his kite dive away from him and of hearing the fading roar of the engines as it fell to earth he did not remember anything at all. He remembered nothing of being angry any longer, or scared, or even in pain.

He knew only that it was a wonderful feeling to be out of the kite, in the air, quite free and at least temporarily safe, in the enormous peaceful space of sky. He could hear nothing except the dying roar of his kite going down to earth and once, above it, a long burst of cannon fire. He knew quite well, and quite intelligently, that he was upside down. It was a little ridiculous; his legs cut off his upward view. His arm was beginning suddenly to pain him very much and because of this he decided to pull the cord. He had been very struck by the notion that he might faint and never pull it at all.

When he went to pull the cord it was not there. For a moment it seemed to him that the chute must have been torn away from him as he left the kite. He was falling upside down and this was the end. He afterwards remembered thinking how very simple it was. You were shot down and you fell upside down and you found there was no chute and really, after all, it was a simpler, less painful, less horrible business than you had always imagined dying to be. You would fall a very long way and would hit the deck with a very hard thud, but the impact and the pain would by that time no longer matter. Your arm would cease hurting for ever and nobody would ever attack you behind again. At home your parents would read the telegram about your death and perhaps there would be a notice of it in *The Times*. Your mother would cry and the real pain of loss and emptiness and sacrifice and despair would not be yours, but theirs, and it would be far away and you would never know.

And finally, thinking this, he made one last effort to see if his parachute was with him. He snatched for the cord and suddenly it was there. He held it in his hands. He pulled it violently, and suddenly it was as if he were being hanged. The upward force of the chute opening seemed to wrench the upper part of his body away from the rest. The harness tightened with great power. He could not breathe and he felt very ill. Waves of darkness began to float over him and blood flashed back into his face, in windy spurts, from the wounded arm. The pain of the arm was savage and the pain of not being able to breathe, stupefying him, was worse. He saw Malta far below him, like a misty map in the sun, and all he wanted now was to be there, to lie on this map like the inanimate mark of a town, peacefully, without movement and without pain.

He must have gone off at this moment into a stupor, perhaps a faint, brought on by pain and shock and the loss of blood. He came out of it to hear the noise of an aircraft. It seemed to be bearing down on him and he had a notion at that moment, once again, that all was over. He was going to be holed like a bloody colander by an M.E. who had followed him down. This, and nothing else, was the experience of being shot down. This was the killing part. You were hung up like a half-dead pheasant on a string and an M.E. who had nothing else to do came down and did circles round you at leisure and fired until your guts ran out like jelly.

He looked up at last and saw not an M.E. but a Hurricane. 'Thank Christ,' he thought. 'Oh! thank Christ for that.'

The Hurricane circled a few times but he was too tired, too weak, and still too much in pain to show his joy. He was holding the raw stump of the wounded arm with his other arm and he could not wave his hands. He shut his eyes and drifted away, swinging, as if he were drunk and the world were spinning round.

When he opened his eyes again the Hurricane had gone and he could see the town more clearly. But it was still far down and once or twice he swung very violently and because of his hands he could not stop the swinging. He felt very sick and then finally he fell faster, not caring much until he looked down and felt that the roofs of the town, hot in the sun, were flying upward like enormous missiles that would hit him and lift him skyward again. Then for the first time he drifted away, more to the edge of the town, and soon it was only the flat roof of a little house that was rushing up to meet him. There was the little house and beside it was a little patch of wheat. The wheat was very green and McAlister saw it wave and shimmer in the wind and sun.

He hit the ground with great violence and rolled over. He lay still and this, at last, he thought, is the moment. I have been falling twenty-five thousand feet for the privilege of this moment, for the sweetness, the calm, the painlessness and the silence of being able to die. There is nothing else now. The chute does not matter, nor the arm, nor the pain. It is enough to lie in the wheat and shut my eyes against the sun and wait for the moment, and myself, to end.

The crowd of gesticulating Maltese who rushed up to him, trampling the wheat and tearing off his chute and holding up his head, made him very furious. They stopped all his thoughts about dying. He was not going to be bumped about like a piece of beef by anybody and he let out with extraordinary strength with his feet. It was as if the Maltese wanted to tear him to pieces for souvenirs. He kicked very hard for a few moments, just to show how very living he was and then his strength slipped out of him and he lay emptily on the earth, too tired to be angry again, only telling the Maltese how to give him morphia and how to bind the torniquet.

A little later they carried him across the little field of wheat to the advanced dressing station, and then to the town. He did not know much what happened. Two days later they took off his arm and in the night he was very restless and used to amuse himself sometimes scaring the Sister by telling her he would die because he did not want her to go away. The arm did not smell very nice in the days before they took it off and he was terrified that, without the arm, he would never fly again. But in fifteen days, from that moment, he was flying solo.

He is still flying solo. He flies beautifully and dangerously and they have fitted him up with an arm that has many intricate devices. You can see the delight of being able to fly in his face. It is one of the faces of those who fight wars they do not make and for whom flying and life are one: the faces of those who should be watched, the faces of the young – not of the young who die, but of the young who are shot down and live – of the young who are at the beginning of things.

I WAS THERE

Nicholas Monsarrat

SHE was a lovely boat, and a thousand times during that long trip across the Channel and up the French coast from Southampton to Flushing I found myself wishing she were mine. But country lawyers in a small way of business don't own sixty-ton diesel-powered yawls like the *Ariadne*: if they are lucky, they get the job of delivering them from their builders to other, more fortunate people. That was what I was doing that June evening, and not hurrying the job either; we had a fortnight to make the trip, ironing out the snarls on the way, and none of us wanted to cut that fortnight short.

'Us' was three people altogether: myself, on holiday from the dry-as-dust legal business of an English market town; George Wainwright, about whom I knew nothing save that he was on the fringe of London's theatrical world, and an excellent small-boat navigator; and Ginger, who tripled as steward, deck-hand, and running commentator. 'Call me Ginger!' he had said in a cheerful Cockney voice as soon as we met on the dockside: 'My mother was scared by a carrot!'

I had left it at 'Ginger'; he was the kind of man who didn't need a second name.

This was the sort of holiday I took every year, signing on with a yacht-delivery service and pulling strings to wangle the best boat and the best trip I could. It was the only way I could get to sea nowadays; the war had taken my own boat, and the post-war my bank balance. George Wainwright told me, airily, that he was 'resting between shows', though I fancy he was glad enough to pick up free quarters and twenty pounds for making what was virtually a pleasure cruise. He was a big man, sinewy and tough. I had the impression that he had done a lot of ocean-racing at one time in other people's boats, though I couldn't imagine him in any conceivable part in any West End play.

Ginger, the steward, didn't volunteer anything about himself. He never stopped talking, for all that.

The crew on these 'builder's delivery' jobs was usually a scratch lot, though it struck me that this time we were remarkably assorted. Middle-aged lawyer, forty-year-old actor, a red-headed Cockney who might have been fresh out of jail – the crew of the *Ariadne* seemed to have been picked at random from the Yellow Pages. But we had made her sail like a champion, all the same.

We had made her sail to such good purpose that now, with two days in hand, we were loafing along on the last hundred miles of the journey. Earlier, we had come smoking up the Channel before a Force 6 gale; *Ariadne*, handling beautifully, had logged a steady ten knots under her storm canvas. But then the wind had fallen light, and the leg from Dover to Calais had become a gentle drifting under hazy sunshine, while the decks and the sails dried out and we made what small repairs were necessary. Nothing had gone wrong that didn't always go wrong in a boat fresh from the builders – a leaking skylight, some chafed rigging, a cupboard door that wouldn't stay shut in a seaway. By and large, she went like a dream – as far as I was concerned, an envious dream of ownership that I would never live in reality.

George Wainwright and I had taken turn-about at the wheel, with Ginger filling in for an odd trick or two to give us an extra margin of sleep. We had lived on tea, corned beef, beans, and something which Ginger called 'cheesy-hammy-eggy', and which, for cold, hungry, and tired men, was a banquet in itself. Rum, twice a day, completed our paradise.

Now, towards the end of that paradise, we were punching eastwards against the ebb tide at six o'clock of a magic evening. *Ariadne*, under all plain sail, could not make much of the light air; we were barely holding our own, creeping up the flat coastline with the sun warm on our backs. I had the wheel, letting the spokes slide through my fingers with a sensual joy. Ginger, standing with his head poking out of the cabin top, was drying cups and saucers. George Wainwright, his elbows planted on the chart, stared landwards through his binoculars.

'We're not making any headway,' he said presently. 'Barely a knot, I should say.'

'Suits me,' said Ginger irrepressibly. He could never resist a comment on anything, from UN politics to juvenile delinquency. 'I've got all year.'

The water gurgled at the bow. The sail slatted, empty of wind.

'We might as well anchor,' I said. 'The tide will be against us for another four hours. What's the depth here?'

George Wainwright glanced at the chart. 'About four fathoms. Sandy bottom. She'll hold all right.'

'We'll anchor till the flood,' I decided. 'Give us a chance to catch up on our sleep.' I eased *Ariadne* up into the wind, and our way fell off. Ginger went forward to see to the windlass. 'How far are we off shore?' I asked George.

'About a mile,' he answered. 'The tide sets us inwards.'

'And where, exactly?'

'Off Dunkirk.'

'Dunkirk . . . As the anchor-chain rattled down through the leads, and *Ariadne* swung and settled to her cable, I was conscious of an odd foreboding. It was true that we were a mile off Dunkirk: I recognized, as if from a hundred photographs, the oily swell, the sloping beaches, the fat mainland enclosing a loose-knit grey town. Here were the waters, full of ghosts, full of sunken ships and dead men, which a decade earlier – no, it was now nearly *two* decades – had resounded to a murderous uproar. In my mind's eye I saw them all again; the straggling lines of men wading through the shallows, crying out for rescue or waiting in dull stupor to be picked up: the burning town behind, the Stukas overhead, and the small boats darting in and out – going in light, coming out laden to the gunwales – on an errand of mercy and salvage that went on hour after hour, day after day. That was what Dunkirk would always mean to me – a name at once grisly and proud, a symbol, a haunting from the past. I was curious to know what it meant to the other two, and I did not have to wait long to find out.

Ginger, having secured the anchor, came aft again. George Wainwright looked up from his chart, where *Ariadne*'s observed position was now marked by a neatly pencilled cross. There was no need to wonder which of them would speak first. It would have been an easy bet to win.

'Good old Dunkirk! said Ginger jauntily. He wiped his hands, greasy from the windlass, on a bunch of cotton-waste, and looked round him at *Ariadne*'s benevolent anchorage. 'Makes you think a bit, don't it?'

'How do you mean, Ginger?' asked George Wainwright.

'All this . . .' Ginger waved his hand round vaguely. 'It's nineteen years ago now, but by cripes it's like yesterday! . . . The bombers coming over as thick as bloody fleas, the lads waiting . . . I'll never forget it, not as long as I live. By cripes, skipper!' he turned to me, his creased leathery face alight, 'I could tell you a yarn that would curl your hair! A yarn – '

. . . a yarn which, as the sun sank to the westwards, and *Ariadne*'s wavering shadow lengthened and faded on the tranquil waters off Dunkirk, recalled all the horrors, terrors, and triumphs of those mortal days. Ginger told it well; I knew that he must have had many audiences, many chances to polish and perfect.

The lads, he said (and we could all see them as lads, beefy Lancashire lads from the mills, grey-faced lads from the Yorkshire coal pits, likely lads from Bermondsey and Bow) – the lads were fed up. The officer had promised them they'd be taken off that night, and they'd been content with that, after a week's dodging the bombers on their way back to the coast, and they'd settled down on the beach to wait. But they hadn't been taken off, not that night, nor the next, nor the next. That was the army for you – waiting about, nobody knowing what was happening, all a lot of bull, put that bloody light out! . . . First they had waited on the beach; then at the water's edge; then chest-high in the water itself.

The straggling line inched its way outwards from the shallows to the deep water. 'Link arms, there!' said the officer; so they linked arms, and with the other hand held their rifles safely above water. 'Because you'll be using those rifles tomorrow,' said the officer. 'Keep them dry, keep them ready for instant action!' ''Ark at 'im,' said the lads . . .

They waited in the shallows and the deeps. It was cold at night; then it was hot; behind them the town was burning, and the perimeter force kept blazing away with everything they'd got, and the Stukas circled, and swooped, and roared away again, leaving behind them a salty human flotsam – men mixed with sand, men mixed with water, seaweed, other men, all draining slowly away as the tide ebbed. 'Where's the bloody Air Force?' asked the lads, scanning the alien sky between waves of noise and pain. 'Tucked up in bed with anyone they can get hold of' . . . 'Heard from your missus lately? . . .'

It was cold at night, then it was burning hot. Men got hit, and dropped out; men got cramp, and floated away; men went mad, and tried to hide beneath the waves. There were other straggling lines within sight, like feelers weaving and groping towards home. Their own line grew thinner; sometimes part of it disappeared altogether, as if by weight of noise and pressure. 'Close up!' said the officer. 'And no smoking there! Might give away our position.'

The officer was the last to go. He was one of the lads himself, only a bit lah-di-dah . . . When it was their turn to be taken off, the boat from the destroyer, bobbing inshore after a stick of bombs had straddled the shallows, drew alongside the wavering line.

'Look lively!' said the sailor at the helm, as cool as fresh salad, and they looked lively – as lively as they could after three days of it. There was one lad going off his head with the noise and the sun, and he tried to clamber on board, suddenly screaming with mingled pain and joy, and the officer came up behind and gave him a heave into the boat, and then himself crumpled up like a sodden newspaper and disappeared without a trace.

They fished around for him, couldn't find him, suddenly abandoned the idea and drew swiftly away. Better to save twenty lives, they reassured themselves . . . But it was funny how surprised he had looked after three such days, just before he faded out.

Dusk came down like a blessing. *Ariadne* rode to her anchor proudly; she was gleaming new, and the white of her doused sails seemed to hold the sunlight long after it had dipped below the horizon. I would have needed a lot of things – a lot of luck, a lot of horse-sense, a lot of drive I had never had – to possess a boat like this. But somehow, sitting relaxed in the cockpit, nursing a rum-and-water, I found it easy to imagine that it had all happened, and that she was mine.

The lights of Dunkirk were coming on one by one. George Wainwright took an anchor-bearing from them, satisfied himself that we were not dragging, and sat down by my side again. He raised his voice against the lap and gurgle of the tideway.

'That was a good yarn of yours, Ginger,' he said. 'I know exactly how you must have felt . . . But it was just as bad for the little ships that had to come close inshore and take the troops off. If you want to hear a story . . .'

. . . a story about a big man in a small boat (and, looking at George Wainwright's broad shoulders as he lounged at the after-end of the cockpit, we both knew that it was *his* story). Hundreds of little ships played their part in the evacuation of Dunkirk; everything from old paddle-wheel ferries to ship's lifeboats, nursed across the Channel by a man and a boy. Their job was to run a shuttle service – to come close inshore, load up with troops, and bring them out to deeper water where the bigger boats and the destroyers were waiting.

Some of the little ships kept it up for three or four days. The two-and-a-half-ton sloop *Tantivvy* was one of these.

Tantivvy (said George Wainwright) was nothing to look at though she was the owner's pride and joy. She'd sailed across from Dover with the rest of the mob, following a call on the radio which asked for every small ship that could stay afloat to report for emergency duty. The motley fleet fanned out like a crazy Armada, then converged on Dunkirk. Dunkirk, with its pall of smoke, its mass of shipping, its hurricane of gunfire, was something you couldn't miss.

Tantivvy, drawing less than four feet, could get within half a mile of the shore; and there she anchored, and presently launched from her upper deck a small pram-dinghy propelled by a large man whose bulk left room for, at the very most, two other passengers . . . All day, and most of the night, the dinghy plied to and fro, taking off two soldiers at a time from the waiting hordes, loading them on to the deck of *Tantivvy*, and then going back for more.

There came a time, towards dawn, when *Tantivvy* had fifty passengers. They sprawled in the tiny cabin, grey-faced, dead to the world; they lay about on the upper deck, soiling it with their blood; they sat with their backs to the mast, staring at nothing, waiting for peace. After his twenty-fifth trip, the big man looked at them, and said: 'Not many more, I'm afraid.'

One of the soldiers, still awake and still able to talk, waited for a lull in the bombing, and called out: 'Let's get going, for God's sake!'

'We might manage two more,' said the big man, resting his swollen, aching arms on the oars.

'Don't be a bloody fool!' said the soldier in a cracked voice. 'You'll lose the lot of us if you do. We're damn' near sinking already.'

A bomb fell with a screaming crump! and a shower of dirty water, close beside them.

'Well . . .' said the big man. His face was deadly tired, his eyes puffy and discoloured.

He climbed on board, secured the dinghy to the stern post, and started up the tiny motor.

'Help me with the anchor,' he said to the soldier.

The two of them shambled forwards, picking their way between half-dead men who, even when kicked out of the way, could not spare them a glance. They heaved on the anchor and finally brought it home. The big man stood upright, and then suddenly stiffened.

'You stupid bastard!' he said to the soldier.

'What?' said the soldier, in amazement.

There was an enormous explosion ashore, and the small boat, gathering way, rocked as the hot shock-wave reached them.

'*Don't you know better,*' asked the big man, with murderous sarcasm, '*than to walk on a wooden deck in those blasted hobnailed boots?*'

There was a breeze coming up from the southward, sending the small ripples slap-slapping against *Ariadne*'s shapely hull. An hour before moonrise, it was now very dark; Dunkirk's glow was reflected in the sky overhead, but between the town and the boat there was a waste of inky black water, deserted, featureless. It was as if the soldiers had all been picked up, and we were free to go . . .

In the glow from the binnacle Ginger's perky face was sombre. Perhaps, for him as well, the ghosts were still thick around us. If only for our comfort I knew that I had to tell them about the triumphant part, the end of the story . . .

. . . the end of the story, which I could see now, as clearly as the others had seen theirs.

She was an old destroyer, a bit cranky in her ways (which were the ways of 1916, not 1940) and bringing her alongside at Dover, feverishly crammed with shipping, was not easy. Not if you'd been on the bridge for thirty-six hours, and made two trips to Dunkirk, and dodged the bombers all the way there and all the way back, and waited off-shore, sweating, while eight hundred and sixty-two men scrambled, clawed, and bullocked their way on board. Not if you had to go back, as soon as this lot was landed, and do the whole thing over and over again till there were no more soldiers showing above water.

The old destroyer slipped between two trawlers leaving for a routine minesweep, stopped in her tracks with a sudden boiling of foam aft, and edged sideways towards the quay. The lines went snaking ashore, the windlasses took in the slack; presently she was berthed, and the hum of the main engines ceased. The captain walked to the back of the bridge and looked aft along the length of his ship.

This was the dividend, this was what the excursion had been for . . . There wasn't an inch of the deck that was not covered with men – men in khaki. On the trip home they had lain there as though stunned or dead; now they were stirring, moving towards the gangway and peering down at the Dover dockside as if they could scarcely believe their eyes. Their uniforms were filthy, their faces unshaven, their many bandages bloodstained; they looked like a wretched scarecrow army in some hollow Shakespearian comedy. About half of them had rifles. There was no other equipment.

The destroyer captain thought: if this is what's left of the British Army, then God help us . . .

They began to disembark, shambling down the gangplank like men sleepwalking in a dream of death. They collected in groups, and then in ragged lines, filling the whole quayside. There was a bunch of them directly below the bridge, standing as if in a shattered trance.

Then suddenly one of them, a small lance-corporal, looked up at the bridge, and then directly at the destroyer captain himself. For a moment they held each other's eyes as if they were seeking some rare, unheard-of element that could bridge the ground between a stunted Cockney soldier and a tall, beribboned Royal Navy captain; and then the small lance-corporal grinned, and looked round at his weary comrades, and shouted, on a cracked note of energy:

'Come on, lads! Three cheers for the bleedin' Nyvy!'

They could hardly be called three cheers; they were like the thin rise and fall of a groan, or a spectral sighing from an army of ghosts. But they did emanate from those bedraggled ranks, and they did reach the gaunt, teak-faced destroyer captain on the bridge.

The captain, when he went ashore, was the elder son of an earl; and, when afloat, an unbending disciplinarian who had been known to deal out exemplary punishment for a sloppy salute. It was a difficult moment, covered by no textbook, no family code, and indeed no war so far. But he also had something important to express, and he did the best he could. He leant over the wing of his bridge, stiff as a rod in spite of his weariness, and enunciated very clearly:

'My compliments to *you*, gentlemen – my *best* compliments.'

They liked my story, I could tell that; it reminded them that the Dunkirk disaster could be read two ways. In the binnacle glow, Ginger's face grew cheerful again, and George Wainwright took a swig of his rum as if toasting Victory herself. The night breeze, from landwards, brought a warm homely smell of Flanders fields. At anchor off Dunkirk we had mourned long enough; for the tragedy had a happy ending after all.

'That's what we tend to forget,' said George, echoing my thoughts. 'We *did* take off more than three hundred thousand of them, and they *did* get back again, in the end.'

Looking up after the long spell of talking, I became aware that the lights of Dunkirk were no longer on *Ariadne*'s starboard beam, but traversing slowly round astern of her. The Channel tide was flooding.

'We're swinging, skipper,' said George Wainwright, noticing at the same moment. 'The tide's with us now. The wind's got some weight in it, too.'

I clicked the switch of the navigation lights, and the friendly red and green eyes brought *Ariadne* to life.

'Let's get under way,' I said.

'Now you're talking!' said Ginger. 'This place gives me the creeps.'

We were all standing up, ready to go about our tasks – hoisting the foresail and the main, getting up the anchor, putting ourselves and *Ariadne* to work again.

'Of course Dunkirk is haunted,' said George Wainwright suddenly. 'But it gave us something to be proud of, all the same.'

Some quality of wistfulness in his voice prompted me to ask a question which had been in my mind ever since the three of us started talking.

'Tell me something,' I said. '*Were* you at Dunkirk?'

It was light enough to see him grin. 'Not actually, old boy,' he answered. Suddenly he *did* sound like an actor, rather a good one. 'I was touring with ENSA at the time. *Private Lives* – eight shows a week. I wasn't actually *at* Dunkirk.'

It seemed right that he did not sound sheepish . . . I turned towards the slight figure clambering up to the fo'c'sle deck.

'Ginger? Were you?'

'Not me!' I might have been charging him with picking pockets. '1940, wasn't it? – I was in the glasshouse already! Asleep on sentry-go, the man said. What a — liberty!'

I knew what was coming next.

'Were *you* there?' George Wainwright asked me.

I didn't want to embarrass either of them; in any case, I couldn't be sure that, even now, they were telling the truth. One of them was an actor, the other a liar; they lived, congenially, in opposite corners of the same dream-world. And I myself led such a dull life nowadays. . . .

'Afraid not,' I answered. 'Bad heart, you know . . . I was doing civil defence work in London all that summer. I wasn't at Dunkirk either.'

But the moment of revelation did not make us ashamed among ourselves, nor were we truly liars, whether we were lying or not. For our last three answers had all been wrong. Every Englishman was at Dunkirk.

OLD BEETHOVEN

Alexander Baron

LISTENING to a Beethoven piano concerto, I remembered Tom Meredith.

Music sets my dreams free; it is nearly always Beethoven. A storm of harmony subsides, leaving a lucent ground-swell of melody. Into the lakelike calm the piano enters with little cascades of music, ripples of high pure notes that fall as softly as tears into the wider flow. The waves run again, surge smoothly, mount and break once more in vast proclamatory chords. All the weight of human passion is crashing down upon the listener, thundering about him. Consciousness is drowned; blind eddies of agitation reach down into the depths; and, all unbidden, memories are drawn up to the mind's surface.

On this evening, as I listened to the fourth piano concerto, it was the forgotten face of Tom Meredith that rose to haunt me.

In nineteen forty-three when he was twenty and I was five years older, our unit was waiting to go overseas. Our past training and the equipment we had received warned us that we were going to take part in an assault from the sea – somewhere. I cannot remember whether we were afraid. It was unlikely, for we were young, fit and too confident. Certainly, however, we were afflicted by a kind of stage fright, an iciness and a rending impatience at the core of our high spirits; and the need to hold this down increased our determination to have a good time in the few days before we left.

At the beginning of the last week three of us, Tom, myself and an ex-bookmaker's runner from Liverpool named O'Toole, drew all our back pay and set out to spend it in town.

On Monday night we went the round of the pubs and lurched back to barracks spewing and singing discordantly.

On Tuesday night we went to the music hall. After the show we went round to the back door and persuaded three of the girls to come to supper with us. We were disappointed to find that, off the stage, they were just three pallid, tired and very cautious working-girls, but we were proud to have talked them into coming with us and we were quite satisfied to be dismissed with a few prim good-night kisses.

On Wednesday night we went, for the first time in any of our lives, to a good restaurant, and ate a black market dinner. We had roast duckling and a bottle of wine. After a rest we had omelets and mushrooms, strawberries and cream and more wine. Then, while Tom and I were drinking little cups of black coffee, O'Toole, who liked to show off, had a lobster salad.

On Thursday night there was a gigantic party in the barracks, which ended up amid a good deal of wrecked furniture.

On Friday –

On Friday the three of us had very little money left and no idea how to pass the evening. We lounged about the town, thinking rather miserably that we ought to find something better than this to do on our last free night in England. We could not afford another night's drinking. We had seen all the films. We were still arguing what to do, vaguely and fruitlessly, when we came to the Civil Hall.

O'Toole said, 'Ah, bloody concert. Come on, there's nothing here.'

Tom and I hung about, looking at the people going in. Tom pointed at a poster. 'Chap playing the piano. I like to hear a chap that's good on the piano. Or the fiddle.'

I said, 'He's one of the best there is.'

'It's only half a dollar,' Tom said. 'We can always come out if we don't like it.'

O'Toole said, 'Bloody ideas you get sometimes!' But when we went in, he followed us.

We stayed to the end of the concert. We sat back in the gallery, arms folded, and frowned down upon the orchestra, not clapping when others clapped, making no comment in the intervals and pushing our way out at the end while the conductor was still bowing.

It was a lovely May night. The streets were full of moonlight.

Each of us waited for the others to say something, but none of us spoke. We swung along, our steel-shod boots crashing loud on the deserted pavements. O'Toole said that there was time for a drink before the pubs closed. Tom said, 'Ah, — you and your drinks!' O'Toole stared at him, but kept loyally in step, and did not ask where we were going even when, instead of returning to the barracks, we strode clear across town, over the Common and back through the silent outskirts. At midnight we walked into the billet. O'Toole looked as if he were still waiting for one of us to say something, but he got nothing except 'Goodnight', and went off to his room looking puzzled.

A few days later we were at sea. For the first few days, in the North Atlantic, the ship was wrapped in mist. All we knew of the rest of the convoy was the sound of sirens. There was no feeling of movement except for the vibration of the decks and the beat of the ship's engines. We still did not know where we were going. It might have been unnerving if we had talked or even thought about this uncanny journey, about the hazards that might strike at us through the mists, or about what must lie at the end of it; but we did not.

We performed wearisome fatigues, attended boat drills, played housy-housy for hours at a time, queued interminably for cups of tea, read and lounged about the decks talking of trivialities. One morning Tom and I were taking a turn on deck. O'Toole was down below tidying the hammock lockers. Tom said, 'That was a week, wasn't it, before we went away?'

'I'll say!'

'Them tarts!'

'Smashing!'

'I could do with one of them right now, couldn't you?'

'Just right for this weather.'

'Just right for any weather.' A pause. 'Here, how do you say that name again? Chap wrote that music?'

'What music?'

'Up the Town Hall that night.'

'Beethoven.'

'Beethoven,' He pronounced the word carefully. 'Long time ago, wasn't he?'

'I reckon so.'

'When?'

'About Napoleon's time.'

'When was that about?'

'About a hundred and fifty years ago.'

'And they still play his pieces?'

'Yes.'

He made a sucking, wondering sound. 'Jus' shows you, eh?' I left him to his thoughts. A few moments later he said, 'About time we got in the tea queue, isn't it? Or we won't get served.'

The days passed; engines thumping; rough weather; the other ships in sight once more, dotted over the wide grey circle of sea; destroyers burying themselves in white masses of water and shaking themselves free; an aircraft alarm, din of guns and the empty sky stained with smoke; card games, concerts, rumours, rumours, rumours. Time become a dream. Into southern waters; sunlight sparkling on a blue sea; the men wearing shorts and bush shirts; a strange, dizzy, holiday feeling; rifles to be cleaned; physical training; the end of the dream approaching.

We came up on deck one day after a good lunch, all three of us. We leaned at the rails, watching the porpoises leap, shed dazzling drops of spray and thump back into the sea. Tom said, 'That was a treat. Tripe and onions for dinner. Not often you get that.'

'It's lucky half the chaps was sick,' O'Toole said. 'I ate till I bust and there was still some left in the tin. It breaks your heart to leave it.'

'I'm not seasick,' Tom said.

'I'm not seasick neither,' O'Toole said. 'What about you?'

'Seasick?' I said. 'Me? You're daft.'

'Who's daft?'

'The pair of you.'

'Well,' Tom said. 'I like that! Here, I was thinking. This feller – '

I said, 'What feller?'

'Old Beethoven.' He uttered the name quite unexpectedly. We had not mentioned it since that morning together on deck; and now he spoke as if of an old friend.

O'Toole asked, 'Who's he?'

Tom answered, 'Chap wrote that music.'

'What music?'

'Up the Town Hall that night, daft!'

'Ha! That night! Bloody night that was!' He glared at Tom. 'Your bloody clever idea, that was!'

'I reckon it was.'

'Reckon it was what?'

'A bloody good idea. Here, look – ' Tom turned to me. 'Old Beethoven, that tune of his they played, that wasn't one tune we heard there, was it? It was about twenty. I was trying to remember it, and first I remembered one tune – well, you know, a bit of it – and then I remembered another. And then I forgot that one and I thought of another one altogether. Here, well I reckon there was about twenty tunes in that piece, at least, and they all went in together, and that sort of made the one big tune.' He waited anxiously for my opinion.

'I reckon that's the idea of it,' I said. 'That's why composers like him are famous. It's not just one tune they write. It's a whole, sort of, pattern of music, and they weave it all together. There's anything from fifty instruments upwards in those orchestras, and he writes a separate part for each of them. Only they all harmonize.'

Tom asked, 'Do you reckon he thinks of them one at a time or all together?'

'Well, I don't know really.'

'Still,' he said, 'it's clever. He must think of them all at once or he wouldn't – ' He broke off, and then exclaimed in a tone of deep awe, 'All that in one man's head!'

'You know what I think?' O'Toole said.

'What, daft?'

'I think we're going to Russia. Through the Dardanelles. Get in behind the Jerries there and finish them off.'

An old argument started again.

A few days later the argument was settled. We swarmed out of the ship's sally ports into a white glare of sunshine, crammed into one of the little landing-craft that wallowed on the slow, sickening swell, crouched helmeted and heavily burdened for hours on a hot steel deck amid the reek of oil and at last landed, tired, ill and sweating, on a beach in Sicily.

A new world, as unreal as the world of the sea; a succession of broken dreams, good dreams and bad dreams; on the move all the time yet not feeling that we were going anywhere; unaware of the things we were doing, only feeling that things were being done to us; blinding sunlight, bright colours, mosquitoes, thirst, muffling, parching white dust; days that were quiet and drowsy and nights that were fearsomely alive, riven by the noise, the racking fear and the firework flashes of war.

Three weeks later the advance along the coast had ended and the three of us were in a slit trench looking out across a broad bare plain. Across the plain, invisible but watching to strike down any man who tried to move forward, were the enemy.

We had a bad time there. The sun beat down upon us and sucked the strength out of us. Our uniforms clung to us uncomfortably, sodden black with sweat. We could not wash to keep cool or drink enough to keep thirst at bay, for water was scarce. The wells stank, for the Germans had polluted them with dead animals, and the water from them tasted evilly of chlorine. The sweet stench of unburied dead, men and beasts, hung upon the air. The white dust drifted and tormented. There were mosquitoes and malaria. The Germans had their snipers everywhere, and it was dangerous to show ourselves above ground by daylight. We huddled, ill and miserable, in our burning little holes in the ground.

The time had to be passed somehow. We talked.

I sat at one end of the trench, my knees up, reading a magazine. Tom was in the middle, staring at the brown wall as if he could see through a mile or two of solid earth into the pits where other men sat facing us. O'Toole was huddled at the other end with his eyes shut, his head lolling on one side, breathing heavily. He had dysentery. He was too weak by now to crawl to a latrine when his spasms came; in any case, with the snipers active, it was hardly worth the risk. He kept a biscuit tin by him, and from time to time one of us would empty it for him. His trousers were soaked with blood and slime. The tin made the close little pocket of overheated air in the trench smell horrible, and it attracted the flies in beastly black swarms, so that whenever we tried to eat we had to brush them off every scrap of food.

Tom said, 'How long we been here?'

I closed my magazine. 'I don't know. About three weeks.'

'What? In this place?'

'I thought you meant in Sicily.'

'Oh,' he said wearily. 'Sicily!' He closed his eyes and leaned his head back against the wall of the trench, swearing softly at Sicily.

'It's Friday. We dug in here Tuesday night.'

We lit cigarettes and blew smoke up at the parapet. Tom asked O'Toole if he wanted a smoke. O'Toole shook his head feebly without opening his eyes and fumbled for his water-bottle. Tom helped him to drink and put the water-bottle away.

In the distance we heard the faint crack of a sniper's rifle. We listened. Silence. Tom said, 'Give us one of your sweets. For him.'

We had a ration of boiled sweets. They were the only food that O'Toole could keep in his mouth without vomiting, and the sugar in them kept his strength up. I passed my pack to Tom. He rummaged, and pushed a sweet between O'Toole's lips. 'What the *bloody* hell are we doing here?' he burst out. 'Call this a war?'

'It's a war all right. Stick your head over the top and find out.'

'It makes you wonder. How did we *get* here? Listen, I'll tell you what. I can't remember *coming* here!'

'I can't remember ever being anywhere else.'

'I – ' He had sat up, straining to think. He relaxed again. 'Phew! It's too bloody hot to remember anything.'

We both went off into a waking doze; for how long, I cannot remember. It may have been an hour or two. I opened my magazine again, but my gaze rested on the words without taking them in.

It was the sound of another shot that roused us; the distant crack and the faint glassy echoing of shouts in the hot stillness of the day. Men were calling for stretcher-bearers.

Tom said, 'I suppose he was one of them.'

'Who?'

'Old Beethoven. He was a Jerry, wasn't he?'

'Yes.' I was too dull and heat-struck to feel any surprise at the casual introduction of the name after all these weeks.

'That's a bloody laugh, eh?' He spoke without interest, not looking at me but continuing to gaze vacantly at the wall of earth in front of him.

'There's good and bad everywhere.'

'That's not what they tell you.'

I said, 'He was deaf.'

'What's that got to do with it?'

'Nothing. I just thought.'

He looked at me, and traces of life came back into his face. 'How could he be, anyway?'

'Why not?'

'A deaf musician? You got the bloody sunstroke or something.'

'It was all in his head. He wrote some of his greatest music, and he conducted the orchestra that played it, but he couldn't hear them. That's another reason why they call him a genius.'

'Genius!' Tom's voice was awake now, awake with pain. 'Bloody torture I call it! Think of writing all that *lovely* bloody music and not being able to hear it. Here, if that was me, my bloody head would burst. All that music thundering away inside. Burst your head, it would.' Wonder lent animation to his eyes, and strength to his voice. 'I tell you what, though, that feller was a Man. A real, bloody Man, eh?' It took him a few seconds to recover from the articulation of his thought. Then he said, 'Of course, we only heard one of his pieces, didn't we?'

'Well, one and a couple of smaller bits.'

'I should like to hear the rest of them. That's what I'm goin' to do one day. Hear all the bloody lot of them, I will. Here – ' he looked at me, and an anguish of puzzlement flitted across his face. 'It's a funny thing I never heard of him before. I mean, I'm twenty! Years of my life behind me. How come I never heard of a chap like that, all those years?'

I shrugged my shoulders. 'Happens.'

'How did you know all this about him?'

'A book.'

'Where'd you get it?'

'Up the library.'

'Library, eh? That's another lark I've never tried.'

'Sounds as if you'll have a busy time when you get back.'

'Ha! I will! I'll – You're right there, I will an' all. What else?'

'About him? Well, he was a very independent chap. He was a bit of a rebel. He was all for freedom, and all that kind of thing. One day, some chap introduced himself, he said, "I'm So-and-so von So-and-so, Landowner." And old Beethoven bowed back, and he said, "And I'm Ludwig von Beethoven, Brain-owner." '

'Ha! There's the kiddie! *He* would, eh? It's gone quiet, hasn't it?' It was ten minutes since we had heard any sound of war.

'I tell you what,' he resumed. 'You were right, what you said. About having a busy time when I get back. When I get back, do you know what I want to do?' His whole body came alive, and before I could restrain him he straightened up, all upright and shining with youth, looking out over the parapet as if beyond the dismal plain was appearing all the bright beauty of the world that he had never seen. 'When I get back I want to – '

Those where his last words.

HAMLETS
OF THE WORLD

Irwin Shaw

THE captain was getting more and more remote every moment. He kept stuffing papers into a heavy saddle-leather bag, whistling tunelessly under his breath. From time to time he looked out over the windy plain, swirling with dust in the late afternoon sun. He would peer thoughtfully into the eye-burning distance, then shake himself a little and resume his packing, a little more quickly each time. He never looked at Lieutenant Dumestre.

Lieutenant Dumestre sat on the edge of the desk, very neat in his expensive uniform. He was a tall, fairish man, who looked too young to be in his lieutenant's uniform, too young to be so serious, too young to be in a war.

He never took his eyes off the Captain. The Captain was a round, solid man, who had been very jovial when they had met in Algiers and had paid for the wine and had sighed gallantly over all the pretty women in the café. There was nothing jovial or gallant about the Captain now, as he prepared in a businesslike way to disappear, each moment seeming more and more remote.

'Do you expect to come back, sir?' Lieutenant Dumestre finally asked, because the silence in the orderly room broken only by the low bumble of the Captain's humming was at last too much to bear.

The Captain stopped his packing and looked thoughtfully out over the plain again, as though there, in the dust and scrub, some answer to a profound although somewhat vague question was to be found. He stood silently, even forgetting to hum.

'Do you expect to come back, sir?' the Lieutenant asked loudly.

The Captain at last turned and looked at the Lieutenant. His eyes were very cool and you would never have thought from looking at him in this moment that he had ever bought a bottle of wine for a lieutenant in his life. 'Come back?' the Captain said. He turned away and sturdily buckled his bag. 'Who can tell?'

'What do I do with the Americans?' The Lieutenant's voice, he noticed angrily, was much higher than it should have been. At Saint Cyr they had been after him all the time to pitch his voice lower. 'An order given in the soprano register, Mister, is not calculated to drive troops to impossible glories.' 'What happens when the Americans arrive?'

The Captain was putting his helmet on very carefully in front of a mirror. 'That is just what I hope to discover,' he said.

'In the meantime?'

'In the meantime your orders are to resist. Naturally.'

The Lieutenant peered out over the plain, hoping painfully that over the rim of the horizon the Americans would appear before the Captain could leave on his personal retreat. But the only movement to be seen was a corporal hurrying to the battery observation post.

'They'll arrive tomorrow morning, at the latest,' the Lieutenant said.

'Quite possibly.' The Captain picked up his bag decisively, marched out and into the command car. The Lieutenant followed him and saluted. The Captain saluted and the car started and the Captain drove down the road.

The Lieutenant plodded slowly up the road toward the forward gun, thinking of the Captain, in the command car, speeding over a macadam road to Algiers, where there would be other men to make the decisions, other men to say, 'We will move to the left, we will move to the right . . .' and the Captain would have to make no decisions himself. No matter how things turned out, he would not be committed and would be a fine fellow with whichever side turned up on top, and would jovially buy wine for his new lieutenants at the second-best restaurant in town . . .

The Lieutenant made his way to the aimless little mud house they used as an observation post and climbed the ladder and stood under the umbrella next to the red-eyed little corporal and peered through his glasses at the plain. He looked until his eyes ached, but aside from the blowing dust there was nothing.

The men who served the forward gun had rigged up a tarpaulin to one side and lay under it, out of the wind. Usually they slept all the afternoon, but today no one was sleeping.

Sergeant Fourier even went so far as to get up and look out across the plain.

'Anything?' Labat asked.

The Sergeant squinted anxiously. 'Nothing.'

'Waiting, everything is waiting,' Labat said. He was a long, ugly man, with a big nose and large ears. He was from Paris and excitable and given to throwing his arms around in rage and was a great patriot of the French Republic. 'In a war you wait for everything! Even the Americans! At last, I thought, things will finally move. The Americans are famous for their briskness . . . We're still waiting . . .'

'Only a day,' said Boullard. Boullard was a big, quiet man, over forty, with a wrinkled, brown, farmer's face. 'They'll be here soon enough.'

'I can't wait,' Labat said. He stood up and peered out. 'For a year I sat in the Maginot Line. Now for two years I sit here. I am finally impatient. A day is too much.'

'Shut up,' Boullard said calmly. 'You'll get us all nervous.'

Labat lay down and put his hands behind his head and looked up at the tarpaulin angrily. Sergeant Fourier came back and sat down.

'More of the same,' Sergeant Fourier said. 'More nothing.'

'It must be worse for Americans,' Corporal Millet said. He was a man who, although he was nearly thirty-five, was still plagued by pimples. His face had raging red blots on it all the time and he suffered meanly under his affliction, taking his misfortune out on the work details in his charge. 'It must be unbearable for Americans.'

'Why?' Labat asked angrily. 'What's wrong with the Americans?'

'They are not a military people,' Corporal Millet said. He had a lawyer's voice, smooth and reasonable and superior, and on bad days it made men want to kill Corporal Millet. 'They are used to sitting back and pushing buttons.'

'Corporal,' Labat said calmly, 'you are perhaps the biggest idiot in the French Army of 1942.'

'The jokes,' Corporal Millet said. 'We can do without the jokes. It is a fact that war is harder on some races than on others. The Americans must be suffering the tortures of the damned.'

'I repeat,' Labat said. 'The biggest.'

Corporal Millet was a devotee of Vichy, and Labat enjoyed making him angry.

'Push buttons,' Boullard said reflectively. 'I could use a few push buttons at the moment.'

'See,' Corporal Millet gestured to Boullard. 'Boullard agrees.'

'See,' Boullard said. 'Boullard does not agree.'

There was silence for a moment, while the men thought of the wind and the ugliness of the men around them and the possibility of dying tomorrow.

'Be more cheerful,' Boullard said, 'or kindly keep quiet.'

The men sat silently for a moment, everyone heavy and gloomy because the word death had finally been mentioned.

'It will be a ridiculous thing,' Labat said. 'To be killed by an American.' Labat had fought at Sedan and made his way bitterly down the length of France, cursing the politicians, cursing the officers, cursing the Germans and English and Italians and Americans. At last he had stowed away aboard a freighter to Algiers and without losing a day had joined up all over again and had since then sat, full of pent-up vengeance, in the gloom of Africa, waiting to fight the Germans once more.

'I refuse,' Labat said. 'I refuse to be killed by an American.'

'You will be told what your orders are,' Corporal Millet said, 'and you will follow them.'

Labat stared gloomily and dangerously at Corporal Millet. His face, which was ugly but usually pleasant enough, now was harsh and his eyes were squinted balefully. 'Corporal,' he said, 'Corporal of the pimples, do you know what our orders are?'

'No.'

'Does anybody know?' Labat looked around, his face still flushed and glowering, angry at Corporal Millet and the government of France and his position in the world that afternoon.

Sergeant Fourier cleared his throat professionally. 'The Lieutenant. He must know. The Captain's gone . . .'

'What a wonderful thing,' Boullard said, 'to be a captain . . .'

'Let us ask the Lieutenant,' Labat said.

'Sergeant Fourier, we make you a committee of one.'

Sergeant Fourier looked around him uneasily, pulling in his round little belly nervously, uncomfortable at the thought of any action that would make him conspicuous, endanger his pleasant anonymous future with the masseuse in Algiers. 'Why me?' he asked.

'Highest non-commissioned officer present,' Labat chanted. 'Channels of communication with the commissioned personnel.'

'I haven't said two words to him,' Sergeant Fourier protested. 'After all, he just got here five days ago. And he's reserved . . . All he's said to me in five days is, "Make sure the men do not smoke in the open at night." '

'Enough,' Labat said cheerfully. 'It's obvious he likes you.'

'Don't joke,' Boullard said sharply. 'We have no more time to joke.'

'I'm only joking,' Labat said soberly, 'because I am willing to slit my throat.'

He got up and went to the edge of the tarpaulin and stood there, his back to the men, watching across the enigmatic plain for the first fateful dust cloud.

'What sort of man is this Lieutenant Dumestre?' Boullard asked.

'It's hard to tell,' Sergeant Fourier said, with the caution born of three years in an army where a hasty approval of a man, before all the facts of courage, sense and rectitude were in, might one day cause your death. 'He's very quiet. Stiff . . .'

'A bad sign,' said Boullard.

'Very rich in the uniform department.'

'Another bad sign.'

'It doesn't pay to be too hurried,' Sergeant Fourier protested.

'It's the Americans,' Boullard said. 'They're in a hurry, not me. Well, there's only one thing to be done.' He rubbed his cheek absently with the back of his hand, like a man determining whether or not he needs a shave. The other men watched him silently, anxious and curious about a definite plan that might have finally bloomed on this last nervous afternoon. 'One thing,' Boullard repeated. 'We kill him.'

★

Lieutenant Dumestre stood in the observation post and felt the headache coming on like an express train. Every afternoon the boredom and misery of the day accumulated in his brain pan and punished him for still living. He stared painfully over the darkening plain, which was silently enveloping itself in blue and purple folds, intangible and deceptive, in which the shapes of men and machines might be capriciously and dangerously lost . . .

Lieutenant Dumestre shook his head and closed his eyes, measuring gloomily the exact extent of the pain in his skull.

How do you do it? he asked himself. How does a first lieutenant hand a battery over to an advancing army, without orders? How does a first lieutenant save his life in a situation like this? In the distance there is a puff of dust and soon the first shell dropping somewhere near you, and all around you doubtful and uncertain men whom you do not know but who, for the lack of a better word, are under your command. Why had he left his post in Algiers? In this one, crazy, fateful week, his transfer had to be granted, this transfer to dilemma, this transfer to death . . . In the days of Napoleon it was said that every French private had a marshal's baton in his knapsack. Today every French soldier had in his knapsack a fatal and insoluble conundrum.

Lieutenant Dumestre had asked to be transferred from Algiers because he had been spending too much money there. It was as simple as that. The bills came in, the monthly reckonings were made, the deductions for the money sent home to his mother and father, who were lean and ailing in Paris, and it became clear that on a lieutenant's salary you could not save money in a gay town, especially if you had been rich all your life and your family rich before you and certain habits of eating and drinking and generosity ingrained in you, war or no war . . .

So, it was too expensive, Algiers. So, the desert would prove to be even more expensive.

. . . Back in Algiers he knew the men of his battery had mimicked him behind his back – his slow, painful way of delivering orders, full of agonized pauses, as he tried to remember to keep his voice down, tried not to sound like a young idiot imposing callously on these veterans of a war that had passed him by . . . They had mimicked him, but he knew them and even felt they liked him, and if he were with them now in this tragedy of a situation he would be able to go to them, talk to them, draw strength and resolution, one way or another from the men who would have to bear the burden of living and dying with him.

But here he was, on the one important day of the last two years, with a group of sullen and bearded strangers, who regarded him only with steady and cool hostility, a newcomer and an officer in an army where newcomers were automatically suspect and officers automatically hated . . .

Lieutenant Dumestre walked slowly out toward the west across the dusty scrub. The sun had set and the wind had died and the walking, he felt, might help somehow. Perhaps, he thought, smiling a little to himself, there will be an American patrol and I am unavoidably captured and there's an end to the problem . . . It's like a child, he thought, hoping that by morning he will have a sore throat so he does not have to go to school and take his examination in arithmetic. What an arithmetic was being imposed upon him now! What a savage and pitiless calculation! He looked toward the last blur of the horizon beyond which the Americans were marching. How simple it was to be an American! In their arithmetic there was an answer to all problems. How merry and dashing a lieutenant in the artillery in the American army must feel tonight, marching beside men whom he could trust, who trusted him, who all believed the same thing, who knew an enemy when they saw one, whose parents were well-fed and healthy, in no one's power, three thousand sweet miles from all battlefields . . .

What a tragic thing to be a Frenchman this year! Hamlet, sword out, killing Polonius and uncle in blind unprofitable lunges . . . Frenchmen, Hamlets of the world . . .

Lieutenant Dumestre stopped and sat down like a little boy on the dark earth and put his head in his hands and wept. He stopped suddenly and bit his lips and neglected to dry the tears from his cheeks. Nonsense, he thought, a grown man . . . There must be an answer to this, too. After all, I am not the only Frenchman afloat on this continent. The thing is, the men. If I knew what they wanted . . . If there was only some way to be present, without being seen. Armies have surrendered before. Detachments have surrendered before. Officers have appeared under a flag of truce and offered their services to their official enemies. The Captain was in Algiers, there was no one to stop him. 'Dear sir, is there anyone here who speaks French? Dear sir, Lieutenant Dumestre, Battery C, wishes to state that he desires to join forces with the American Army in North Africa and put himself under the flag of the United States for the duration against the common enemy . . .' There must be a technique to surrender, just the way there was a technique for everything else in the army. His mother and father would have to look out for themselves. Now, if only the men . . .

Lieutenant Dumestre slapped his thigh briskly as he stood up. At last he had reached a decision. He had faced the arithmetic and at least he knew what answer he wanted. There only remained going in frankly to the men and putting the situation up to them, in words of one syllable, simply . . . He started back toward the forward gun, walking more swiftly than he had walked for a week.

'Men,' he would say, remembering to keep his voice pitched low, 'this is the way it is. You may or may not know it, but tomorrow an American army will appear.' You never knew how much the men knew, what rumours had reached them, what facts confirmed, what punishments and discharges and prophecies and movements were peddled at the latrine or over a morning cigarette. 'I am under orders to resist,' he would say. 'Personally, I do not believe we are bound by those orders, as I believe all Frenchmen to be on the side for which the Americans are now fighting.' Perhaps that was too heroic, but it was impossible to fight a war without sounding from time to time a little heroic. 'I intend to go out under a flag of truce and give over the guns of this battery.' Now the question of dissenters. 'Anyone who does not wish to join me in this action is free to leave toward the rear . . .' No, they'd go back and talk and by morning a troop of cavalry would come up and Lieutenant Dumestre would be finished in thirty minutes. Keep them with him? How do that? Supposing they were all Vichy men? After all, they were being paid by Vichy and there were thousands of Frenchmen in Africa who had staked their lives on a German victory. They'd shoot him in cold blood.

Once more he cursed the trick that had landed him at this moment among two hundred strangers. In his old company he would have been able to take Sergeant Goubille aside and talk honestly and get an honest answer. Sergeant Goubille was forty-five years old and there was something fatherly and tolerant of young officers in his bearing, and a man like that would be worth a man's life on this harsh and doubtful plain tonight. Well, there was no Sergeant Goubille at hand . . . Perhaps that Breton, that farmer, Boullard. He was an older man and he looked honest and pleasant.

He took a deep breath and walked swiftly, not knowing exactly what he would do but knowing he had to do something, toward the forward gun . . .

Under the tarpaulin, Boullard was talking, his voice low and harsh, all the kindly, old countryman's lines somehow vanished from the set, desperate face. 'There will be a token resistance,' he was saying to the men, who were all sitting up, looking at the ground most of the time, looking up only occasionally at Boullard with a kind of deep embarrassment. 'In a token resistance there are token deaths.' He looked around him calmly from face to face, his thought plain in his eyes. 'A token corpse feeds as many worms as any other . . .'

Jouvet, the young one, was the only one who could not manage to sit still. He rubbed his heels back and forth, making marks in the sand, and studying them intensely.

'Kill the pretty Lieutenant,' Boullard said, 'and we have our own lives in our own hands. We dispose of them as we see fit.'

'Let us look at it from the political angle,' Labat said. 'Politically, we are fried if the Germans win . . .'

'Perhaps,' Sergeant Fourier said uneasily, his voice full of the nagging pain of having to make a decision. 'Perhaps we ought to wait and see what happens.'

'We will wait and see ourselves buried,' Boullard said.

'At least,' said Labat, 'we ought to talk to the Lieutenant. Sound him out.'

'I was on the Meuse,' said Boullard. 'I know better than to talk to a lieutenant. I'll take the responsibility. If you're all afraid . . .' He looked around him with savage, peasant contempt. 'There're a lot of men still to be killed in this war. I don't mind making it one more or less, personally . . .'

'We have to talk to him first,' Labat said stubbornly.

'Why?' Boullard asked loudly.

'Maybe he's with us. Maybe he wants to fight with the Americans, too . . .'

Boullard laughed harshly. Then he spat. 'I'm surrounded by children,' he said. 'If he's still an officer in the French Army after two years, he is not fond of the Americans. I am. At this moment, I am crazy about Americans. If there is any hope for anybody in this stinking year, it is in the Americans. I'm forty-four years old and I've fought in two wars. The third one, I want to pick my own side . . .'

'Still,' Labat said, his voice low and persistent, 'still, we ought to talk to him.'

'For myself,' Corporal Millet said briskly, standing up, 'I am on duty at the observa – '

He let his hands fall gently to his sides as Boullard brought his rifle up and touched his chest lightly with the bayonet.

'You are on duty here, Corporal.' Boullard moved the bayonet tenderly on a breast button. 'There is a question before the house that must be decided by a full membership.'

Corporal Millet sat down carefully.

'I don't care,' Labat was saying, grinning at Corporal Millet, 'what you do to the fighting Corporal, but nothing happens to the Lieutenant until we talk to him.' He patted Boullard's shoulder, in a small reassuring gesture. Boullard slowly took his eyes off Millet and the Corporal sighed.

Boullard looked around him searchingly at the men caught in this hour on this desert with him. Sergeant Fourier, haunted by dreams of a pension and his masseuse and still troubled by some obscure, painful sense of patriotism and honour, refused to look at him. Jouvet, faced at the age of twenty with the ancient, tangled threads of a bloody and complex century, looked ready to weep. Labat was smiling but stubborn. Corporal Millet was sweating, and was making a great effort to look like a man who did not intend to rush to the nearest officer and announce a mutiny.

'All right,' Boullard said wearily, 'if that's what you want. Although I tell you, two words too many and we are all against a wall, looking at a firing squad.'

Jouvet fumbled with his handkerchief quickly and Boullard looked at him curiously and impersonally.

'It is not necessary to commit ourselves,' said Labat. His long, workman's arms waved in argument. 'We approach the subject, we skirt it, we take soundings like a boat coming into a harbour . . .'

'Better!' Sergeant Fourier said loudly, happy at all deferment. 'Excellent! Much better!'

Boullard stared at him coldly and Sergeant Fourier became quiet and nervously took out a pack of cigarettes.

'It's possible,' Labat was saying, convincing Boullard, 'to judge a man without a direct question . . .'

'Possibly,' Boullard said with no enthusiasm. 'Possibly.'

'I'll do the talking,' Labat said. 'I'm used to things like this. I have talked at union meetings for seven years and nothing could be more delicate . . .' He looked around him anxiously, hoping for a little laughter to take some of the deadly tension away, but only little Jouvet, who was always polite, smiled nervously because he realized Labat had meant it as a little joke.

'All right,' Boullard said. He fingered his rifle gently and let it dip almost imperceptibly toward Corporal Millet. 'I will judge. And you . . .' The rifle dipped very clearly toward Corporal Millet. 'You will not open your mouth. Is that clear?'

Corporal Millet sat up stiffly at attention, feeling sorrowfully within him that his honour demanded some show of resistance and that his life would not be worth a great deal if he was incorporated in the army of the United States. He looked at Boullard's huge crushing hands, calm on the rifle. 'It is your affair,' he said faintly. 'I wash my hands of it.'

Boullard laughed.

Sergeant Fourier lighted his cigarette, gift of his plump wife the masseuse, eating her dinner comfortably, all unknowing, in the curtainy little apartment in Algiers with three exposures. He sighed and stood up and walked between Boullard and the limp Corporal Millet and stood at the edge of the tarpaulin in the full darkness, pulling with small comfort at his cigarette, while behind him, under the tarpaulin, there was no sound from the waiting men.

Lieutenant Dumestre made his way slowly across the rough black ground toward the gun position, turning over in his mind his possible opening sentences to the gun crew. 'Men,' he could say, 'I am going to be absolutely honest with you. I am putting a white flag up beside this gun and I am delivering this battery over to . . .' Or he could say, 'There is a possibility that tomorrow morning American troops will appear. Hold your fire until I give the word . . .' while silently swearing to himself that the word would never be given. There was much to be said for this method, as it was indefinite and seemed less dangerous and didn't tip his hand until the last moment, when it would probably be too late for anyone to do anything about it. Of course there was always the possibility that he could stand up in front of the men and pour his heart out to them, remind them in ringing words of their country's shame, call upon them with blood and passion to forget themselves, forget their families in France, remember only honour and final victory . . . He could see himself, pale and fluent, in the dim light of the moon, roaring, whispering, his voice singing in the quiet night air, the men listening entranced, the tears starting down their cheeks . . . He shook himself, smiled wryly at the dream, remembering his harsh, slow way of speaking, plain, indefinite, without the power to move men to the nearest café, much less throw themselves grandly and thoughtlessly upon a doubtful and possibly fatal cause . . .

Oh, Lord, he thought, I am the wrong man for them, the wrong man, the wrong man . . .

He turned the corner of the tarpaulin, seeing the watchful, hateful shape of the gun outlined stubbornly against the starlit sky.

Sergeant Fourier was smoking pensively in the open and the other men were sitting, strangely quiet, under cover. When Sergeant Fourier saw him he started guiltily and threw his cigarette away as unostentatiously as possible. He stood at attention and saluted and with his right heel tried to douse the glowing speck in the dirt. Somehow, the sight of the small man with the comfortable little pot belly trying to pretend, like a vaudeville comedian, that he hadn't been smoking, irritated Lieutenant Dumestre, who all morning and all afternoon had been grappling bitterly with war and fratricide and tragic, bloody policy . . .

He returned the Sergeant's salute curtly. 'What's wrong with you?' he asked sharply, his high voice making all the men in the tarpaulin turn their heads coldly and automatically to watch him. 'You know there's to be no smoking.'

'Please, sir,' Sergeant Fourier said stupidly, 'I was not smoking.'

'You were smoking,' Lieutenant Dumestre said, weeping inside because inside he knew how ridiculous this charge and countercharge was.

'I was not smoking, sir.' Sergeant Fourier stood very straight and formal and stupid with the problem of the evening, almost happy to have a simple little idiotic argument to worry about at least for ten minutes . . .

'You've been told, you've been told!' Lieutenant Dumestre shrieked in his highest voice, mourning deep within himself for that womanly timbre, for his military insistence upon form and truth at this unmilitary hour, but somehow unable, with the Captain's departure and the imminence, potent and desperate, of the Americans over the horizon, to stop the high noise of his tongue. 'At any moment we may be bombed. A cigarette glows like a lighthouse in a black desert at ten thousand feet! Why don't you draw a map of the gun position and publish it in the morning newspapers?' He saw Labat look at Boullard and shrug coldly and turn away with an air of dangerous significance and something within him clutched at his throat, but now there was no stopping that high, silly tongue, freed for a moment from the locked agony and doubt of the day's decision making. Here at least was familiar ground. Troops disobeying orders. Troops endangering security of the post or station. Troops slightly insubordinate, lying . . . His weary, ragged mind, terribly grateful to be relieved of its unaccustomed task of painful exploration, relapsed into the formal, years-long grooves of Saint Cyr, of countless garrisons, countless lectures . . . 'There will be double security tonight, two-hour watches for everyone,' the voice still high, but with the three-thousand-year-old bite of military command. 'An extra half day's ammunition will be drawn up from the battery dump by three this morning.' He saw the men's faces bleakly collapse and also something else in them, although he couldn't tell in the rush of his commands what it was. Even as he spoke he hated himself for what he was doing, knowing that a better man would have ignored the cigarette or joked about it . . . He hated Sergeant Fourier, standing there, pained and stupid and impassive, but in a way he was grateful to him, because he had given him the opportunity at this late hour once more for postponement.

He turned on his heel and strode away. Later, perhaps at midnight, he would come back, he told himself, and finally get this question of the Americans settled. He pulled his shoulders high in disgust as the sound of his own voice squalling about the cigarette sounded in his ears, but there was nothing to be done about it and he walked without looking back. Midnight, he thought, midnight is still time . . .

Back under the tarpaulin, Boullard looked around him at the men. Their faces were grave, but except for Millet, there was consent in all of them.

Boullard walked out from under the tarpaulin with his rifle.

Midnight, Lieutenant Dumestre was thinking, when the bullet struck, midnight is still time . . .

They buried him quickly without marking the grave and sat down in front of the gun to wait for the army of the Americans.

GOLD FROM CRETE

C. S. Forester

THE officers of HMS *Apache* were sizing up the Captain D. at the same time that he was doing the same to them. A Captain D. – captain commanding destroyers – was a horrible nuisance on board if, as in this case, the ship in which he elected – or was compelled by circumstances – to hoist his distinguishing pendant was not fitted as a flotilla leader. The captain needed cabin space himself, and he brought with him a quartet of staff officers who also needed cabin space. Physically, that meant that four out of the seven officers already on board the *Apache* would be more uncomfortable than usual, and in a destroyer that meant a great deal. More than that; morally, the effect was still more profound. It meant that with a captain on board, even if he tried not to interfere with the working of the ship, the commander and the other officers, and the lower deck ratings as well, for the matter of that, felt themselves under the scrutiny of higher authority. The captain's presence would introduce something of the atmosphere of a big ship, and it would undoubtedly cut short the commander's pleasure in his independent command.

So Commander Hammett and his officers eyed Captain Crowe and his staff, when they met on the scorching iron deck of the *Apache* in Alexandria Harbour, without any appearance of hospitality. They saw a big man, tall and a little inclined to bulk, who moved with a freedom and ease that hinted at a concealed athleticism. His face was tanned so deeply that it was impossible to guess at his complexion, but under the thick black brows there were a pair of grey eyes that twinkled irrepressibly. They knew his record, of course – much of it was to be read in the rows of coloured ribbon on his chest. There was the DSO he had won as a midshipman at Zeebrugge in

1918 – before Sub-lieutenant Chesterfield had been born – and they knew that they had only to look up the official account of that action to find exactly what Crowe had done there; but everyone knew that midshipmen do not receive DSOs for nothing. The spot of silver that twinkled on the red-and-blue ribbon told of the bar he had received for the part he had played at Narvik last year – not to many men is it given to be decorated for distinguished services twenty-two years apart and still to be hardly entering on middle age. There was the red ribbon that one or two of them recognized as the Bath, and a string of other gay colours that ended in the Victory and General Service ribbons of the last war.

The introductions were brief – most of the officers had at least a nodding acquaintance with one another already. Commander Hammett presented his first lieutenant, Garland, and the other officers down to Sub-lieutenants Chesterfield and Lord Edward Mortimer, RNVR – this last was a fattish and untidy man in the late thirties whose yachting experience had miraculously brought him out of Mayfair drawing-rooms and dropped him on the hard steel deck of the *Apache* – and Crowe indicated his flotilla gunnery officer and navigating officer and signals officer and secretary.

'We will proceed as soon as convenient, Commander,' said Crowe, issuing his first order.

'Aye, aye, sir,' said Hammett, as twenty generations of seamen had answered before him. But at least the age of consideration given to omens had passed; it did not occur to Hammett to ponder on the significance of the fact that Crowe's first order had been one of action.

'Get yourselves below and sort yourselves out,' said Crowe to his staff, and as they disappeared he walked forward and ran lightly up the bridge.

Hammett gave his orders – Crowe was glad to note that he did so without even a side glance out of the tail of his eye at the captain at the end of the bridge – and the ship broke into activity. In response to one order, the yeoman of signals on the bridge bellowed an incomprehensible string of words down to the signal bridge. It passed through Crowe's mind that yeomen of signals were always as incomprehensible as railway porters calling out the names of stations in England, but the signal rating below understood what was said to him, which was all that mattered. A string of coloured flags ran up the halyards, and a moment later yeoman of signals was bellowing the replies received. The flagship gave permission to proceed; the fussy tug out there by the anti-submarine net began to pull open the gate. The bow was pulled in, the warps cast off. The telegraph rang, the propeller began to turn, and the *Apache* trembled a little as she moved away. Everything was done as competently as possible; the simply operation was a faint indication that Crowe would not have to worry about the *Apache* in action, but could confine his attention to the handling of his whole flotilla of twelve destroyers, if and when he should ever succeed in gathering them all together.

A movement just below him caught his attention. The anti-aircraft lookouts were being relieved. At the .50-calibre gun here on the starboard side a burly seaman was taking over the earphones and the glasses. He was a huge man, but all Crowe could see of him, besides his huge bulk and the top of his cap, was his cropped red hair and a wide expanse of neck and ear, burned a solid brick-red from the Mediterranean sun. Then there were a pair of thick wrists covered with dense red hair, and two vast hands that held the glasses as they swept back and forth, back and forth, over the sky from horizon to zenith in ceaseless search for hostile planes. At that moment there were six seamen employed on that task in different parts of the deck, and so exacting was the work that a quarter of an hour every hour was all that could be asked of any man.

Commander Hammett turned at that moment and caught the captain's eye.

'Sorry to intrude on you like this, Hammett,' said Crowe.

'No intrusion at all, sir. Glad to have you, of course.'

Hammett could hardly say anything else, poor devil, thought Crowe, before he went on: 'Must be a devilish nuisance being turned out of your cabin, all the same.'

'Not nearly as much nuisance as to the other officers, sir,' said Hammett. 'When we're at sea I never get aft to my sleeping cabin at all. Turn in always in my sea cabin.'

Perfectly true, thought Crowe. No destroyer captain would think of ever going more than one jump from the bridge at sea.

'Nice of you to spare my feelings,' said Crowe, with a grin. It had to be said in just the right way – Crowe could guess perfectly well at Hammett's resentment at his presence.

'Not at all, sir,' said Hammett briefly.

Sub-lieutenant Chesterfield gave a fresh course to the quarter-master at this moment and changed the conversation.

They were clear of the minefields now and almost out of sight of the low shore. The myriad Levantine spies would have a hard time to guess whither they were bound.

'We'll be in visual touch with the flotilla at dawn, sir,' said Hammett.

'Thank you. I'll let you know if there's any change of plan,' replied Crowe.

He ran down the naked steel ladder to the deck, and walked aft, past the quadruple torpedo tubes and the two pairs of 4.7s towering above him. On the blast screen a monkey sat and gibbered at him, gesticulating with withered little hands. Crowe hated monkeys; he liked dogs and could tolerate cats; he had been shipmates with pets of all species from goats to baby hippopotamuses, but monkeys were his abomination. He hated the filthy little things, their manners and their habits. He ignored this one stolidly as he walked past it to the accompaniment of screamed monkey obscenities. If he were in command of this destroyer he would have seen to it that the little beast did not remain long on board to plague him; as it was, he thought ruefully to himself, as he was in the immeasurably higher position of commanding a flotilla, he would have to endure its presence for fear of hurting the feelings of those under his command.

Down below, Paymaster-Lieutenant Scroggs, his secretary, was waiting for him in the day cabin. Scroggs was looking through a mass of message forms – intercepted wireless messages which gave, when pieced together, a vague and shadowy picture of the progress of the fighting in Crete.

'I don't like the looks of it at all, sir,' said Scroggs.

Neither did Crowe, but he could see no possible good in saying so. His hearty and sanguine temperament could act on bad news, but refused to dwell on it. He had digested the contents of those messages long ago, and he had no desire to worry himself with them again.

'We'll know more about it when we get there,' he said cheerfully. 'I shan't want you for a bit, Scroggs.'

Scroggs acted on the hint and left the cabin, while Crowe sat himself at the table and drew the notepaper to him and began his Thursday letter:

My dear Miriam,
There has been little enough happening this week –

On Thursdays he wrote to Miriam; on Mondays, Tuesdays and Wednesdays he wrote respectively to Jane and Susan and Dorothy. On Fridays he wrote to old friends of his own sex, and he kept Saturdays to clear off arrears of official correspondence, and he hoped on Sundays never to take a pen in hand.

He often thought about using a typewriter and doing four copies at once, but Miriam and Dorothy and Jane and Susan were not fools – he would never have bothered about them in the first place if they were – and they could spot a carbon copy anywhere. There was nothing for it but to write toilsomely to each one by hand, although it did not matter if he repeated the phraseology; not one of those girls knew any of the others, thank God, and if they did, they wouldn't compare notes about him, seeing what a delicate affair each affair was.

Scroggs re-entered the room abruptly. 'Message just arrived, sir,' he said, passing over the decoded note.

It was for Captain D. from the vice-admiral, Alexandria, and was marked 'Priority'. It ran:

MUCH GREEK GOLD AWAITING SHIPMENT MERKA BAY. REMOVE IF POSSIBLE. END.

'Not acknowledged, of course?' said Crowe.

'No, sir,' said Scroggs.

Any acknowledgement would violate standing orders for wireless silence.

'All right, Scroggs. I'll call you when I want you.'

Crowe sat and thought about this new development. 'Much Greek gold.' A thousand pounds? A million pounds? The Greek government gold reserves must amount to a good deal more than a million pounds. If Crete was going to be lost – and it looked very much as if it was going to be – it would be highly desirable to keep that much gold from falling into the hands of the Germans. But it was the 'if possible' that complicated the question. Actually it was a compliment – it gave him discretion. It was for him to decide whether to stake the *Apache* against the gold, but it was the devil of a decision to make. The ordinary naval problem was easy by comparison, for the value of the *Apache* could be easily computed against other standards. It would always be worthwhile, for instance, to risk the *Apache* in exchange for a chance to destroy a light cruiser. But in exchange for gold? When she was built, the *Apache* cost less than half a million sterling, but that was in peacetime. In time of war, destroyers might be considered to be worth their weight in gold – or was that strictly true?

There was the question of the odds too. If he took the *Apache* into Merka Bay tomorrow at dawn and risked the Stukas, what would be the chances of getting her out again? Obviously, if he were quite sure of it, he should try for the gold; and on the other hand, if he were sure that she would be destroyed, it would not be worth making the attempt, not for all the gold in the Americas. The actual odds lay somewhere between the one extreme and the other – two to one against success, say. Was it a profitable gamble to risk the *Apache* on a two-to-one chance, in the hope of gaining an indefinite number of millions?

He had only to raise his voice to summon the staff that a thoughtful government had provided. Three brilliant young officers, all graduates of the Naval Staff College, and the main reason for their presence on board was to advise. Crowe thought about his staff and grinned to himself. They would tell him, solemnly, the very things he had just been thinking out for himself, and, after all that, the ultimate decision would still lie with him alone. There could be no shifting of that responsibility – and Crowe suddenly realized that he did not want to shift it. Responsibility was the air he breathed. He sat making up his mind, while the *Apache* rose and fell gently on the Mediterranean swell and the propellers throbbed steadily; he still held the message in idle fingers, and looked at it with unseeing eyes. When at last he rose, he had reached his decision, and it remained only to communicate it to his staff to tell them that he intended to go into Merka Bay to fetch away some gold, and to look over the chart with them and settle the details.

That was what he did, and the flotilla gunnery officer and the signals officer and the navigating officer listened to him attentively. It was only a matter of a few minutes to decide on everything. Rowles, the navigating officer, measured off the distance on his dividers, while the others asked questions that Crowe could not answer. Crowe had not the least idea how much gold there was in Crete. Nor could he say offhand how much a million sterling in gold should weigh. Nickleby, the gunner, came to a conclusion about that, after a brief glance at his tables of specific gravities and a minute with his slide rule. 'About ten tons, there or thereabouts,' he announced.

'This is troy weight, twelve ounces to the pound, you know,' cautioned Holby, the signals officer.

'Yes, I allowed for that,' said Nickleby triumphantly.

'But what about inflation?' demanded Rowles, looking up from the map. 'I heard you say something about an ounce being worth four pounds – you know what I mean, four sovereigns. But that's a long time ago, when people used to buy gold. Now it's all locked up and it's doubled in value, pretty nearly. So a million would weigh twenty tons.'

'Five tons, you mean, stupid,' said Holby. That started another argument as to whether inflation would increase or diminish the weight of a million sterling.

Crowe listened to them for a moment and then left them to it. There was still a little while left before dinner, and he had to finish that letter. As the *Apache* turned her bows towards Merka Bay, Crowe took up his pen again:

> . . . but it is most infernally hot and I suppose it will get hotter as the year grows older. I have thought about you a great deal, of course –

That damned monkey was chattering at him through the scuttle. It was bad enough to have to grind out this weekly letter to Miriam, without having monkeys to irritate one. The monkey was far more in Crowe's thoughts than the Stukas he would be facing at any moment. The Stukas were something to which he had devoted all the consideration the situation demanded; it would do him no good to think about them further. But that monkey would not let Crowe stop thinking about him. Crowe cursed again.

> – especially that dinner we had at the Berkeley, when we had to keep back behind the palms so that old Lady Crewkerne shouldn't see us. I wonder what the poor thing is doing now.

That was half a page, anyway, in Crowe's large handwriting.

He had only to finish the page and make some appearance of a wholehearted attempt on the second. He scribbled on steadily, half his mind on the letter and the other half divided between the monkey, the approach of dinner-time, Hammett's attitude and the heat. He was not aware of the way in which somewhere inside him his mental digestion was still at work on the data for the approaching operation. With a sigh of relief he wrote:

Always yours,
George

and added at the foot, for the benefit of the censor:

From Captain George Crowe,
CB, DSO, RN.

The worst business of the day was over and he could dine with a clear conscience, untroubled until morning.

The dark hours that followed midnight found the *Apache* in Merka Bay. She had glided silently in and had dropped anchor unobserved by anyone, apparently, while all around her in the distance were the signs and thunder of war. Overhead in the darkness had passed droning death, not once or twice but many times, passing by on mysterious and unknown errands. Crowe, on the bridge beside Hammett, had heard the queer bumbling of German bombers, the more incisive note of fighter planes. Out on the distant horizon along the coast they had seen the great flashes of the nightmare battle that was being fought out there, sometimes the pyrotechnic sparkle of anti-aircraft fire, and they had heard the murmur of the firing. Now Nickleby had slipped ashore in the dinghy to make contact with the Greeks.

'He's the devil of a long time, sir,' grumbled Rowles. 'We'll never get away before daylight, at this rate.'

'I never expected to,' said Crowe soothingly. He felt immeasurably older than Rowles as he spoke, immeasurably wiser. Rowles was still young enough to have illusions, to expect everything to go off without delay or friction, something in the manner of a staff exercise on paper. If Rowles was still so incorrigibly optimistic after a year and a half of war, he could not be expected ever to improve in this respect.

'The bombers'll find us, though, sir,' said Rowles. 'Just listen to that one going over!'

'Quite likely,' said Crowe. He had already weighed the possible loss of the *Apache* and her company against the chances of saving the gold, and he had no intention of working through the pros and cons again.

'Here he comes now,' said Hammett suddenly; his quick ear had caught the splash of oars before anyone else.

Nickleby swung himself aboard and groped his way through the utter darkness to the bridge to make his report.

'It's all right,' he said. 'The gold's there. It's in lorries hidden in a gully half a mile away and they've sent for it. The jetty here's usable, thank God. Twelve feet of water at the end – took the soundings myself.'

'Right,' said Crowe. 'Stand by to help Commander Hammett con the ship up to the jetty.'

Merka Bay is a tiny crack in the difficult southern shore of Crete. It is an exposed anchorage giving no more than fifteen feet of water, but it serves a small fleet of fishing craft in peacetime, which explains the existence of the jetty, and from the village there runs an obscure mountain track, winding its way through the mountains of the interior, over which, apparently, the lorries with the gold had been brought when the fighting in the island began to take a serious turn. Crowe blessed the forethought of the Greeks while Hammett, with infinite care in the utter blackness, edged the *Apache* up the bay to the little pier, the propellers turning ever so gently and the lead going constantly.

They caught the loom of the pier and brought the *Apache* alongside. Two seamen jumped with warps, and as they dropped clove hitches over the bollards, Crowe suddenly realized that they had not had to fumble for the bollards. The utter pitchy blackness had changed into something substantially less; when he looked up, the stars were not so vividly distinct. It was the first faint beginning of dawn.

There was a chattering group on the pierhead – four women and a couple of soldiers in ragged khaki uniforms. They exchanged voluble conversation with the interpreter on the main deck.

'The gold's coming, sir,' reported the individual to Crowe.

'How much of it?'

'Forty-two tons, they say, sir.'

'Metric tons, that'll be,' said Holby to Nickleby. 'How much d'you make that to be?'

'Metric tons are as near as dammit to our ton,' said Nickleby irritably.

'The difference in terms of gold ought to amount to something, though,' persisted Holby, drawing Nickleby deftly with the ease of long practice. Let's have a rough estimate, anyway.'

'Millions and millions,' said Nickleby crossly. 'Ten million pounds – twenty million pounds – thirty million – don't ask me.'

'The knight of the slide rule doesn't bother himself about trifles like an odd ten million pounds,' said Holby.

'Shut up!' broke in Rowles. 'Here it comes.'

In the grey dawn they could see a long procession of shabby old trucks bumping and lurching over the stony lane down to the jetty. All except one halted at the far end; the first one came creeping towards them along the pier.

An elderly officer scrambled down from the cab and saluted in the direction of the bridge.

'We got the bar gold in the first eight trucks, sir,' he called in the accent of Chicago. 'Coins in the other ones.'

'He sounds just like an American,' said Rowles.

'Returned immigrant, probably,' said Holby. 'Lots of 'em here. Made their little pile and retired to their native island to live like dukes on twopence a week, until this schemozzle started.'

'Poor devils,' said Rowles.

Sub-lieutenant Lord Edward Mortimer was supervising a working party engaged in bringing the gold on board the *Apache*.

'Where do you propose to put the stuff?' said Crowe to Hammett.

'It's heavy enough, God knows,' was the reply. 'It's got to be low and in the centre line. Do you mind if I put it in your day cabin?'

'Not at all. I think that's the best place at the moment.'

Certainly it was heavy; gold is about ten times as heavy as the same bulk of coal.

The seamen who were receiving the naked bars from the Greeks in the lorry were deceived by their smallness, and more than once let them drop as the weight came upon them. A couple of the bars, each a mere foot long and three inches wide and high, made a load a man could only just stagger under. It gave the hurrying seamen a ludicrous appearance, as if they were soldiering on the job, to see them labouring with so much difficulty under such absurdly small loads. The men were grinning and excited at carrying these enormous fortunes.

'Hardly decent to see that gold all naked,' said Rowles.

'Don't see any sign of receipts or bookkeeping,' said Nickleby. 'Old Scroggs'll break a blood vessel.'

'No time for that,' said Holby, glancing up to the sky. The action recalled to them all the danger in which they lay; each of them wondered how long it would be before the Stukas found them out.

The first lorry was unloaded by now, and driven away, its place being taken by the second. An unending stream of gold bars was being carried into the *Apache*. The second lorry was replaced by the third, and the third by the fourth. And then they heard the sound of dread – the high incisive note of a fighting plane. It came from the direction of the sea, but it was not a British plane. Swiftly it came, with the monstrous unnatural speed of its kind, not more than five hundred feet above the water. They could see plainly enough the swastika marking on the tail and the crosses on the wings.

'Open fire,' said Hammett into the voice tube.

Crowe was glad to see that there was no trace of hurry or excitement in his voice.

All through the night the gun crews had been ready for instant action. The long noses of the 4.7s rose with their usual appearance of uncanny intelligence under the direction of Garland at the central control. They they bellowed out, and along with their bellowing came the raving clamour of the pom-poms and the heavy machine guns. The plane swerved and circled. The .50-calibre gun under the end of the bridge beside Crowe followed it round, its din deafening Crowe. He looked down and noticed the grim concentration on the face of the red-haired seaman at the handles.

But that plane was moving at three hundred and more miles an hour; it had come and gone in the same breath, apparently unhit. It seemed to skim the steep hills that fringed the bay and vanished behind them.

'It's calling the bombers this very minute,' said Holby, savagely glaring after it. 'How much longer have we got to stay here?'

Crowe heard the remark; naval thought had not changed in this respect at least, that the first idea of a naval officer should be now, as it had been in Nelson's day, to get his precious ship away from the dangerous and inhospitable shore and out to sea, where he could find freedom of manoeuvre, whether it was battle or storm that threatened him.

'That's the last of the bars, sir,' called the English-speaking Greek officer. 'Here's the coin acoming.'

Coins in sacks, coins in leather bags, coins in wooden boxes – sovereigns, louis d'or, double eagles, napoleons, Turkish pounds, twenty-marks pieces, dinars – the gold of every country in the world, drained out of every country in the Balkans, got away by a miracle before the fall of Athens and now being got out of Crete. The bags and sacks were just as deceptively heavy as the bars had been, and the naval ratings grinned and joked as they heaved them into the ship.

The first lorry full of coin had been emptied, and the second was driving onto the jetty when the first bombers arrived. They came from inland, over the hills, and were almost upon the ship, in consequence, before they were sighted. The guns blazed out furiously while each silver shape in turn swept into position, like the figures in some three-dimensional country dance, and then put down their noses and came racing down the air, engines screaming. Crowe had been through this before, and he did not like it. It called for nerve to stand and look death in the eye as it came tearing down at him. He had seen men dive for shelter, instinctively and futilely, behind the compass or even the canvas dodger, and he did not blame them in the least. He would do the same himself if he were not so determined that the mind of George Crowe should be as well exercised as his body. To watch like this called for as much effort as to put in a strong finish after a twenty-mile run, and he leaned back against the rail and kept his eyes on the swooping death.

At the last possible second the hurtling plane levelled off and let go its bomb. Crowe saw the ugly black blob detach itself from the silver fabric at the same second as the note of the plane's engine changed from a scream to a snarl. The bomb fell and burst in the shallows a few yards from the *Apache's* bows and an equal distance from the pier. A colossal geyser of black mud followed along with the terrific roar of the explosion. Mud and water rained down on the *Apache*, drenching everyone on deck, while the little ship leaped frantically in the wave. Crowe heard and felt the forward warp that held her to the jetty snap with the jerk. He could never be quite sure afterwards whether he had seen, or merely imagined, the sea bottom revealed in a wide ring where the force of the explosion swept the water momentarily away. But he certainly noted, as a matter of importance, that bombs dropped in shallows of a few feet did not have nearly the damaging effect of a near miss in deeper water.

The second plane's nose was already down and pointing at them as the *Apache* swung to her single warp – Mortimer was busy replacing the broken one. Crowe forced himself again to look up, and he saw the thing that followed. A shell from one of the forward guns hit the plane straight on the nose; Crowe, almost directly behind the gun, saw – or afterwards thought he had seen – the tiny black streak of not a hundredth of a second's duration, that marked the passage of the shell up to the target. One moment the plane was there, sharp and clear against the pale blue of sky; the next moment there was nothing at all. The huge bomb had exploded in its rack – at a height of two thousand feet the sound of the explosion was negligible, or else Crowe missed it in his excitement. The plane disappeared, and after that the eye became conscious of a wide circular smudge widening against the blue sky, fringed with tiny black fragments making a seemingly leisurely descent downward to the sea. And more than that; the third bomber had been affected by the explosion – the pilot must have been killed or the controls jammed. Crowe saw it wheel across his line of vision, skating through the air like a flipped playing card, the black crosses clearly visible. Nose first, it hit the sea close into the shore, vanished into a smother of foam, and then the tail reappeared, protruding above the surface while the nose remained fixed in the bottom.

It was a moment or two before Crowe was able to realize that the *Apache* was temporarily safe; one bomber had missed and the other two were destroyed. He became conscious that he was leaning back against the rail with a rigidity that was positively painful – his shoulder joints were hurting him. A little sheepishly he made himself relax; he grinned at his staff and took a turn or two along the bridge.

Down on the main deck Mortimer had made fast again. But somehow one of the containers of gold coins had broken in the excitement. The deck was running with gold; the scuppers were awash with sovereigns.

'Leave that as it is for now!' bellowed Hammett, standing shoulder to shoulder with Crowe as he leaned over the rail of the *Apache*. 'Get the rest of the stuff on board!'

Crowe turned and met Hammett's eye. 'It looks to me,' said Crowe, with a jerk of his thumb at the heaped gold on the *Apache*'s deck, 'as if this would be the best time in the world to ask the Admiralty for a rise in pay.'

'Yes,' said Hammett shortly, with so little appreciation of the neatness of the jest that Crowe made a mental note that money was apparently a sacred subject to Hammett and had better not in future be made a target for levity – presumably Hammett had an expensive family at home, or something. But Hammett was looking at him with a stranger expression than even that assumption warranted. Crowe raised his eyebrows questioning.

'There's mud on your face, sir,' said Hammett. 'Lots of it.'

Crowe suddenly remembered the black torrent that had drenched him when the bomb burst in the shallows. He looked down; his coat and his white trousers were thinly coated with grey mud, and it dawned upon him that his skin was wet inside his clothes. He put his hand to his face and felt the mud upon it; the damp handkerchief that he brought from his pocket came away smeared with the stuff; he must be a comic-looking sight. He tried to wipe his face clean, and found that his day-old beard hindered the process decidedly.

'That's the lot, sir!' called the Greek officer.

'Thank you,' replied Hammett. 'Cast off, Mortimer, if you please.'

Hammett strode hastily back to the engine-room voice tube, and Crowe was left still wiping vainly at the mud. He guessed it had probably got streaky by now. He must be a sight for the gods.

Those idiots on his staff had let him grin at them and walk up and down the bridge without telling him how he looked.

The *Apache* vibrated sharply with one propeller going astern and another forward, and she swung away from the pier.

'Good luck, sir!' called the Greek officer.

'Same to you, and thank you, sir!' shouted Crowe in return.

'The poor devils'll need all the luck that's going if Jerry lays his hands on them,' commented Nickleby. 'Wish you could take 'em with us.'

'No orders for evacuation yet,' said Holby.

The *Apache* had got up speed by now and was heading briskly out to sea, the long v of her wash breaking white upon the beaches. Hammett was as anxious as anyone to get where he had sea room to manoeuvre before the next inevitable attack should come. Soon she was trembling to her full thirty-six knots, and the green steep hills of Crete were beginning to lose their clarity.

'Here they come!' exclaimed Nickleby.

Out of the mountains of Crete they came, three of them once more, tearing after the *Apache* with nearly ten times her speed.

Hammett turned and watched them as the guns began to speak, and Crowe watched Hammett, ready to take over the command the instant he should feel it necessary. But Hammett was steady enough, looking up with puckered eyes, the grey stubble on his cheeks catching the light.

The bombers wasted no time in reconnoitring. Straight through the shell bursts they came, steadied on the *Apache*'s course, and then the leader put down its nose and screamed down in its dive.

'Hard-a-starboard!' said Hammett to the quartermaster.

The *Apache* heeled and groaned under extreme helm applied at full speed, and she swung sharply round. Once a dive bomber commits itself to its dive, it is hard for it to change its course along with its target's. Crowe's mathematical brain plunged into lightning calculations. The bomber started at about fifteen thousand feet or more – call it three miles; three hundred miles an hour. The hundredth of an hour; thirty-six seconds, but that's not allowing for acceleration. Twenty-five seconds would be more like it – say twenty before the ship began to answer her helm. The *Apache* was doing thirty-six knots. In twenty seconds that would be – let's see – almost exactly one-fifth of a mile, but that did not mean that she would be one-fifth of a mile off her course, because she would be following a curved path. A hundred and fifty yards, say, and the bomber would be able to compensate for some of that. A likely miss would be between fifty and a hundred yards.

Crowe's quick brain did its job just in time. The bomber levelled off as it let go its bomb, the thing clearly silhouetted against the sky.

'Midships!' ordered Hammett to the quartermaster. The bomb hit the water and exploded seventy-five yards from the *Apache*'s port quarter, raising a vast fountain of grey water, far higher than the *Apache*'s stumpy mainmast.

'Well done, Hammett!' called Crowe, but softly, so as not to distract the man as he stood gauging the direction of the second bomber's attack.

The *Apache* was coming out of her heel as she steadied on her new course.

'Hard-a-port!' said Hammett, and she began to snake round in the other direction.

The crescendo scream was repeated, but this time the pilot had tried to out-think the captain of the destroyer. The bomb fell directly in the *Apache*'s wake and not more than forty yards astern. She leaped madly at the blow, flinging everyone on the bridge against the rail. And the pilot, as he tore over the ship, turned loose his machine guns; Crowe heard the bullets flick past him, through all the din of the gunfire.

The *Apache* was coming round so fast that soon she would be crossing her own wake. The third bomber was evidently so confused that he lost his head, and the bomb fell farther away than the first one did. Now all three were heading northward again, pursued vainly for a second or two by the *Apache*'s fire.

So they were safe now. They had taken the gold and had paid nothing for it.

Crowe looked aft to where a sailor began to sweep the remaining gold coins into a little heap with a squeegee, and he wondered whether any destroyer's scuppers had ever before run with gold.

Then he looked forward, and then down at the crew of the .50-calibre gun. It was with a shock that he saw that the red-haired sailor was dead; the limp corpse, capless, lay neglected, face in arms, on the steel plating, while the other two hands were still at work inserting a new belt. He had been thinking that the *Apache* had escaped scot-free, and now he saw that she had paid in blood for that gold. A wave of reaction overtook him. Not all the gold in the world was worth a life. He felt a little sick.

The first-aid detachment had come up now, and were turning the body over. A heavy hand fell to the deck with a thump; Crowe saw the reddish hair on the wrist that he had noticed earlier. And then his sickness passed. Forty-two tons of gold; millions and millions sterling. Hitler was starving for gold. Gold would buy the allegiance of Arab tribesmen or neutral statesmen, might buy from Turkey the chrome that he needed so desperately, or from Spain the alliance for which he thirsted. That gold might have cost England a million other lives. Through his decision England had given one life for the gold. It was a bargain well worth it.

REUNION

Miles Noonan

THE introduction of computers might by now have made a difference and the contraction of British overseas commitments has certainly reduced the scope, but it was not unknown for the War Office to post the wrong man to the wrong place at the wrong time.

An example of this occurred in 1951 during the Korean War. It became evident to a brigade headquarters that an improvement in the coordination of their arrangements with their allies would be achieved if they were to be given an additional officer, charged with looking after liaison with the South Koreans on a fulltime basis.

Realism dictated that the finding of an ideal candidate for the job, a speaker of Korean, would be unlikely. An acceptable second-best, it was suggested, would be somebody with Far Eastern experience.

The War Office found somebody with Far Eastern experience. He was an able officer who had served in Hong Kong in the late 1930s and had been captured by the Japanese in Singapore in 1942. His time as a prisoner-of-war had, of course, deprived him of the operational opportunities that had been open to luckier contemporaries. It was felt that an active appointment in Korea would help him to catch up in this respect.

He was flown out immediately. He reported himself, eager for work, at the brigade headquarters housed in a requisitioned school. The brigade major welcomed him hospitably and said the brigade commander would see him as soon as he could. At the moment the brigadier was talking to his Korean liaison officer, whose English was none too good and who was inclined to verbosity. There might be quite a wait. Have a cup of tea.

Over the tea the brigade major, who had himself drafted the job specification, put some tactful research into the newcomer's Asian background. It was impressive. Among other things he was an enthusiastic linguist who had qualified in Cantonese and Malay. He would start on Korean at once.

Had he come across any Koreans before?

Only on the railway.

The railway?

The Burma–Siam railway. Prisoners-of-war of the Japanese had been put to work building the bloody thing. It had been unpleasant. For obvious reasons, nobody at the time had been able to keep an overall count of casualties, but he'd seen the figures recently. Sixty-one thousand POWs had been sent there. Sixteen thousand had died. All the guards had been bastards. The biggest bastards of the lot had been Koreans.

The brigade major was beginning to wonder whether there might not be a touch of reserve in the new man's attitude to his allied opposite numbers, when the brigadier's door opened and the Korean liaison officer came out.

The brigade major rose to his feet to make the introductions. 'This is . . .' he started.

The newly joined member of the brigade staff drew his pistol and shot the Korean dead.

'Recognized him at once,' he explained later. 'He was one of the bastards on the railway.'

His replacement matched exactly the requirements redrafted jointly by the brigadier and the brigade major. He was a qualified Finnish speaker who had never before set foot out of Europe.